The
GREATEST
GUJARATI
STORIES
EVER TOLD

In the same series

The Greatest Bengali Stories Ever Told (ed.) Arunava Sinha
The Greatest Urdu Stories Ever Told (ed.) Muhammad Umar Memon
The Greatest Odia Stories Ever Told (ed.) Leelawati Mohapatra, Paul St-Pierre, and K. K. Mohapatra
The Greatest Hindi Stories Ever Told (ed.) Poonam Saxena
The Greatest Tamil Stories Ever Told (ed.) Sujatha Vijayaraghavan and Mini Krishnan

The GREATEST GUJARATI STORIES EVER TOLD

selected & edited by
RITA KOTHARI

ALEPH

ALEPH

ALEPH BOOK COMPANY
An independent publishing firm
promoted by *Rupa Publications India*

First published in India in 2022
by Aleph Book Company
7/16 Ansari Road, Daryaganj
New Delhi 110 002

This edition copyright © Aleph Book Company 2022
Copyright for individual stories vests with respective authors/proprietors.

Introduction copyright © Rita Kothari 2022

The Acknowledgements on p. 239 constitute an extension of the copyright page

All rights reserved.

While every effort has been made to trace copyright holders and obtain permission, this has not been possible in all cases; any omissions brought to our attention will be remedied in future editions.

This is a work of fiction. Names, characters, places and incidents are either the product of the authors' imagination or are used fictitiously and any resemblance to any actual persons, living or dead, events or locales is entirely coincidental.

No part of this publication may be reproduced, transmitted, or stored in a retrieval system, in any form or by any means, without permission in writing from Aleph Book Company.

ISBN: 978-93-91047-48-1

3 5 7 9 10 8 6 4

Printed in India

This book is sold subject to the condition that it shall not, by way of trade or otherwise, be lent, resold, hired out, or otherwise circulated without the publisher's prior consent in any form of binding or cover other than that in which it is published.

CONTENTS

Introduction vii

1. Saubhagyavati: The Fortunate Wife DWIREF 1
2. A Letter K. M. MUNSHI 10
3. Jumo Bhishti DHUMKETU 14
4. The Death of Maaja Vela SUNDARAM 18
5. A Drop of Blood JAYANT KHATRI 29
6. Once Upon a Time in Naimesharanya SURESH JOSHI 43
7. Vaadki BHUPEN KHAKHAR 49
8. Pyre RAGHUVEER CHAUDHARY 66
9. Indubhai Gaayab ANJALI KHANDWALLA 72
10. The Invasion DALPAT CHAUHAN 77
    (Translated by HEMANG DESAI)
11. Name: Nayana Rasik Mehta VARSHA ADALJA 92
12. Doors HIMANSHI SHELAT 100
13. The Unblemished One MOHAN PARMAR 105
14. The Stairs CHANDRA SHRIMALI 128
15. Creamy Layer NEERAV PATEL 139
16. Congratulations BINDU BHATT 146
17. Nightmare MINAL DAVE 153
18. The Bilge Water NAZIR MANSURI 158
    (Translated by SACHIN KETKAR)
19. Nandu DASHRATH PARMAR 189
20. The Black Horse MONA PATRAWALLA 197
    (Translated by SACHIN KETKAR)

21.	Maajo PANNA TRIVEDI	206
22.	The Twenty-first Tiffin RAAM MORI	217
23.	Chunni ABHIMANYU ACHARYA	226

Notes on the Contributors   233
Acknowledgements   239

INTRODUCTION
RITA KOTHARI

'Vaarta re vaarta' is a common Gujarati expression that invokes many associations. It could be said by a child demanding a story from an adult. It could also be used to mock the false reassurances of the state. Apart from such colloquial ways in which the word vaarta (stemming from vaat, or baat in Hindi) has been used, it also simply means a short story. At times the short story is also referred to as 'toonki vaarta' or 'navalika', or even 'laghu-katha'. These are perhaps more self-conscious labels that refer to the short story genre as it is understood in the Western canon. Along with poetry, the short story has been the Gujarati community's most used form. It is a vibrant tradition, both in terms of quantity and continuity. Its history also shows how experimental it has been, and all this is evidence of it being a lively, living form. From the point of its inception in the early decades of the twentieth century, it has reflected some of the most dominant concerns of the Gujarati people. The newly educated class formed under the aegis of colonialism turned to many forms of art, but chiefly the story, to articulate its ambivalence about gender, modernity, social class, inequities, etc. For instance, the very first published Gujarati short story 'Govalini' by Malaynil is about a woman from the cowherd community and her autonomy and wit that puts the educated narrator to shame and causes him great embarrassment. K. M. Munshi's early stories also have a satirical streak that exposes the hypocrisy of the upper-caste Gujaratis in Bombay Presidency. Gandhi's followers in the literary world wrote about the concerns of the poor, in modes that were Gandhian—gentle but condescending. A well-known story, 'Khemi' (not included here, for it exists in multiple translations), by Ramnarayan Vishwanath Pathak written in the late 1920s remains a site of discussions and disagreements.

Even to this day, readers of magazines and periodicals such as *Navneet Samarpan, Parab, Shabdasrishti,* and others wait eagerly for Diwali special issues that feature new short story writers. Institutions like the Sahitya Parishad continue to hold workshops and meetings to help new writers hone their skills at short stories. Mainstream newspapers too carry stories, sometimes in the form of serialized novels. And not unlike many other literary traditions in India, the genesis of the short story in Gujarat also owes its origins to both 'folk/lok' stories as well as colonial modernity*. In this collection, the nature of this mixed genesis is best exemplified by Suresh Joshi's story, 'Once Upon a Time in Naimesharanya…'. The ellipsis in this title suggest both antiquity and continuity, while the story itself is a tussle between divergent truths of both the traditional and modern kind. 'Once upon a time in Naimesharanya, there was a sage who had immersed himself in penance for a thousand years.' Did the story begin in the hoary past of *Singhasan Battisi* or does it belong to the period of colonial modernity in Gujarat? Did the dark forest—the naimesharanya—exist then? As a writer of high modernism, Joshi challenges the teleology from the traditional, oral, collective tale to the written and individually owned short story. However, before we launch into the stories and their translations—two acts that might be seen as one—we might ask: what is the point of this anthology?

To the world at large, Gujarat has come to be associated with a set of signs—specific food, specific politics, mercantilism and, in recent times, the political power of Hindu majoritarianism. There has also been, in the last two decades, a deafening amount of rhetoric, regarding the success and dangers of the muscular nationalism associated with the region. This present-ness is likely to shape our responses to both the production and reception of its literature, if at all we think of Gujarat in the context of literature! But it is in this realm of the literary that some of the most fascinating stories lie, confirming and defying the

---

*For an excellent introduction to the journey of the Gujarati short story, refer to Krupa Shah, *Translation as Reflective Praxis: Three Narratives from Twentieth Century Gujarat,* unpublished dissertation, Indian Institute of Technology, Gandhinagar, 2018.

perceptions that form the common sense about Gujarat. One hopes that this act of translation and the discussions surrounding Gujarati literature will nudge Gujarat to own up to its own multiplicities. At the same time, it might help a non-Gujarati reader to appreciate the less acknowledged aspects of Gujarat. Meanwhile, the stories in this volume are not a product of a pre-conceived framework to include the most known or the lesser known. It is their relationship with each other, despite their differences, that may perhaps be an explanation of what was essentially an intuitive choice. If inequality of caste and gender remains a recurring phenomenon, it is a reflection of how, as a society, we continue to be assailed by this reality.

The Aleph series 'The Greatest Stories Ever Told' invites a translator to curate and translate stories from a region that form, in his/her mind, the 'greatest' repertoire. While the semantics around the word 'greatest' is left unsaid, it is implicitly understood to be stories that meet literary and subjective standards of the translator, that appear to the translator to be unusual or fresh in their themes or styles. This subjective context makes me want to begin a discussion on the stories included in this volume by first talking of a writer from Gujarat I have held in the highest regard, but whom we unfortunately lost too soon to cancer. Neerav Patel gave me his story 'Creamy Layer' a few months before he passed away and both the story and the poignancy of those months have left a mark on me. The tragic effect of 'Creamy Layer' is slow, almost imperceptible. It does not have an upper-caste perpetrator or a rural landowner who wreaks havoc in the life of a Dalit tiller. The upper-caste person is mostly missing and only present as a normative standard of life in the psyche of the Dalit protagonist. This leads to a psychic rupture in the life of a well-to-do, modern, and upwardly mobile Dalit, Mr Vaghela. Torn between his community in the village that he has escaped from and the urban upper-caste world which his daughter is about to marry into, Mr Vaghela's predicament is very complex. When Mr and Mrs Vaghela go to their village to invite their extended family to their daughter's wedding, they realize the chasm that lies between the politicized, urban and upwardly mobile Dalit and his counterparts in the village. The paragraph below is one of the most unusual that one encounters in fictional and non-fictional accounts of caste identity:

> The paternal cousins had quite the same attitude. They were not very literate, but the youngest one had been tempted to go to school, lured by the prospect of a mid-day meal. He had haltingly learnt to put letters together. With arduous effort he managed to read out the kankotri to everyone. On hearing their own names among some two hundred hosts they felt pleased: Dhulabhai Punjabhai Vaghela, Kalidas Punjabhai Vaghela.... But then the Mota Bhabhi turned the kankotri over, and snapped: 'What, bhai, you forgot to put our kuldevi Chavanda Ma on it? It is through her blessings that our clan survives. Have you become such a savarna that you cast aside our own mother? You have included the picture of your kind of coat-pant wearing God, but abandoned our ever-present mother goddess.' With a broom over her shoulder, she muttered on her way to the village, 'Go get your daughter married into a rich family, our presence will not bring any glory to your aangan.'

With this one story, Patel manages to bring questions of caste from the outer to the inner world, shifting our focus from identifiable tormentors in the social world to forms of torment in the mind, and the rupture of psychic cohesion. 'Creamy Layer' is a valuable script of selfhood, assailed by splits hitherto undocumented in literature. I want to record my gratitude to and love for a writer-friend who was my first adviser on this anthology. This brings me to the rest of the stories in the collection and some discussion on how and why they find themselves in this book. Frankly speaking, my role as a translator-editor-curator of anthologies (poetry and short stories) has evolved over time. In the 'common sense' world view of the well-heeled Gujarati Banias and Jains as well as those who see the region superficially, Gujarat appears entirely urban and affluent and comprised of its vegetarian mercantile population. The fact that the state comprises a large number of Dalits and Adivasis or the Denotified Tribes remains invisible. The first anthology that I co-edited and translated, *Modern Gujarati Poetry: A Selection* (1998), reflected this narrow and blinkered view of Gujarat. As a researcher-translator in my mid-twenties, I had taken literature to mean what got passed on and transmitted over and over again. The politics surrounding the production and reception of literature, especially in Gujarat, unfolded itself in subsequent years. Since then, my attempt has been to not allow any dominant pattern to emerge in an anthology, except for the one of many Gujarats, both visible and invisible. This diffusion of region-making and anthology-making go hand in hand because anthologies also masquerade as exhibition panels on which are hung stories of a language. So what are the sins of omission and commission in this anthology? It does not include, for instance, a well-known story like 'Khemi' or Munshi's famous 'Shaamaldas no Vivaah'. Instead, it has other unexpected ones by the same writers. Similarly, it could have included stories by Gulabdas Broker or Jhaverchand Meghani, writers much acclaimed and very significant, but room had to be made for certain contemporary voices. The aim is heterogeneity, so that no one discourse dominates the flavour. The stories are selected from across different time periods, with styles as different as the epistolary one by Munshi to the high modernism of Suresh Joshi, the colloquial world of Mona Patrawalla and Nazir Mansuri to the genteel world of Varsha Adalja. The Gujarati Dalit short story is also a rich genre that covers divergent approaches to caste and this anthology includes a significant number of Dalit writers. In sum, the underlying theme or logic of selection is a negative one—to not have only one kind of voice or theme.

In the discussion that follows, some stories from the anthology emerge and I put them in conversation with each other. Since this is not meant to be a comprehensive guide on how to read this anthology, the selection of stories I speak about is arbitrary. For instance, an early-twentieth-century story in this anthology is by the famous writer K. M. Munshi. Written in an epistolary format, it is, titled 'A Letter'. Munshi, who is remembered for tales of valour and the concept of asmita (the essence of Gujarati-ness, a sense of pride), was also a child of social reform in Gujarat. The story carries the stamp of the concerns of the educated elite about the 'plight' of women in the late nineteenth and early twentieth centuries.

The subject of a child-bride who is made to labour all day in Munshi's story may seem archaic from our vantage point. However, a life of dignity and sufficiency is not an archaic matter for certain bodies, especially when caste, class, and gender intersect. So in 'Maajo', written by contemporary writer Panna Trivedi at least eighty years after Munshi, we encounter once again the absence of minimum resources. The protagonist is not an upper-caste woman (as Munshi's young bride was), therefore her struggles are rather more severe. Maajo doesn't ask for much. As she stands on a railway platform watching trains go by or sits on the floor in a dark and overcrowded room watching TV, she longs for a butter-like softness to her skin, a Shah Rukh Khan-like glance from a young man, an escape from her reality. The change that has occurred in society is restricted to a certain group and has not yet reached Maajo. The search for a dignified life and the annihilation of desire are a common theme across the stories. Shaili (in Abhimanyu Acharya's story), on the other hand, has no prison-houses of the kind Maajo does. This story could have been in any language, inhabiting as Shaili does the spaces of the metropolis, picking and discarding relationships on Tinder.

'Maajo' by Panna Trivedi and 'Chunni' by Abhimanyu Acharya are not very far from each other in terms of time. Both Acharya and Trivedi are contemporary writers but map very different lives. Shaili does not live in an urban slum, in fact, she does not even live in Gujarat. Like her cat, Chunni, she also lacks a named language. Both these stories remind us in different ways how fantasies of togetherness end in violence.

Let's go back in time again and look at the celebrated short story writer R. V. Pathak's 'Saubhagyavati: The Fortunate Wife', written in the early decades of the twentieth century. Pathak, popularly known as Dwiref, goes a few steps further than Munshi in pointing out the selfish and non-consensual nature of sexual relations in marriage. In a story ironically called 'Saubhagyavati', he manages to show how oppressive marital sex is in Mallikaben's upper-class life, a shackle that Jeevi (the pastoralist woman) had managed to shrug off. Between the early years of Munshi, followed by Dwiref and other contemporary writers, is Varsha Adalja, a very reputed name in Gujarati literature. The protagonist in her story 'Name: Nayana Rasik Mehta', an upper-class South Bombay woman goes to a police station to file a complaint against her husband. The banality of the questions asked in Marathi, the naming of the act in English, and the affective memory of the Gujarati-speaking household make this multilingual story very real and convincing:

> 'See, madam, you seem to be from a respectable family. Khandaani ani sanskari ghar. You must be educated too, right? By doing this you are jeopardizing your family's honour, do you understand?' Jadhav continued.
> 'But...but will you at least hear me out?'
> 'Woman, you listen to me. Have you informed your family that you are coming to a police station?'
> 'No, no....'
> 'Bas then. It's not too late. Go. Go home. Married life madhe sagda hote, all kinds of things happen in a marriage.'

Somewhat younger than Varsha Adalja is another reputed writer, Bindu Bhatt. The narrator in Bindu Bhatt's story 'Congratulations' does not seem like one ravaged by guilt. Her relationship with Prashant, a married man, has lasted for years, and the judgemental remarks by the rest of the world only irk her. But we don't know this for sure, do we? It's very likely that an element of self-doubt assails her, for it is one thing to get used to an unnamed commitment and quite another to name it, and stake a legal claim on it. Bindu Bhatt is an unusual writer of the usual stuff of relationships. For a sampling of her attempt at understanding homosocial relationships, readers may also wish to read her novel *Mira Yagnik nee Dairy*.

Sparsely yet vividly told is 'A Drop of Blood' by Jayant Khatri. Well known as Kutch's short story writer, Khatri has a distinct place in Gujarati literature. 'A Drop of Blood' gets to the heart of violence and looks at how violent acts engender violence. Bechar's righteous indignation at discovering his son's violent tendencies makes him demand whose blood is running through the veins of that young man. His wife's retort 'Even I want to ask, whose drop of blood?' hangs in the air, challenging the self-image of men who suffer from convenient amnesia about their own actions.

One of the finest stories in this volume is Minal Dave's 'Nightmare'. Two women, Hindu and Muslim, and probably belonging to different classes, are locked in a precarious nightmare during communal riots. Dave writes honestly of a well-meaning, upper-class/caste woman who sees herself as a secular person, making a herculean effort not to let the demons of her mind judge her Muslim co-passenger. The internal monologue of fear and paranoia is remarkable as a document of the middle class and elite Hindu who needs very little to believe that she is under threat.

> You never know what she might do, this woman. She could pull a knife out of her bag and stab me and no one would see. Arre, she only has to kick me and I will collapse. Look at her hands, how big and masculine they are! Is there a hardened criminal hiding behind that burkha?

To my mind, this story is unique in representing forms of segregation and solidarity with poetic and poignant understatement.

I want to draw attention now to Chandra Shrimali. Belonging to a community of Dalits in Gujarat, but also occupying among Dalits a relatively high position by being a Garoda (a Brahmin caste among the Dalits), Shrimali is also the only woman writer of that constituency. Her much acclaimed story 'The Stairs' seems like a banal account of living in a dilapidated chawl with a rickety staircase. Caste figures more subtly in this tale in the set of practices, in the distortions of names, in avoiding being seen by certain people, and general levels of indifference towards the self. We see this through the life of newly wed Chandan who goes through her new life with charm and optimism, but is rendered bereft of an offspring because of the stairs, which are both real and symbolic. The 'self' in Gujarati is 'jaat'. 'Jaat maate atlu karvu pade.' You have to do a little something for the self. But the word 'jaat' also stands for 'caste', and the resources available to the self and the caste are not different. In fact, in Dashrath Parmar's 'Nandu' we see this duality. The narrator refuses to answer insistent questions about his caste. He hides his self, his jaat, or caste. In the coded world of caste society, questions don't need to be asked or answers given directly; they have a way of making themselves present.

A rare treat in this anthology is the story 'The Black Horse' by Mona Patrawalla (translated by Sachin Ketkar). Patrawalla explores the world of the tribal region of the Dangs in Gujarat and provides a hair-raising picture of the violent forms of power wielded by the Parsis there. The landscape, the tone, and the man and animal relationship in this story (in contrast with 'Jumo Bhishti') leaves the reader distinctly disturbed and arrested. The opening paragraph of this story takes an urban Gujarati (like me) to a terrain rarely seen in Gujarati literature.

> Deep in the dense foliage and the bamboo groves of Ahwa-Dang lies the village of Vansda. Inhabited mainly by Adivasis, the village also has Koli, Kandi, and Anavil communities. About five miles from Vansda is the village Manpur, where Bamansha Daruwalla lived in his timber and bamboo mansion. In Manpur, among the five to seven Parsi households, Bamansha's was the richest. He owned an enormous liquor shop in Vansda as well as more than a hundred bighas of land. In his large house, set amidst thick bamboo groves, Bamansha lived on his own like a huge owl.

Meanwhile, the delightful glimpse into the life in a chawl (Bhupen Khakhar's 'Vaadki') where exchanges of poha tell the story of who slept with whom; or the powerful character Natho (in Dalpat Chauhan's 'The Invasion', translated by Hemang Desai); or the sexual and caste politics of Mohan Parmar's story ('The Unblemished One') and many more add to the rich fare in this volume. It is neither possible nor desirable for me to talk about each of them; however, the reader will find a fairly large and diverse collection here.

The real and imaginary world of literature provides a subtext to the many meanings of Gujarat. This anthology aims to contribute to an understanding of the region, add nuance to the idea of Gujarat, both to its inhabitants as well as readers outside. This collection also hopes to hint at the differences in the realm of the social and personal and provide a variegated and unsettled picture of Gujarat, showing how Gujarat itself is constituted by multitudes, each with challenges of its own; and how, on some days, being human is an aspiration, not a fact. And one may even ask after reading Dhumketu's classic 'Jumo Bhishti': what do the distinctions between human and non-human even mean?

Finally, anthologies such as this one invite a set of expectations. The reading communities they emerge from expect their social memory to be supported through them. The Gujarati literary community would look for signs of familiarity in this anthology, totems of association, and nostalgia for the stories they grew up on, had conversations with, and remembered as great. Whether a selection such as this fully confirms that memory is an open matter, for it has been done with a view to making the stories speak to each other, and sometimes disagree with each other. Despite the series title, although each story may not subjectively conform to the superlative claim, each one shows us a new aspect of Gujarat—ranging from a tentative genteelness to the well-meaning Gandhian reformist mode to a gamut of articulations regarding caste and gender. The idea of the canon (for want of a better word) is more a juncture rather than a destination in this collection. The departures aim to show how Gujarat is a discursively formed concept, and that every interpretation of Gujarat and its people and the land is great, if not the greatest.

SAUBHAGYAVATI: THE FORTUNATE WIFE
DWIREF

The moment Mallikaben arrived amidst us, she and I became friends. I was drawn to her, more than anyone else around me at that time. I had never seen a woman that delicate and beautiful. It's not that she was particularly young. She must've been on the wrong side of thirty, maybe even in her forties. But her face did not show her age. Granted, she had not borne any children, but you know how it is with some faces: they are simply ageless.

And what drew my attention was how compatible she and her husband looked, how happy and lively. Vinodrai was also quite good-looking, and he had such a well-maintained body! I clearly remember how we got to know each other. At ten o'clock one night, they suddenly appeared at our door, calling, 'Doctor sahib, Doctor sahib.' My husband, the 'doctor', and I were sitting on chairs under the moonlight. We sort of knew that our new neighbour was an excise inspector. We welcomed both of them, seated them, and enquired after them. He said, 'See, doctor, my cheek is injured.'

Doctor flashed the torchlight on his cheek and noticed an inch-deep wound. He dressed the wound. Once they left, Doctor said to me, 'If there was a conscription policy in the army, this man would have adorned the force.' And, truly, that's how regal Vinodrai looked. He would participate in horse racing and compete with the British, and even managed to bag prizes!

I must have found the couple attractive because I probably saw them as a romantic pair. And it was a contrast to my own life; maybe that's what attracted me to them. My husband and I are low-key people, while this Vinodrai! He seemed so passionate. He had come over just once, but soon we got to know each other quite well. Doctor once asked him, 'Vinu bhai, what made you race a horse on a dark night and run into thorny hedges?' and I still remember

Vinodrai's reply, made only half in jest:
'My camel rider used to sing a doha:

> *If the rider stays miles away*
> *Either the maid is not winsome,*
> *Or the lover not so constant*

Wouldn't I be the inconstant lover if I stayed away? You can be certain I'd come back from wherever I was to spend the night here!'

This was the passionate bond between the husband and wife.

I would often spend time with Mallika, especially when Vinodrai was away on work. We were chatting one day during one such period when I heard him swiftly climbing the stairs to his house, singing loudly, '*Either the maid is wanting, or the lover shameless.*' He entered the room like a torrent. Mallika's face went pale. Thankfully, Vinodrai saw me, and promptly disappeared, with the excuse that he had to freshen up. I excused myself and left.

I came away thinking, you know, it's different with people like me and the Doctor. But separation among other couples must surely reduce the drudgery of everyday life and add some spice to their relationship. However, there was something that I could not understand. Mallika seemed to carry a deep sorrow within her. She did not have children, but she didn't seem the kind to mourn childlessness. And it must be real misery because she was also not the kind to cook up imaginary problems. I did not have the temerity to ask her though. She was the kind who preferred enduring her pain without having anybody's sympathy. As the days went by, I was more and more convinced that she was unhappy, and my curiosity grew.

Once, Vinodrai was away and Mallika was at my place. At about three o'clock in the afternoon, the servant came to inform that 'sahib' had arrived. I could not help joking, 'Congratulations winsome maid, your constant lover is here!' But the moment these words came out of my mouth, I noticed such an expression of disdain and misery on Mallika's face that I was dumbfounded. Was she offended that I had taken the liberty to treat her like a younger person, although we were the same age? Or did my frivolity remind her of her childlessness? I couldn't fathom what I had done. I was about to ask for her forgiveness and enquire as to what had bothered her so much, but she left without a glance in my direction. She returned to meet me after a few days and by then she seemed her old cheerful self. So I dismissed the thought from my mind.

On another late evening, she was with me at my home again. We were both sitting on the sofa. Just then Jeevi, who sells milk to me, appeared with her six-year-old daughter. Jeevi has an impressive personality. She's tall and stately, full-bodied and strong. Her gait is regal, like she had taken birth to become the queen of some state. Her eyes sparkled, although on a closer look you could see lines caused by age and the vagaries of life. She had first come to our house about three years ago. We needed milk for our house and the patients at the hospital, but we had not been satisfied with the quality of milk we bought. It was then that Jeevi became our supplier of milk. Her rates were also reasonable.

'How come you are here at this time, Jeevi?' I asked her.

Mallika said, 'Is this the person you keep talking about?'

'Yes,' I said to Mallika, and then to Jeevi, 'You've brought milk very early today.'

Jeevi replied, 'Ben, I haven't brought milk with me. I will bring it at the regular time. My buffalo gave birth to a new calf, so I thought I'd get you some new whey. Make bari out of it and feed sahib and your children. This is the same buffalo that I had bought with the money you had lent me. See how tasty the bari turns out to be when you use this milk.'

'Great, is it a she-calf or a he-calf your buffalo gave birth to?'

'Ben, it's a girl!' Jeevi replied with a smile.

I stood up to go to the almirah and get some money. Jeevi knew that's what I was going to do, so she immediately began to say, 'Upon my life, ben! Thanks to you, I found a life here. If I was in my village, and you were coming to visit me, I'd wash your feet with milk. I have fed many with milk and ghee by now, what with the many buffaloes I have there.'

'Alee, which village are you from?'

'Oh Jeevipar, it's only eight gaus from here.'

'Did you leave behind all the animals you had there?'

'No, ben, everything's there. There are four buffaloes, and an ox.'

'So who's looking after all that?'

'Why, my daughter-in-law! I have four sons, two are married, and another one will get married soon. I also have a daughter, who's now old enough for the aanu ceremony. My Patel is also around.'

My interest was piqued. I said, 'Jeevi, since you have come early today, please sit. Wait till I finish making the bari.' I went inside, instructing the domestic help to make the bari, and sat down on the sofa once again. I put away the teapot that stood between Jeevi and me, and offered her a place to sit. 'Here, Jeevi, sit peacefully. Tell me, why did you leave such a full-fledged home and come here?'

'It's nothing, ben, just came, what else....'

'Why, did you not get along with your daughters-in-law or were you dissatisfied with the children's marriages? Tell me.'

'Arre, ben, I dote over my daughters-in-law. There's not a shade of conflict between us. They are all the same to me.'

'Oh ho, look at her! You are such a forceful person; I'm sure you did what you wanted to and put them off!'

'No, ben, nothing like that.'

By this time the bari was ready and brought to the table. Jeevi said, 'Ben, eat it while it's warm. Add some jaggery to it.'

But I was my mischievous self today so I said, 'No, I will do that only after you tell me your story. Let the bari go cold otherwise. I refuse to touch it, hanh!'

Jeevi laughed. 'Ben, you are being difficult!' She turned to her daughter, and said softly, 'Go, beta, take this pot and go home, it's time to feed the buffaloes. I will join you shortly.'

I said, 'Let her be for a moment.' I sliced four or five pieces of bari and a lump of jaggery and gave it to the girl. 'Be careful, don't drop this, okay?' I told her. The girl left. I turned to Jeevi and asked,

'How old was she when you brought her here?'

'She was two.'

'Now tell me, why did you leave your home? If you hadn't fought with anyone, that is. Did your Patel chase other women once you were old?'

'No, ben, it wouldn't be fair to him to say that. He's not like that.'

'So are you upset about something? I can talk to your Patel. He will woo you and take you back! Someone like you is a jewel to any family.'

'Arre, I only have to mention going back and he'd happily take me home. He said, "Tell me what kind of clothes and jewellery I can buy for you" when I told him about the new calf. He said he has two hundred rupees saved up, tied in a knot. "You ask for what you want and come home with me." But I refused.'

I was really surprised. Jeevi was clearly very fond of Patel, and yet in her middle age, she had chosen to stay alone! I simply couldn't understand what was going on. 'So what made you move away? Tell me, or I'll die!'

Jeevi said, 'Ben, don't make me take an oath like that. You are very dear to me, may you live long.'

'Now you have to tell me, I made you swear!'

'Look, ben, I am an old woman now. I cannot bear children any more, so after this last girl was born, I came away.'

'But I can make sure you don't get pregnant any more. That's what all these big people do now. Don't you know? You know Desai sahib? He has three children. The youngest one is eight years old, and that's the end of it.'

'But, ben, I don't want any of it. I have had enough. I became old, but he continued to remain a demanding young man. He's exactly like he was when I came to the house as a twenty-year-old. Wretched me, had I died, he could have brought a young wife and fulfilled all his desires. But, ben, with this old body now, I find even being touched loathsome. God knows why he's not repulsed by my miserable body! I understand men are particularly like that, and I was also like that once, but there's an age and time for everything, no?'

I watched Jeevi with my mouth agape. After a while, I said, 'Look, Jeevi, if this is the case, you should explain to your husband. What's there to feel shy about? You should speak plainly that this is your problem.'

'Dear ben, do you think I haven't done that? How many times? Told him at home, in the fields, with words and gestures. My little boy was sucking on a mango seed after having eaten the fruit one day, and Patel says to him, "Alya, leave it alone now, what's left of the mango that you keep sucking and sucking?" My older children were not at home, so I said to Patel, "That message should be for you." He understood and laughed but when night fell, he was exactly the same. And with so many older children around, how do I yell and scream at him at night? Our homes are also small, you have to be careful. And, ben, can I be honest? The more I resisted, the more he insisted. He refused to understand. He was like a twenty-five-year-old boy. I tolerated for so many years; sometimes I found it terribly disgusting. But what could I do? It's unfortunate to be born with a female body. Sometimes I let him do what he liked to my body like it wasn't mine at all. Finally, when it became unbearable, I decided that I was going to raise this little girl myself and that was that. Thank God, ben, that I had some gap between the births of my last two children, otherwise imagine what condition I would have been in! Ben, when I simply couldn't endure any more, I left. To leave my home, land, social relations, my children, and such comfort...why would anyone do that otherwise? And we are such a respected family in the village. I am considered to be auspicious because I have not lost a single child, so newly-wed women in the village would come to seek my blessings. God has given me so much, but this thing has left me so very tired....'

I was in awe of this woman and kept staring at her. Her wisdom and her courage astonished me. A little later I said, 'Alee, you are remarkable. What a woman you are! Weren't you worried about fending for yourself?'

'No, ben. We are not fortunate like you, to afford such thoughts. We know that we do back-breaking work and we get a day's meal. In our community, a widow can survive with a single buffalo. What do I have to worry about? Once this girl grows up, I will get her married. We belong to the labourers' community, we know we can work and survive.'

Mallika had been quiet all this while. Now she spoke, 'Arre, bai, you are truly fortunate to have escaped. It's the so-called fortunate ones like us who can't escape.'

Jeevi said, 'Ben, people like you don't have these problems. We are uneducated people, we are illiterate, and our lives are so different. But never mind, eat the bari now…it has gone cold, hasn't it? You had to unnecessarily listen to the silly stories of our lives.'

I tried to make her taste the bari, but she refused to eat in our presence. Finally, when I kept insisting, she took a bit as 'shukan' and left. I went up to the door to see her off, and she walked away with the gait of an authoritative officer, fearless and firm. I returned to the sofa to sit next to Mallika and found her looking very despondent. I commented, 'Poor thing, how many things these people have to go through, isn't it?'

Mallika snapped, 'What makes you think only they do? The fortunate ones she refers to also go through them. They are the truly unfortunate ones. They cannot escape.'

'Is that so, Mallika?'

'I have experienced it.'

'What are you saying?'

'Yes, she was telling my story. I also loathe being touched. I have also offered up my body with the same disgust and disdain I would have if I were giving it to a dog. Like her, I had also thought of running away. But I could not. Today, I have understood two things that I had doubts about. I thought that since I didn't have children and was not occupied in raising them, I was in this condition. But today, I realized that that is not the issue. Secondly, I thought that old age was going to be my liberation; when my body would have ceased to be attractive. But that has been proven wrong as well. In fact, I can't see an end to my misery—except after death.'

Her sorrow erupted like a volcano. I took her in my arms. She wept uncontrollably. I gave her water, made her wash her face, and forced her to eat some bari. But she said, 'I can't. Not today. When I am in this state, I feel like I am choking.' I gave her a cup of coffee and, after a while, sent her home.

Doctor returned home after a while. He saw the plateful of bari on the table and said, 'Wow, you have made preparations for my arrival.'

I said, 'This bari is cursed, if I were to tell you the story that came with it. I had thought of eating it while it was hot, but it's been lying like this for over two hours. Such are the horrors I heard today.'

'Why, what happened?'

'You eat first, I will tell you later.'

'Arre, we doctors are used to eating even after slicing a corpse. We eat after opening up a living body in the operation theatre.'

'I'm telling you, you eat first.'

'No, I must hear you out first, otherwise I will not eat.'

Since Doctor would not budge, I told him about Jeevi and Mallika. At the end I said, 'You know, when he recited that doha, I thought there was poetry in his life.'

'An incompetent man can ruin both woman and poetry.'

He took a piece of bari, seeming somewhat uninterested. But he kept thinking. 'I will talk to Vinodrai.'

'Won't he feel offended when he finds out that Mallika has talked about it?'

'We doctors manage to bring up anything under the guise of clinical matters. I can always talk to him about infertility.'

He must have talked to Vinodrai, but I did not see any visible change in Mallika's sadness. When after eight months or so they were transferred to another place, Mallika came to see me. She couldn't stop sobbing that day. 'I may not live too long, and perhaps I may not be able to write to you. But I'll be thinking of you even when I die.'

How helpless are human beings, I thought; can nothing be done to help her?

In a year's time she brought an end to her life. Vinodrai was at work when she passed away. People we both knew came to my house for the mourning ritual. All of them said things like, 'What a beauty!' 'How lovely she was', 'How lucky', 'Oh she was so fortunate, I always thought of the word "saubhagyavati" when I saw her', and 'It was auspicious that she courted death as a married woman'.

Truly saubhagyavati, I said to myself, saubhagyavati indeed!

A LETTER

K. M. MUNSHI

My lord, my master! I wish to lay my head in your lap once again, while I am on my deathbed. I had considered not writing this letter. Thousands of my heart-rending entreaties amounted to nothing, why would this one have any effect now? I have no doubt that nothing is going to change. But voicing my thoughts, my experiences, will liberate me from pain. Also, if your future wife turns out to be lucky because you finally grow wiser, she will be spared the suffering I went through, and not wither away before blossoming.

In my lifetime of sixteen years, there's so much I have gone through. God alone knows who might be responsible for my miseries, but I do need to say this at least once—abandoning shame, or the maryada of the older generation—if at all there was one person responsible for my suffering, and one person who could have alleviated it—then that person was you, my master, my lord. The world handed you an inexperienced, delicate little girl, but you didn't even think about her. This is what happened to me. I am about to lose my life, my very breath is ebbing away from me.

Do you remember the time I came into your house as your wife? Despite being the adored child of loving parents, it was you I sought and pined for. Even when I went to school before we were married, just looking at you made me feel things I hadn't felt before, and I couldn't wait to meet you. I couldn't wait to serve you and feel fulfilled. Later, you found many faults with me; you even laid the cruel charge of my being indifferent to you. How could that even be possible? In a Hindu universe, the lordship of the husband is considered greater than that of even God. Little girls start worshipping their husbands even before they meet them. The difference, however, is this: that this husband, lord of the lords, has even more pretentions than God and much less affection for his devotees.

A Letter

When I came into your home, how small I was! A month before that, I was going to school and prancing about like a deer in a forest. A mother-in-law's rage and slavery to the husband were unknown concepts to me. I did not have the foggiest notion that in six months' time I was going to feel muffled and lacerated. No matter what I said or did, it became an unnecessary opportunity to accuse my parents. Why? If I did not know certain things, it was sasuji's duty to teach me. I was hardly a demoness who refused to learn. If a man is expected to have regard for his parents, should a girl not have any towards those who gave birth to her, raised and nurtured her? If someone were to say to you, 'Your mother and your father and your kind', you would slap that person. But an innocent young girl listens to all the aspersions cast on her parents and merely suffers in silence.

After a few months, when I finally braced myself to endure these comments, a new thing began. Dear one, what kind of strength did you expect from the body of a thirteen-year-old? How did you expect a naïve child to know what the customs of your house were? Just as your sister was dear to your mother, so was I to mine. Your sister, however, was simply not bothered about my fragility. Are you saying that a twenty-year-old sister would be damaged by work while I, a thirteen-year-old, would not?

Does Hindu culture not teach the mother-in-law and husband to have any sense of fairness? I, too, was a body, not a log of wood. And after a day's arduous labour, what care did I receive from my husband? None, right?

I have endured all my life, but I shall speak today. Did you not know that I was also a young, foolish, and fragile child? That I slogged like a beast of burden every day? That I could neither sleep nor sit? You played cricket and went to office. Do you think people like us sleep at home? We worked every minute, endured abuse, filled our stomachs with leftovers, spent our lives longing for more. At the end of a hard day, when I came to you expecting a word of affection, you couldn't manage any. I was immediately made responsible for fetching every small thing you needed. A moment's delay and you began yelling. Your strong, manly feet ached from sitting in one place in your office, and you needed my weak hands to press them. If you perspired at night, I had to fan you with my small trembling hands. Did you not think at that time, even for a moment, how was this young girl to withstand such burden? But why would you? I was a slave, wasn't I?

A daughter-in-law is like a mere cat in the house. But a cat gets to sleep and eat twice a day. What do you men know of what we go through? There were so many days when after back-breaking work I could barely sit; I also had to be deprived of sleep. Yet, I served you even during such times. Silently, I stole a wink here and there, only to be reprimanded, threatened, and even slapped. But shedding tears was also a crime.

Forbidden from going to my natal home, victimized by a perpetually enraged mother-in-law, you lording over me, cruel and heartless. You made a fifteen-year-old go through all this? I did what thousands of my kind do.

I inadvertently blurted out something to my mother one day. She sent word to your mother, who made a mountain out of a molehill and instigated you. That night, you beat me up. Do you remember? I sobbed into the pillow and asked for death. Let those women of earlier days—who filled pots with water from the river and carried them on their heads, or those dumb, thickheaded women who helplessly went through life—suffer if they will. But how could a delicate, young, educated girl have to go through this?

Had you shown affection, some concern for the courtesan who entertained you, the slave that fed you—some sense of fairness—then I would have made you the sovereign of my soul, not merely my husband, the owner of my body. I would have sprinkled your path with flowers and made you experience heaven. But all that remained unspoken and undone. I did not find justice, affection, nor happiness with you. I withered and wilted inside—so did my body. Finally, your words and actions managed to murder me.

At least for a day you could have talked to me about something other than your concerns. For one moment, couldn't you have allowed me to taste genuine love? At least after your meal you could have asked me, 'Is there food left for you, or mere crumbs?' At least for a day you could have exposed me to some aesthetic pleasure or a higher plane of being. But what was I expecting? Why would you care beyond gorging on food and fattening yourself? Those ideal women, the satis, prayed to have the same husband in their next birth. I could pray too, but have you proven yourself worthy of that prayer? Those pious women had husbands who were worthy of their sacrifice. I am done with you in this birth. May God never bring us together.

Do tell sasuji not to bring an educated daughter-in-law into her home again.

The Unfortunate Woman

JUMO BHISHTI

DHUMKETU

Anyone who passed by Anandpur noticed the three identical squalid structures that stood in a corner, with an ancient, tired-looking tamarind tree casting its shadow over them. Here, the stink of sewage mingled with the dust in the air. The three hovels were patchwork constructions—made of tin, wood, and jute bags—and the entrance to the structures remained permanently open. Inside, Jumo Bhishti sat on a tattered mat, smoking his hookah. Throughout his life, Jumo had witnessed the sharp vicissitudes of fortune—from food being served in golden vessels to nibbling from chipped pots, he had seen it all. He had been born into wealth, the cherished child of well-to-do parents with everyone doting on him. He probably still remembered how, at the age of ten, he had sat atop an elephant for his wedding procession. This was around the same time he had been gifted a buffalo as a pet. Now, after experiencing all the vagaries of life, Venu, the buffalo, and Jumo lived together. Venu was an unusual name for an animal. In more prosperous times, Jumo had many friends, one of them being a Hindu who had a weakness for literature. He had affectionately christened the buffalo Venu, and the name had stuck.

Once wealthy, today all his possessions fit into the three ramshackle hovels. Venu occupied one of them, and Jumo, another. The third structure was used to store grass. Jumo and Venu gazed at each other all day long through the opening between their structures. Friends had come and gone. Now the only ones who remained were Jumo and Venu, bound to each other since childhood.

Every morning at five o'clock, Jumo loaded the large mashaq on Venu's back and set out. The bell around Venu's neck would tinkle gently and Jumo would follow, singing a ghazal. After delivering water from door to door, the master and servant would make their way back home. Jumo would buy carrots for a few paise, and at times, tomatoes and greens for his sabzi, and an armful of fresh fodder for Venu, which the buffalo would nibble on the way as he followed his master home. This was their daily routine. Jumo would never haggle for more than what he was offered, and he never sought a new customer if he lost an existing one. From noon till evening, Jumo would pull at his hookah. Venu, lost in the hum of the hubble-bubble, languidly flapped his ears to drive away flies and drifted in and out of slumber. Later in the evening, the two friends would take a walk to the banks of the river. Occasionally, if the workload was light, they went to the riverbank in the morning as well.

One day, at five in the morning, they set out for the river. Jumo thought it would be a good idea if the buffalo chose to graze on the plants that grew by the river, but Venu disliked eating out in the open. Every time Jumo encouraged him, he would stop and bellow, as if saying, 'No, I will not eat.'

Finally, Jumo gave up, 'Very well, you can eat once we reach home. I think you enjoy being spoilt.'

The buffalo mooed victoriously, swished its tail, flapped his ears at Jumo, and turned around. He was so pleased by his triumph that he scampered a little on the way back.

'There, there…stop running, or I'll not take you home,' Jumo scolded. But Venu had already clambered onto the main road. It so happened that a railway line cut across the road. In his haste, Venu got his foot stuck between the tracks. He tried to free himself in vain and collapsed on the tracks. The more he struggled, the more firmly he was stuck. Jumo rushed to him. He held the buffalo's foot and tried to pull it out, but to no avail. In the hazy light of dawn, Jumo saw that the semaphore arm of the signal had been lowered. Terror gripped him as he wondered, what if the train….

Before he could complete the thought, he began rushing towards the road. He saw two young men out for their morning stroll. Each one had a walking stick in his hand which they swished about. They had removed the hats from their heads to enjoy the morning breeze.

Jumo ran up to them like a mad man.

'Bhaisahib...my Ve...my buffalo will be cut to pieces right now. Look, he's trapped in the tracks.' The two young men looked in the direction Jumo was pointing. They could make out a dark form struggling.

'What is that?'

'My Venu...my buffalo'

'Oh ho, go quickly, run, run to the gate, man.'

'If you honourable people help me, we can save him.'

'Us? No, no, you run. Inform the gatekeeper,' they said and walked away.

Jumo ran towards the gatekeeper's hut but there was no one around. All he could hear was the sound of someone working a grinding stone inside the hut. Just then, the distant whistle of an approaching train could be heard. Jumo cast a despondent glance around him, but there was no sign of anyone. He ran up to the signal post and pulled the chain and kept yelling for help. The hut beside him was deaf to his cries, which were drowned out by the clamour of the grinding stone. Jumo now kicked the hut door.

'Who is it?'

'Bhai-ben, please change the signal. My animal will be crushed.'

'There's no man in the house.' With that indifferent response, the grinding resumed.

The sound of the approaching train grew closer and closer.

'Run, run, my animal will be cut to pieces,' Jumo cried out as loudly as he could, but except for the harsh echo of his own voice, there was not a sound to be heard.

Jumo looked up at the sky. The last star was about to disappear. Soon, dawn broke, not with light, but with the haziness of a fog. The train was getting closer. He flung his stick away.

'Ya parwardigaar,' he called out loudly and ran. Venu lay panting from his efforts to free himself. Jumo sat by his side and gently scratched Venu's back.

'My friend, my brother, my Venu, we are together, okay?' Jumo said, and lay down by him.

With each passing moment the pounding of the train grew louder, its whistle shriller, and the clatter of its wheels came closer. Jumo hugged Venu tightly. But before the train could run over them, before he lost all his senses, Venu suddenly raised his head and struck at his master, flinging him away from the tracks!

The train ran over Venu. Jumo's clothes were soaked in Venu's warm blood. When he recovered and sat up, the only sign of his beloved friend were disjointed parts of his body lying in a pool of blood.

✧

To this day, every morning, Jumo returns to the spot where Venu had died, holding a flower in his hand. Calling out desperately for his friend, he places the flower on a stone before making his solitary journey back.

THE DEATH OF MAAJA VELA
SUNDARAM

Maaja Vela sat with the air of a patriarch of an ancient clan. Tall buildings cast their shade over him like the branches of trees in a sacred forest. Around him lay three to four generations of his family. The young twins of his daughter's daughter clung to his shoulders. His sixty-year-old son sat on his haunches next to him. The wives of his second son's two sons sat at some distance, breastfeeding their babies and simultaneously serving food from the earthen pots onto battered plates. And the various members of his extended family whom Maaja Vela neither cared to remember nor could keep count of sat scattered around the area like stars in a constellation.

It was about seven on a winter evening, and like the smoke of a yagna in a sacred forest, the smoke from the factories permeated the air. Like the smoke of the yagna, it made their eyes smart. Like the smoke of the yagna, it too had a distinct smell, but it was the smell of the gutter, not that of fragrant offerings. Maaja Vela's progeny had gathered, as always, on a footpath by a tall tower. The tower was situated near a garage outside the city's walls.

Every evening, as the people living in the pols were about to finish dinner, Maaja Vela's progeny would traverse the narrow lanes of the city with small earthen pots on their heads, calling out in sweet, high-pitched, ringing voices, 'Ma-baap, give us something.' When the pots were full they would head languidly towards their usual haunt by the tower. The menfolk would have arrived earlier with their wicker baskets of vegetables or pots and pans, and would be waiting. As the earthen pots arrived, justice would be done to their contents. Finally, what remained would be taken for the elderly who had stayed behind in the quarter.

Today, Maaja Vela had a slight fever but had insisted on going out despite everyone's attempts to dissuade him. Based on the items that had been collected from a wedding the previous night, Maaja had formed a high opinion of the event. He was eager to see for himself the wedding, the gathering, and the feasting.

'Maaja Dada, you are suffering from low fever, why do you want to come?' his nephew had asked as they were leaving.

'Bugger the low fever,' Maaja Vela had scoffed and, with the help of a stick, he had crossed the crowded roads, taking in the flashy lights of the hotels until he reached a wall around the tower. He squatted, slightly breathless, but his breathing returned to normal in a while.

The twins frisked around him like puppies, now pulling at his moustache, now climbing onto his shoulders, now lying in his lap. God knows why he was overcome with new enthusiasm to see the city once again. Maaja Vela gazed at the trucks and the scooters and the cars going past as he played with the children and overheard the conversations of the women in his family. A man stood smoking at the garage adda. Its sweet smell tickled Maaja Vela's nostrils. His mouth watered. He stared at the man. The smoker threw away the cigarette after a few drags. Maaja Vela turned to one of the boys and said, 'Go, Laliya, go bring that bidi.'

'Cigarette, Dada,' the boy quipped.

'Yes, yes, shigrate. Such citywallahs they have become,' Maaja Vela grumbled with affection. The boy brought the cigarette and Maaja Vela smoked, occasionally offering a drag to the boy while commenting and questioning from time to time, 'I haven't seen Viji yet' or 'Where have you sent Makla?', 'Vhaldi, you look like a proper Bania woman', 'Arre, Bhanki, why is your daughter crying so much?', 'Is old woman Kali ill?', 'That Magiyo died in the hospital?' His children who ranged till the age of sixty answered his queries briefly and went back to their conversations. But one of his questions startled everyone, 'And why are none of you telling me anything about those fellows on a heist?' Maaja Vela's son, sitting by him, perked up his ears and said, 'Bapu, speak softly. There's a policeman in the vicinity.'

Just then, a large car, as large as a house, pulled over. A tall policeman alighted, and walked away, swinging his baton. Maaja Vela gave him a scornful look and mumbled, 'I don't give a damn about your uniform and baton. I used to carry seventeen of you in my pocket at one time.'

'Dada, tell us the story of your heist,' one of his great-grandchildren came up to him. And Maaja Vela began to narrate a story he had told many times before: of the heists he had taken part in. The older ones had heard it many times before so they continued chatting. All they said was, 'Old man, keep your voice low.' Maaja Vela lowered his voice but there was such flourish in his storytelling that even those chatting with the others found themselves drawn to his tale.

Maaja Vela began to rake up the past, 'When we came to the city from the village, we used to stay outside these walls. We would sell datan, collect leftovers, and occasionally at night, we would shake down a solitary wanderer. But not at this gate, hanh. This city has seventeen gates, right? So at some other gate. At this one we have to live like meek cows, you see. Do you see this tower? There was nothing here, just a large pit. People would come here to relieve themselves, to throw their garbage and leftovers. We had decided that we wouldn't do anything at this gate. But it was the marriage season. And your grandmother came with the news that an oil-presser woman was coming to dispose of leaf plates but she had ornaments worth about a thousand rupees on her. I tried to dissuade her, but that Nagudiyo wouldn't listen and robbed her. Unfortunately, the oil-presser began to create a ruckus and scream and shout. What could we do then? We strangled her, threw her in the pit, and ran away. Yes, but one of us was caught while trying to sell his share of the ornaments. I, of course, had melted them down. Still, I had to serve two years in jail. That was our first big heist.' Then Maaja Vela continued with the stories of the second, third, and fourth adventures.

The children listened to him with astonishment writ large on their faces, 'So, Dada, really? There was no tower here?'

'No.'

'And, Dada, not even that big street light?'

'No, bhai, there were no roads. Only dust. And dogs. How many of them! They barked all the while. But they knew us, okay? And people, they knew how to eat. They knew how to wear clothes. Bhai, what do they eat nowadays? What use are feasts without ghee? And the women are all flash and bling. But the ornaments are all fake. Only for show. Even if we shook one down, you would hardly get anything that is worth ten rupees.'

'And, Dada, there were no cigarettes either?'

'No, bhai, people used to smoke hookahs. My brother and I had once filched one from the home of a Lohana. We sat in the vaas, smoking it through the night. You see, one could be caught smoking it in the daytime. For seven nights we enjoyed the hookah. But one day, there was a fight over whose turn it was and we ended up smashing the damn thing.'

'And, Dada, we've heard that you used to mint coins?'

Maaja Vela was about to speak, but his son stopped him. 'Bapu, shut up. Not that matter here.'

Maaja Vela fell silent. One of the children who had been lost in the narrative suddenly said, 'Mother, I am hungry.' Going towards his mother, he turned back to say, 'Dada, tell us the story about the coins when we go home.'

'Yes, child! Go and see what your mother has brought.'

'And, Dada, how many coins did you make?' another child asked.

'This many.' Maaja Vela spread his arms wide and then lifted the child.

'Dada, your moustache is white like the coins, isn't it?' The child played with his moustache. Maaja Vela laughed. 'No, beta, they are like suttarpheni. The suttarpheni of Khambat.'

'What is that, Dada?' the child asked.

'Oh my, you haven't tasted suttarpheni yet?' Maaja Vela sighed, lamenting the times they lived in. 'Arre, you will probably not even get to see what we ate. What do today's people know of eating?' He called out to the group sitting at a distance.

'Oye, if your collection has a suttarpheni, bring it along.'

His request was met with the ringing laughter of women. One of the men said softly, 'Such desires with one foot in the grave!'

'Arre people, did you hear me or not?'

'We'll give it when it comes, Dada. It's only dal and rice we've got so far.'

'Okay, okay. Bhai, I don't want it. I wanted to show it to the children.'

And until the real suttarpheni arrived, Maaja Vela gave in to the children's insistence that he describe what it looked like.

'You know how you make dung pats? It's like a small dung pat.'

'Chhee chhee!' the children exclaimed.

'Arre listen, but it is white. Pure white. Like milk.'

'Really?' The children's eyes widened with surprise.

'And sweet! And if there's saffron inside, it'd be yellow.'

'Yellow? Like khichdi?'

'Exactly. And it would have in it cardamoms, almonds, pistachio, mace, and many such things.'

'Dada, what is all that?'

'Arre, you haven't seen any of this yet?' Maaja Vela was shocked. He felt contempt towards his children who had not imparted this knowledge to their children. He felt like breaking into a grocer's shop and bringing these dry fruits for the children.

'One day I will show you, beta, if I live long enough,' he said.

'Dada, why is your moustache quivering?' a child asked.

'Dada's shoulders are also shaking,' another said.

'Will it go away if you eat suttarpheni?' a third one said. 'Wait, I'll get it for you.' And the child went to his father and said, 'Father, why don't we give Dada some suttarpheni? He's shivering.'

The father, who was one of Maaja Vela's sons, said, 'Old man, is your fever rising now? Didn't I warn you?'

'Oh it's nothing, son. I am just a bit cold. You carry on with your work, children.'

But his nephew, Vana, came up to him and felt his body. The

fever was rising. Removing the green blanket from his own body, he wrapped it around the old man. 'Here, rest a bit. Don't talk too much.' He began to shoo away the children.

But Maaja Vela said, 'Let them stay with me.'

The children, playing with the edge of the blanket, began to speak. 'Dada, you still have to tell us the story of those coins. When you make the coins, give us one each, okay? We want them. And that thing...to eat...what did you say its name was...uttar...utt....'

Maaja Vela laughed out, 'Suttarpheni. How will you eat it? You can't even say it right.'

He leaned against the tower wall and glanced at the activity around him. His daughters and daughters-in-law were busy, now sitting, now standing. Someone emptied a pot and headed back to the city gate. From a distance the faint sound of a band could be heard. Far away, through the city gate, one could see the night sparkling with lights of the celebration. The atmosphere buzzed with the swelling presence of people.

Vana, who had earlier tried to dissuade him from coming, had a soft corner for Maaja Vela. He came to him and said, 'Dada, would you like to eat something in particular?'

'No, bhai, I will eat whatever comes.'

'No, no, you mentioned suttarpheni a while ago.'

'No, bhai, that was only to show the children.'

'Very well. You want something else?' And, picking up a wicker basket and his staff, and setting it right on his turban, he walked away.

Maaja Vela was startled at seeing him go like this. The boy was bold. And if he got a chance he'd bring something. But what if he got caught? The police nowadays were much smarter. No, no, he should hold off for today. And Maaja Vela called out loudly, 'Vana, eh Vana, come back. Come back.' But his voice did not reach Vana.

Under the street light by the gate, he saw Vana disappearing into the city.... Maaja Vela suddenly felt tired. He curled up on the ground.

The children moved away from him and leaned over the contents of the earthen pots. Some of the food had been emptied into the plates. The children ate with both hands and if they came across something that they could not identify, they would call out, 'Alya, uttarpheni, uttarpheni.'

The tower clock struck ten. The policeman standing at the gate moved away. Seeing him go, Maaja Vela felt relief flooding over him. He was angry at himself. Old man, you are scared of a sentry now? No, no. He could still go on a heist. He thought of Vana again—of his back as he went through the gate. What if he was caught by the police? As such he could be a terror to hundreds, but today it felt like that boy ought to be next to him.

'Alya, is there something I can use as a pillow?' Maaja Vela asked.

'Dada, use this wicker basket,' a girl replied as she placed the basket under his head.

Maaja felt comforted and lay down. 'The stones feel particularly cold today.' But he lay quietly, watching the children enjoying their meal.

A young woman with a swaying walk came up with a pot on her head. She was Vana's daughter and one of his favourites. She had barely put the pot down when the children surrounded her, saying, 'What have you got for me, Khudi? Khudi, give me.'

'Hold on. I've got something very nice. Just have some patience,' she said, as she covered the pot with one hand, and with the other, held the children at bay. The children surrounded her with their dirty plates in their hands. With the grace of a queen, Khudi said, 'Listen, sit down lanbandh, in a line. Each one will get something. Okay?' But first, she went to her beloved 'Dada'.

'Dada, are you asleep? Do you want something to eat?'

Maaja Vela awoke with a start. Seeing Khudi in the faint light, affection rushed into his eyes. 'Is it Khudi? What is it, beta? What have you got?'

Khudi whispered into his ear, 'Ice cream!'

'Ice cream on a night like this!'

'Yes, Dada, I landed near a kalub. There were tons and tons of leaf plates with ice cream left on them. Have a little please, Dada.'

'No, no, I don't feel so good.'

'You'll be all right, Dada, have a little. For me.' And Maaja Vela gave in to Khudi's insistence. He sat up a bit and drank the melted ice cream from a leaf bowl. Every now and then he wiped his luxuriant moustache with his hand that was covered with ice cream.

The children who were also enjoying this treat noticed this and laughed uproariously, 'Look, look at Dada's moustache.'

Once he was done with the ice cream, Maaja Vela found the stones beneath him colder. He asked, 'Girls, is there something I can spread here?'

Khudi came up to him, and seeing him shivering, she felt his body with her hand and called out, 'Dada, you have a really high fever. Let us go back to the vaas.'

'It will come down. We will go back once your father returns.'

Other men came closer to Maaja Vela and said, 'Kaka, aren't you well? Why did you come in this condition? Just see how hot you have become.' They sat around him, talking among themselves, and doing justice to the food that had arrived. Khudi grabbed some of the old clothes from the women selling pots and pans, and spread them beneath her Dada. Maaja Vela felt better.

'Daughter, may you live to be a hundred. Sit, child, sit by me for a while.' And he gently caressed her head. To himself, he said, 'Mother Khodiyar, oh my mother Khodiyar.'

Khudi was a blessing from Goddess Khodiyar. The old man had managed to keep her alive after all sorts of appeasements to the mother goddess. The old man loved her more than his own children and grandchildren.

'Beta, do you see your father anywhere?' His discomfort had begun to grow. Khudi stood up and looked towards the gate.

Almost everyone had finished eating. The children were still eating. They called out the names of the items as they ate. Maaja Vela smiled to himself as he heard them. 'Wretched ones, starving all the time. Their fathers hardly bring anything for them.'

The movement of passers-by had reduced to a trickle and the

shops around had begun to pull down their shutters. One by one, the lights of the shops were extinguished. Only a street light at a distance cast its light. Only now did it feel as if night had fallen.

Maaja Vela's glance suddenly went to the tower. 'Oh how tall have they made this. What if it crashes?' Maaja Vela felt as if the tower was shaking. 'You've begun to get old, Maaja Vela,' the old man said to himself. 'There was a time when you could leap down from such a place and run. A time when you leapt down from running trains.'

And thrilling scenes from his life flashed before his eyes. How cowardly was this generation when compared to his? Broke into this house, or picked someone's pocket, or picked up something from somewhere. That's it. Yes, Vana was different. He was really bold, someone who'd keep Maaja Vela's name alive. This reminded him that Vana had not yet returned, and he called out, 'Hasn't Vana come back?'

'He'll be here shortly. Come, let's go.' The men got up. 'Come, Dada, we will drop you to your house. How much you are shivering, old man.'

'Go if you want to. Vana and I will come together.' The old man turned his face towards the tower as he lay down.

'Here he is. He has come, my father has come,' Khudi called out. The old man turned his head. From the gate, Vana could be seen walking swiftly yet cautiously. They all waited eagerly for him.

Vana arrived and uncovered a wicker basket wrapped in a cloth. The children surrounded it. 'What is it, what is it?' they asked.

'Everything,' Vana said, irritably.

'Does it have uttarpheni?' one of the twins asked.

'Yes,' Vana laughed and began to open the basket.

He took out a fragrant item that looked like a white dung pat. He distributed it among the children.

'Alya, did you feed Dada or not?' Vana asked around. 'Fed him ice cream, Khudi? Wah re wah. Go on, give Dada a plate.'

He took a plate and filled it with a little bit of each item in the basket. He took it to the old man and said, 'Dada, will you taste something?'

Maaja Vela sat up. As was his habit, he sat on his haunches, held the plate in his right hand, and with the left began to feel each of the items. 'It has turned dark. I can't see properly. What have you got?'

'Why don't you identify each item, Dada?' Vana laughed.

'All right then.' Maaja Vela smiled back at him and took a bite of each of the items. 'This is jalebi. And this is halwa. This is Mysore pak. And this is boondi laddu. And what is this? Magas or mohanthal. Arre, you also got suttarpheni?' He called Vana and whispered, 'Where did you get all this from? Is everything all right?'

'Mother Khodiyar will take care of everything. Don't worry. Enjoy yourself.' Vana got up, distributed all the items, and threw away the basket in a garbage bin some distance away.

Sitting on his haunches, Maaja Vela ate with deep satisfaction. As was his habit, he caressed his moustache with the back of his hand. While eating the suttarpheni, he was reminded of Khambat. He saw the rising tide of the sea. Yes, that was the biggest heist of his life. After the heist in Khambat, they had escaped to Kathiawad in a boat and throughout that journey by sea they had lived on suttarpheni. Finally he addressed his children, 'Alya, did you eat the suttarpheni?'

'Yes, Dada, this, isn't it?' Three or four children came up to him with suttarpheni in their hands and offered it to their grandfather.

'I've eaten enough, beta. Now you eat. It's your time.'

Suddenly, he called Vana. His voice had changed.

Vana rushed towards him, 'What is it, Dada?'

'Hold me, beta. Something is happening to me.' Vana sat by the old man. 'Give me something to lean against,' the old man said. His entire body was trembling.

Vana wrapped a blanket tightly around Maaja Vela and said, 'Dada, lean on me.'

'Where is Khudi? My mother Khodiyar?'

'Here I am, Dada,' Khudi came up to him.

Maaja Vela said, 'Come, my child, may you live to be a hundred.'

He put his hand on her head. 'Vana, find a good husband for my Khudi.' And saying 'Khodiyar, Mother Khodiyar', he placed his head in his nephew's lap.

Vana took the plate from Maaja Vela's hand and put it down. The old man had eaten almost everything. Vana cleaned the old man's whiskers.

'What happened? What happened?' Everybody gathered around.

'Nothing,' Vana said in a firm voice. 'Nobody should weep. The old man has gone in peace.'

A pall of silence fell over the gathering. A couple of people tried to lift Maaja Vela, but Vana said, 'You will not be able to manage.' He lifted the old man onto his shoulders and began to walk.

Accompanying him was Maaja Vela's progeny, numbering almost thirty, walking along slowly and talking among themselves in low voices, 'Maaja Vela had a grand death. A peaceful death. A glorious death.'

A DROP OF BLOOD
JAYANT KHATRI

Despite two days of rain in the month of Ashadh, the skies had not cleared. And yet, it wasn't heavily overcast either. It was the night of Poornima. At times, the dark clouds engulfed the moon, and at times, they rose mist-like and wafted across the moon, making it look slimmer. The night was quiet and sombre. Yet sleep eluded Bechar—not that it really bothered him. Never before had he gone over the events of his life. When he summed up his life, it did not make him happy. His mind was agitated, and it was slipping away from his control. He fell prey to his own thoughts.

Generally speaking, he was not the kind of person who would fall prey to anything or anyone—his personality was made of fire and brimstone.

Today, he was returning home after having served his term in jail. So, he went over his life in his mind:

He had married—that was usual. But his father died at a critical time, and his house was immediately confiscated. He could not pay off his father's debts. His small home and smithy had also been taken away from him owing to debts. He had consumed alcohol for the first time at the age of seventeen. By twenty, he had managed to steal without getting caught. When he was twenty-eight years old, he went to prison for the first time. At thirty-six, he had hit Jethubha, the village headman. When Jethubha grovelled at his feet, he was overcome with contempt. He had gone with the intention of killing him; instead he chopped off Jethubha's nose. From that point, he went back to blacksmithing. And four years went by. His son was twelve years old. Even his daughter was old enough to be betrothed. This was when an old companion said to him, 'Bechar, there's a great opportunity that we will never get again. There's a merchant carrying stolen goods with him. He is expected to bypass the taluka police station and come via the canal. And he is accompanied only by Kheemo, his servant.' He paused meaningfully, and then added, 'We should not miss this opportunity.'

Bechar firmly turned down the idea, 'No way. No more heists.'

'Bechar,' his accomplice said, 'you see these hands? These hands don't have the strength they used to have. You think I would wait for you otherwise? I am merely asking for your hands. I will take care of the rest. If I mess up anything in my planning, I promise to let you get away. I am asking only for your hands. It's shameful for me to beg like this, but what do I do? At least you manage to work and earn a living. But I do not have the blood for business flowing through my veins. And I need to refill the empty vessels in my house; never mind what happens to me in that process. Do you understand? I don't care what happens to me.'

Bechar did not say anything. The iron rod in the furnace had turned red-hot.

Bechar drank alcohol after almost seven years. He drank like never before. 'What? Oh yes, yes, yes!' He put his arm around his accomplice.

Whatever might have been the reason—poor planning by his accomplice or Bechar's lack of strength—the plan did not go through. Not just that, his accomplice deceived him in the end.

Bechar's eyes sparked. But they both belonged to the same clan of thugs. Keeping with the principles of his clan, he did not squeal on his accomplice, but while coming out of the court, he did give him a piece of his mind: 'May God keep you alive until I come out of jail. I will settle my score with you, make no mistake.'

His eyes remained fiery until he reached the prison gates. At some distance from the gates, he saw someone who had walked eight miles to get there, standing quietly and calmly. The fire in his eyes subsided. His tension drained away and he lowered his head in embarrassment. It was his wife. He had thought she would chastise him and say, 'So you will not listen to anyone's advice, will you? On what basis did you swear by your beloved son's life...?'

But she said nothing of the sort and watched him with cold eyes. Bechar was disconcerted. His wife asked him with equanimity, 'How many years?'

'Five-and-a-half.'

'How will you manage? Your body is not that resilient any more. Why did you do this?'

'Stop worrying about me,' Bechar said, 'Listen to me. Kanaiyo is grown up and he is my own blood, after all. I might have stolen and participated in heists, but I have the mind that is required for the job. Kanaiyo is a fool; he has some of your tenderness. Do you understand? You keep an eye on him. He is half-baked and dangerous. I am not worried about you. Nor am I worried about myself. But you take care of him. Make sure that my blood that is flowing through his veins does not heat up. Understood? And....' Bechar hesitated, 'And don't look at me like that.... Understood? Say something at least.'

The prison gates had closed behind him, but that steady and cold gaze stayed with him for days. She returned to meet him after two months. She made a couple of more visits over the next few months. When she visited Bechar after six months, Bechar held her by her shoulders and asked, 'Why did you take so long to come? Kanaiyo…is he all right?'

'Yes, he's fine. He wanted to come and meet you so—'

'No, no,' Bechar did not let her finish, 'don't bring him here.'

'That's why I couldn't come. I made an excuse that I was going to Dwarka and somehow managed to come and see you. I may not be able to any more.'

'What do you mean you may not be able to? Why?'

She hesitated.

'You are hiding something from me. How is Kanaiyo? What is that swine up to? How is the smithy doing?'

'The smithy is gone.'

'What?'

'Yes. Kanaiyo has started to trade.'

'Trade? Trade what? An ironsmith's son is into trading? That scoundrel, bloody thief....'

'Why are you hurling abuses at him? Watch your own doings first; at least compared to you....'

Bechar stood up. His eyes brimmed with fire. 'I am a thief, I am a scoundrel, right? Did you just realize that? So why do you come knocking here? Go on then, look for another man.'

'What did you just say?' She straightened her back. 'Say it again, will you? Worms will crawl out of your tongue if you speak like that, understood?'

Bechar looked down, ashamed. 'I...I....' He could not speak further. 'But why are you provoking me?'

Neither said anything for the next few minutes. Then his wife stood up. 'I am leaving. And I will take proper care of your son, all right? But by the time you are out, make sure your temper is reined in. I will not be able to tolerate it much more.'

Bechar noticed that she had choked down a sob. He sat and watched her as she left, light and firm-footed.

Years went by. He was released from prison.

Bechar was now done going over everything that had happened in his life. But it did not satisfy him. Something was amiss. Something nagged at him. He had not yet found an answer to certain questions. His discomfort increased.

It was a rainy night in Ashadh. A gust of wind blew every now and then before all went still, as if the panting and heaving night had slipped into a restful languor.

When Bechar came out of the dharamshala, the sky was clear. The leaves of an imli tree rustled softly in the distance. The waters of the river, brimming with youthfulness, gushed noisily.

About ten to twelve carts were waiting for the waters in the river to subside, but the river continued to flow, brimming from bank to bank. Today, even the camel carrying the post had not been able to cross.

The dharamshala was occupied by a strange assortment of people—a Brahmin family, servants, a Bania bride with stars in her eyes, waiting to meet her husband's family, peasants, couriers, and now, even the postman.

This evening, the river had abandoned all restraint. Its waters overflowed the embankment and inundated the fields on the far side, ruining the harvest of jowar.

But that evening a girl arrived—a potter! She must have walked a mile or so. She seemed most impatient to cross the river. On seeing the river in spate she sat down under a peepul tree and began to weep. Bechar went and stood before her. At first, he didn't know what to say, as the girl continued to weep.

'What is all this fuss?' Bechar asked.

'I want to go across the river,' she replied.

'Hmm. You think the rest of us want to sit here and twiddle our thumbs? You will only be able to cross when the river calms down. Cry all you want.'

But the girl continued to cry, and kept saying, 'I want to go... please, I want to go....'

Darkness had begun to descend, and the wind had dropped.

Bechar steadied his gaze upon the girl. Such delicate situations were very rare in his life. And in such situations, his wife would always take charge. Bechar was truly at a loss. He struggled to make light of the matter.

'All right, enough is enough. Get up now.'

The girl did not.

'Are you deaf or what?' Bechar retreated to his old habits, and harsh words escaped him, 'Do you want to go to the dharamshala or not? Or you want to spend the night on this otla? You're being foolish.'

'The dharamshala has all Brahmin–Bania people,' the girl responded amidst sobs.

'So what? You think their ancestors built the dharamshala! Who will dare to object? On your feet, now. Let's go.'

The girl stood up and walked ahead, as the rainy evening reluctantly dispersed its hues around her. In the fading light of the evening, Bechar observed the young woman's silhouette, as she walked with her head downcast, and it occurred to him that the girl had a shapely body. The thought was a fleeting one. But it triggered such memories that Bechar muttered to himself, 'What is the bloody matter with me today?'

While entering the courtyard of the dharamshala, Bechar asked her, 'What's your name?'

The girl blurted out hastily, 'Halima'. Bechar felt that there was a faint smile on her face as she spoke, 'Halima, the daughter of Nathu Haasam. Do you know my father?'

'No,' Bechar replied as he climbed the steps of the dharamshala. He was distracted. Upon entering one of the rooms, he pointed to a corner and said loudly so that everyone could hear, 'Stay there now, and if someone bothers you, shower them with colourful abuses.'

He lay down against a pillar some distance away. Everyone was busy eating. He looked at Halima carefully under the light of the Bania's lantern. She was quite beautiful. She must be barely sixteen years old. He could not see her eyes clearly. But Bechar felt that when she wasn't crying, her face looked radiant.

Bechar fell into thought. Halima ate something she had carried with her and went out to wash her hands. Lost in his thoughts, Bechar did not notice Halima pass by him.

Halima jolted him out of his reverie, 'Kaka, did you eat?'

Kaka? Bechar sat up and managed to say gruffly, 'No, I don't want to eat.'

'I can give you some food.' She stood next to him. A sudden gust of wind made her dupatta fly, and one end brushed against Bechar's face.

'Oh really? Now off you go… "I can give you", she says,' Bechar made a feeble attempt to laugh.

Halima ran to her corner and turned her head ever so slightly to look at him with an alluring smile. Had it not been dark, Bechar would have been embarrassed at his own laughter. He felt somewhat sheepish. In his awkwardness, his turban fell off his head. Bechar propped it up as a pillow and lay down to rest.

All the lights in the dharamshala went off and a thick layer of darkness descended upon everything. Bechar was far from being asleep. He peered into the soothing darkness. Initially, his thoughts did not disturb him. But gradually, they pushed him to the edge. It was past midnight by then and Bechar had become very restless. He lit one bidi after the other. His chest felt constricted and his head became heavy.

He ventured out of the dharamshala for some air.

The earth was pregnant with the weight of Ashadh. Black and white clouds moved in the breeze and the full moon played hide-and-seek among them. The breeze, the play of darkness and light, the fecund and capricious earth created an atmosphere that made one want to curl up under a blanket.

Bechar leaned against the parapet and stood for a while, looking at everything around him until the cool breeze made his eyes droop. Still standing, his head dropped and he almost dozed off. When his eyes flew open, he noticed that someone was fast asleep on the mattress next to him.

When he realized that it was Halima, he was filled with dread and immediately turned his face away. But that feeling was transient. For the second time that night, he turned to look at her with confidence.

She had used a stone slab as her pillow. The breeze had moved her dupatta, leaving her chest and stomach uncovered, and baap re, how unruly her blouse was! Hanging by a zari thread with one golden bead, a large square and silver pendant went up and down on her heaving chest.

This time, Bechar could not take his eyes off her. Eventually, he stopped thinking. He had no idea what he was doing. Halima hadn't stirred yet. One leg lay on another outstretched leg. The fingers of her right hand seemed inches away from her lips as they lay on her cheek. Her left arm, curled like a snake, lay by her side. Bechar was lost in this scene. For some time, the world around him ceased to exist. The minutes flew by. His eyes drooped.

When they reopened, his eyes had changed colour. The lines around them deepened. A five-and-a-half-year-old unfulfilled hunger was rekindled.

Such beauty—such youthfulness! And such tender youth it was. An ugly smile played on Bechar's lips and his eyes lost restraint. His chest felt warmer. His muscles tensed.

With the stealth of a cat, Bechar jumped across the parapet and cast a careful glance at the dharamshala. Then, before focusing on Halima's body, he inadvertently looked at the horizon where the sky and the earth met.

The atmosphere was filled with indolence. When his eyes turned back to Halima, he felt a current course through him. He was now a slave to his sight.

Halima's body seemed to drip like water from the stone slab she was resting against. Her soft eyelids, her rosy lips, and her.... Bechar's demonic body felt taut and....

The agility of a thief and the firmness of a bandit came naturally to Bechar, and he was not one to hesitate or retreat.

The seconds ticked by. Yet Bechar stood, unmoving. The imli tree whispered gently. The moon had not re-emerged from behind the clouds. All was conducive. The world around seemed lost in this intoxicating atmosphere.

But something had happened to Bechar. His desire refused to be nudged this way or that. It seemed frozen, almost dead. When had he bothered about being judged, worried about what was appropriate and inappropriate, and who cared if somebody saw him, who really cared? So what was stopping Bechar then? What was this? What kind of a strange state was this! Had something happened to him? Bechar looked at Halima yet again. That innocent girl was oblivious—she continued to lie like that—she wouldn't be able to let out a peep. Bechar felt like laughing, and the same desire welled up inside him again.

The moon came out from behind the clouds now, and the imli tree shrugged its leaves and grunted. Bechar smiled deviously. He bent down further, then stopped. Baap re! That heaving chest, that pendant swinging delightfully over it, like a bird on a swaying branch. So beautiful, so soft, so pure! He would bend over it and that would be the end of that softness and beauty. His eyes reflected the gamut of emotions flickering through his mind.

Fear gripped him. He straightened himself. His body lost its tension. He turned his face away, and he lifted his gaze high, very high. His eyes went beyond the imli tree, beyond the clouds gathering and dispersing, even beyond the moon, stars, and constellations—far away, lost in the ever-expanding vastness.

Something was forming, or had already formed, he realized. He let out a sigh.

He meant to walk away, but changed his mind and came back. He gently covered, without a touch of desire, Halima's body with her odhni. He did not need to see anything. The image had inhabited his consciousness, and it stayed there.

Halima's odhni brushed against her body and woke her up. Startled, she exclaimed, 'Oh…oh.'

Bechar looked at her with an indulgent and amused eye.

'See the way you were asleep, I thought I should put your….' Bechar found it difficult to continue.

Halima looked at her dishevelled clothes and stood up with lightning speed, hiding her body behind her odhni. 'What are you doing here?'

'I was not able to sleep so I came out and when I saw you like this….' Bechar again became tongue-tied.

'Oh come on!' Saying this, Halima leaned against the banister, and laughed lightly. 'You neither want to eat nor sleep, right, Kaka?'

'Look, girl, stop calling me kaka, all right?'

'Arre!' Halima made a coquettish gesture, 'Why, is that an abusive word? If not kaka, should I say son?' her dulcet voice merged with other sounds of nature.

'Say Bechar.'

'No, no, Bechar kaka.' And in the hours past midnight a melodious laugh merged with a gruff one.

'Go on, Kaka, go to sleep.'

'And you?'

'I will sleep here.'

'You are so naïve, girl. Aren't you scared?'

'Of whom? And if something happens to me, you are hardly far away.'

Bechar went inside and placed his turban on the ground. He encountered the same darkness, the same wakefulness, and the same stock-taking of his life, but he no longer felt tormented. He felt satisfied with his conclusions. He fell asleep.

The next morning, the sky was somewhat overcast, and the breeze of a receding cyclone had begun to blow. Bullock carts were poised to leave, queued up in the courtyard of the dharamshala. The river had receded enough for people to cross, and the bank was crowded with people waiting to undertake the journey across the river. Bechar woke up quite late. His first thought was about Halima. He swiftly tied his turban and ran out. He saw the carts leaving. But Halima was not to be seen. He washed his hands at the well, and spotted Halima at some distance, washing clothes. Bechar immediately went up to her and asked her indulgently, 'So very efficient of you! Could you not have washed the clothes near the stepwell instead of coming this far?'

Halima quickly hid the clothes she was washing behind her. Her eyes were downcast. Bechar noticed that Halima's eyes seemed sore, as if from weeping continuously. Her cheeks and her hands had marks on them, and she quivered. Before Halima could stop him, he leapt and snatched the clothes from her. They were stained with blood. Her blouse had been torn to pieces.

'Who was the monster?' Bechar bellowed. 'Just tell me the name, and I will smash his bones to smithereens.'

Halima broke down. With her head bent, almost touching her shaking knees, she cried inconsolably, without any inhibition. Fury was writ large in Bechar's eyes.

'Has the bastard cut off your tongue? Speak up, woman, who's that son of a swine?'

Embarassed, Halima looked up and said, 'Speak softly, please. My honour has been defiled, now why do you want to announce it to the world?'

An unsteady Bechar went and sat down on a stone and lit a bidi. With downcast eyes, Halima said, 'I don't know exactly what but it happened at dawn. Before I could wake up and call out for help, someone had pressed his hand on my mouth and gripped both my hands, I....' She began weeping again. 'There were two of them, and I...I fought back a lot, less worried about losing my life than.... But "it" did take place. I didn't recognize him; in fact, I didn't even see his face. But he was wearing a silk kurta, he had a ring on his finger, and his little finger had been cut off...the monster...oh mother....'

Bechar was infuriated. He clenched his fists. His chest, wide like that of a king's stallion, jutted out. 'If only you had recognized him,' he said, 'I would have pulled his entrails out.'

'What's the point now?' Halima stood up. Bechar continued to sit. For a few minutes neither spoke.

'All right, come now,' Bechar said, 'My house is across the river, you can rest there and then go your way.'

Halima followed him, but her gait had lost the nimbleness of before.

Most people had left by now and had crossed the river. A solitary bullock cart of a low-caste man waited for a customer. Bechar negotiated a rate with him and he and Halima climbed atop the cart. The bullocks moved into the waters that had receded, but a vast expanse stretched before them. Far away, guava, jamun, and mango trees in a Patel's orchard fought against the blowing winds. The sky looked stifled by the restless clouds that covered it.

Bechar couldn't find the words any more. Halima sat behind him, with her hand on his shoulder. 'You know, Kaka,' she said softly, 'I am just unfortunate, I have wretched luck. The moment I was born, my mother passed away. By the time I was thirteen, our little house had been mortgaged, my brother had passed away, and of the thirteen donkeys we had, only one was left. Now my father is on his deathbed.' She sighed, 'If this wasn't enough, my husband has thrown me out of his house.'

Startled, Bechar turned around and looked into her eyes. He saw that those eyes reflected a lot of pain, nearly congealed over time. But he blurted out, 'What? Threw you out? But you are such a looker!'

'Yes, and smart too! That's the problem. I have a cheerful disposition, and like all human beings, sometimes I get carried away. At my parents' home and at my in-laws', there's abject poverty. So I felt I needed to tread carefully and keep myself under check. Else, they'll conclude all kinds of things; peoples' tongues also wag....' Halima's eyes brimmed over. 'But I turned out to be my own enemy, and had to leave my in-laws' home as well. People carried tales about me wherever I went. That was what I had feared, and it came true. My own nature let me down. Even when my husband lost his temper, I took it lightly and laughed it off. He kicked me and threw me out. I am cursed.'

Bechar felt despondent. Soon they reached the other bank. Bechar jumped out of the cart, Hamila followed.

'Be careful, hanh. The earth is slippery that side,' he told her.

They climbed a hillock from where they could see Bechar's village.

'See that? That lane and that house with a huge mango tree? That's mine,' Bechar smiled wanly, 'I'm seeing it after five-and-a-half years today.'

'Really? Were you away for business in some foreign land?'

'No,' Bechar replied, 'I was in prison! He he he,' he forced a hoarse laugh, but the next moment his flippancy was gone. Halima walked alongside him as he slowed down. His face turned grim again. 'I am a thief, do you understand? You are not afraid of me, are you?'

'Afraid of whom? You, Bechar kaka?' Halima looked at him steadily, 'You are not a thief in my eyes.' She looked at him and smiled a sad smile. That was her first smile of the day. Bechar's heart brimmed with happiness. He laughed, 'Of course I am a thief, and a very distinguished one.'

By this time they had reached his house. The little gate at the entrance was open. Bechar noticed a horse tethered in front of the house.

'What is this?' he said, 'A horse in my front yard? It looks like an empire was set up in my absence!'

Upon hearing his voice, his wife rushed to the door, 'It's you! I was sure that it was your voice I had heard!' Bechar sprung up to the otla of the house and stood right next to her. 'Hmm...you look well! What is this naatak going on here? Whose horse is this?'

Halima came up and stood behind Bechar unobtrusively.

Bechar's wife laughed. 'It's Kanaiyo's horse. He just crossed the river and came home. Didn't he meet you at the dharamshala across the river?'

'But where the hell is that ass?' Bechar became impatient.

'He's eating in the kitchen.'

'Here I am!' Just then Kanaiyo came out of the kitchen, smiling. His eyes fell upon Halima, and his expression changed to shock. He stood wide-eyed, frozen.

Halima let out a scream, and collapsed against Bechar. The heap of clothes she was carrying fell and her wet clothes lay scattered, the faded blood stains still visible on them. Bechar's eyes flew towards them. With the speed of a veteran thief, his eyes went to Kanaiyo and he noticed that his son was also looking at her clothes. He also realized that Kanaiyo was wearing a silk kurta, he had a ring on his finger, and his little finger was missing.

Bechar gritted his teeth in anger, 'You...you scoundrel, you devil!' Before anyone could stop him, he struck Kanaiyo. When his hand descended, it made a heavy thudding sound. Kanaiyo collapsed to the floor and blood spurted from his mouth.

'Arre! What have you done? Have you returned thirsting for blood now?' His wife bent over Kanaiyo like an Ashadh cloud over the earth. 'What crime has he committed? What has he done to you?'

Bechar held his wife's hand and pushed her away brutally. 'You are asking me? Ask this swine what he's done.'

Kanaiyo stood up, blood dripping from his mouth, and ran into the house with lightning speed. Bechar made to chase him, but almost toppled over Halima, who had fallen at his feet. With tears rolling down her cheeks she said, 'Kaka, please, let him go, Kaka please.'

'Shut up,' Bechar disentangled his foot. 'Kaka, she says!'

'You return after years and....' His wife had a stream of tears on her face, 'and this gem of a son is....'

'Gem?' Bechar roared. 'Here, look at her, this bud of a girl whom he raped.... I say whose son is he, that scoundrel, whose drop of blood is in him?'

The meaning of his own words dawned upon Bechar and he muttered to himself, 'Whose drop of blood?' The Ashadh clouds flashed before his eyes. Gone was the fury—his eyes were lifeless now. An image appeared before him, the alluring atmosphere of the previous evening—the whistling of the wind, the sensuousness of a rainy night, a pendant swinging on a heaving chest, a night that you could lose yourself in.

Bechar collapsed to the floor with a thud. His eyes had never shed a tear, but today they welled up and overflowed. His wife sat down beside him and gently ran her fingers through his hair, saying, 'I want to ask as well, whose drop of blood?'

ONCE UPON A TIME IN NAIMESHARANYA
SURESH JOSHI

'Once upon a time in Naimesharanya, there was a sage who had immersed himself in penance for a thousand years. His face was suffused with divine light. In this universe filled with the infernal sufferings of the mind, the body, and the environment, this sage was a fount of serenity. The leaves did not sigh in despair as they fell from the trees above him. They came down, instead, like flowers reciting Vedic hymns not heard before.' He realized he was letting his imagination run wild. He paused as if for breath and looked at the woman sitting in front of him. Her eyes were rimmed red and tears glistened on her lashes. He could hear her long, warm sighs. Grief had turned the face of this middle-aged woman almost ugly.

He resumed, 'Once, it so happened that in the city of Shravasti, a wealthy merchant, Parmanandas, set out on a voyage and never came back. Seasons came and went, but there was not a trace of him. The sun rose in the firmament every day but its bright rays did not succeed in drying the tears of the sethani—Ratnalakshmi, the merchant's wife. Every year, as monsoon set in and dark clouds gathered, the darkness that enveloped her heart grew deeper, so much so that even the light of the winter moon could not dissipate it. Whether the gods had turned away from her or her good deeds had amounted to nothing or the sins of her past lives had caught up with her, the merchant's wife collapsed with the pain of her suffering after her only son suddenly disappeared one day. High and low they searched, but not a trace of him was to be found. What was to be done now? Astrologers were summoned. They came, consulted their charts, collected their fees, and left after giving false assurances. Witch doctors arrived, as did practitioners of the dark arts. They also gave assurances to the sethani, but she did not see the face of her son for many years. Pain echoed in all the corners of their mansion which was filled with servants and slaves. The light slowly dimmed in the sethani's eyes. She fell at the feet of God and prayed, "O Lord, before you take away the light of these eyes, let them rest on my beloved son once." Days passed, as did the nights, but the halls of their mansion remained empty. The courtyard stood desolate and her heart continued to ache.

'At that time, an accomplished yogi arrived in the city of Shravasti. He set himself up in an ancient Shiva temple outside the city. The sethani ran to him with a platter of precious stones. Tearfully, she entreated him, "Please find my son so that I may see his face." The yogi did not open his eyes. He drew something in the dust with his fingers, pointing in a direction, but no one understood what he meant. The yogi's disciple took pity on the woman and explained to her, "If you walk in the northerly direction for seven days and seven nights, you will come to Naimesharanya. There, underneath a large banyan tree, sits a sage who has immersed himself in penance for thousand years—do not ask him anything. Do not disturb his meditation. Be patient. If fortune smiles on you, he will help you find your son."

'The sethani set out immediately with her retinue. She braved rain and sun until she reached a dense forest, where the sage sat in meditation. Without a murmur, she fell at his feet, watching him. The sethani's luck transformed. On the tenth day, the sage said, "In the period of the pushya nakshatra, your son will come from the west. But only if you recognize him will he enter your house. If you fail to do so, he will disappear once again." The sethani's joy knew no bounds.

'Suddenly, the sage stopped. He became circumspect, "What am I saying? Why am I lying that this woman's son will come back? Can you lie to someone out of pity? Don't I know that he has drowned in the sea at Juhu? Don't I also know that this woman's husband ran away with another woman and has started a new life in a city in the south? But what can I offer someone who has no use for the truth and whose only source of support is that which is false?"

'The woman asked, "Why have you stopped? What has happened? Please tell me quickly." This insistence baffled him. He continued, however. The sethani was filled with joy but the next moment a thought crossed her mind, "How many years have passed since I last saw my son? Who knows what he looks like now.... He must be a young man now.... The scars on his knees where he had scraped himself in childhood would have disappeared. How will I recognize him?"'

The woman listening to his story spoke up. 'Is it possible for a mother not to be able to recognize her son? If my son came back I would recognize him immediately. I would smell his head and caress his face....'

The woman was speaking as if her son were standing before her! He grew angry at himself once again. Why did I even start this story? Let me quickly wrap this up and escape from here. He rushed towards the conclusion, 'The sethani thought for some time and then she remembered an important detail. Her son's little finger on one hand was shorter than the little finger on the other. This recollection brought her immense joy. After that the sethani began looking out of her window in the city of Shravasti. The auspicious period of pushya nakshatra arrived. A young man turned up one day and stood in the courtyard. The servants were on the verge of driving him out when the sethani rushed in. She grabbed the young man's hand and upon inspecting his little finger, she hugged him tight. Her son had returned after so many years. The atmosphere was filled with festivities.'

As he concluded his story, a sharp jolt of pain coursed through his body, as if his insides had cramped. He broke out in sweat. He stood up suddenly, looked at this watch, and exclaimed, 'Oh it's already ten. They must be waiting for me at home. So you heard, right, that everything will be fine? Your Hemant will return.' Without saying anything more, he quickly descended the stairs. He felt as if his strength was draining away. That man with the short little finger could have been an impostor. To what lengths would someone go for such wealth? Cursing humanity, he barely managed to reach home and almost collapsed at the door. His wife came down holding a lamp. Seeing his condition, she became worried. 'Where were you? Where could I have looked for you? And what has happened to you? Look how cold your body has become!' He barely managed to sit down, repeating, 'It's nothing, it's nothing.' But his wife did not believe him. 'How many times have I told you that this town is full of witches? Someone has cast an evil eye on you. Look at your eyes. At least tell me where you were. Who did you meet?'

Once again he replied, 'It is nothing.'

His wife conducted a ritual to mitigate the effect of the evil eye. She sat wondering how to uncover the mystery of what had happened. Her persistence irked him even more. For some time, he sat with his eyes shut. He prayed to God, to that fictional sage of Naimesharanya, 'Turn this whole thing into a mirage, human beings cannot handle the truth. Just turn everything into an illusion.' Helped by his wife, he lay down on his bed. Obediently, he drank the potions his wife gave him. He shut his eyes and went to sleep. He kept hearing the same questions even in his sleep, 'When will I find my son? What has happened to you? Where were you? Speak, speak, speak....'

And in that trance, he mumbled, 'It is nothing. It is nothing.'

Day broke. When he woke up, his wife enquired, 'How are you now?'

He replied brusquely, 'Much better.'

His wife insisted once again, 'So, tell me now, who did you meet? Who cast a spell on you?'

Once again he replied, 'Nothing happened. It's nothing.' But seeing the suspicion in his wife's eyes, he felt that he would have to create something out of this 'nothing'. Only then would she be satisfied. Once again, he entered that forest of stories, Naimesharanya. 'Once upon a time in Naimesharanya, there lived a sage. His penance was of a thousand years. His fame had spread far and wide. Stories of his miracles abounded. It so happened that in the town of Chandrapur there lived a young, happy couple. They were like Kamdev and Rati incarnate. The wife was her husband's shadow. Wherever he went, she followed. The sight of this couple was a treat for the eyes.'

'One day, a yogi arrived in the town, his face glowing with a divine radiance. The entire town came to see this resplendent figure. The yogi was passing through the main street. The husband and wife stood in the balcony, looking down. The husband was saying something, but the wife's attention was on the yogi. The husband was offended. Dhaddhaddhad...he stomped down the stairs and walked out of the house, leaving the door ajar. His wife raced after him, huffing and panting, but how was she to find her husband in the swarming crowd? Her feet ached. Her eyes saw black. At midnight she went all by herself to where the yogi was staying. She said, "Yogiraj, if you are a true sage, bring my husband back." Yogiraj said, "Ben, be patient. Sit down. Listen to what I have to say. I know about your previous birth. In your last birth, your husband was the sage Subadhra, you were the princess Ratnamala. One day, you went into the forest with your friends. You were separated from the group and ended up where Subhadra was meditating. You screamed in desperation. The sage's meditation was disrupted. His eyes fell on you and he was smitten. Your eyes met and the inevitable happened. Then you were married with great pomp and enjoyed all the royal pleasures. One day you asked your husband, "We will be husband and wife in our next life as well, won't we?" At that time your husband said, "Yes. But I have to complete my penance. The moment it's over, we will meet once again. Have patience. At the end of five years, when the sun moves to the south, go to the forest 750 kilometres from the city. There you will see a sage meditating by an old, decrepit Shiva temple. And if you recognize him immediately, he will open his eyes and embrace you. If you delay even slightly in recognizing him, then you will have to wait one more birth to be reunited with him."'

He was still speaking when he was interrupted by a knock on the door. His wife hurriedly got up and opened the door. A distraught woman stood outside. She entered and asked, 'Is Hemant here? I had dozed off when I thought someone knocked on the door. By the time I opened the door, he was quite far away. But I recognized him immediately. It was the same gait, the same shape. He turned this way. Has he come here, my Hemant?'

He stared at her for a while. Then he said, 'Sit. Listen to what I have to say. Once upon a time in Naimesharanya....'

VAADKI

BHUPEN KHAKHAR

Jamna lay flat on the bed, staring blankly at the white ceiling above her. She was miserable. Usually, she looked after her home with meticulous care. Since only two people lived in the house, she had chosen to do the sweeping, mopping, and washing of clothes and utensils herself.

Jamna and Jamnadas had drawn up an agreement soon after their wedding. The agreement contained clauses and subclauses regarding the rules and norms of their married life. It was drawn up on a stamp paper and had been duly signed by both parties. Jamna and Jamnadas each had a copy of the document.

> If Jamna, carried away by sensuousness late one night, suddenly longed for a child, Jamnadas would bring out his copy of the agreement and read out to her: We, the undersigned, Jamnadas Bapapal and Jamna Jamnadas agree to abide by the following:
>
> Section 11, Clause (a)
> If our intimacy, embraces, kisses, foreplay, or reading aloud of pornographic books result in the desire for an offspring, we shall suspend such activities, take a bath in cold water, and thereby bring an end to such desires.

After hearing this, Jamna would be brought back to reality, and desires for a (male) offspring would wither away.

After much deliberation and discussion, Wednesdays and Saturdays had been decreed to be the days for lovemaking. Jamna would, ideally, have liked three days allotted to the purpose instead of two. Prior to the signing of the document this dialogue ensued:

Jamna: If you don't have an objection, can we amend Section 10, Clause (b)?

Jamnadas: What amendment do you propose?

Jamna: You recommended Wednesdays and Saturdays for physical intimacy. I feel we could increase that to three days a week. It will give the body more opportunity for sexual pleasure since we are both in the bloom of youth. I am keen on Thursdays, Saturdays, and Sundays.

Jamnadas: You do have a point about our current state of youthfulness. However, when my father, Bapalal, reached the age of fifty, he called for a carpenter. In our very presence, he made the carpenter divide his double bed into two.

Jamna: Why?

Jamnadas: He had stopped feeling attracted to my mother. His virility had diminished. From that day Bapuji's bed was placed next to the window in the drawing room, while my mother's was left inside the bedroom.

Jamna: So what are we supposed to do?

Jamnadas: This is to say that if we want to make our intimacy last, we should restrict our days allotted for lovemaking to two—Wednesdays and Saturdays, in particular.

Jamna: Why have you chosen those days in particular?

Jamnadas: The late night activities and experiments of a Saturday night may delay our going to bed, but considering the fact that Saturday is followed by Sunday, it does not matter. Furthermore, Monday and Tuesday are not distant from Saturday.

Jamna: Why not Thursday then?

Jamnadas: Thursday is a day of fasting. A weak body cannot generate the strength needed for sensuality.

After such deliberation, Jamna agreed. Jamnadas had just turned fifty-two, but the couple had not felt the need to bring in a carpenter to split their double bed. It was Jamnadas's far-sightedness that had made them last this long. The couple continue to celebrate intimacy on Saturdays and Wednesdays.

Section 10 (a) was constituted as follows:

> We hereby do declare that until Jamnadas Bapalal turns fifty, we will celebrate physical relations on Wednesdays and Saturdays. Thereafter, we will take stock of the situation, keeping Jamnadas's capacity and virility in mind, and should the need arise, a carpenter will be called to split the bed into two. The signatories of this Agreement will also abide by subsection (b) and thereby mutually agree to consider physical pleasure optional on days of the full moon, new moon, moon-in-the sixth phase, and birthday nights.

Jamna and Jamnadas have spent their lives in bliss, following the agreement in word and spirit. However, the golden thali of their life was sullied by an unseemly object: Jamna lost her vaadki, a small bowl.

⸺

On most Saturdays, Jamna's heart jumped with anticipation as she waited for Jamnadas to return. But today, she lay flat on the bed, staring blankly at the white ceiling above her. A tidal wave of sorrow rose within her. Jamnadas came home for lunch. While sipping the kadhi with audible pleasure, he winked at Jamna, happy at the thought that it was a Saturday. He chatted about how the prices of stocks and shares had come down. After lunch, he extracted a Cavanders cigarette from his pocket and blew clouds of smoke all over the room. Jamna's face did not break into a smile. On a normal day, she enjoyed Jamnadas' smoking. She would say, 'When you wear "goggles" and blow rings of smoke, you look exactly like Ashok Kumar!'

Jamna lay on the bed, thinking it was her neighbours in Bhadrikashram who were the source of her unhappiness. How many families did she maintain good relations with? Really, they could be counted on the fingers of one hand. There were thirty families living in Bhadrikashram and yet she was friendly with only six. Among those, the closest relationship she had was with Savita, 'just-like-home', as they say. Savita had been gone for the past two days, ostensibly visiting her natal home, where her brother and his wife lived. God knows if that was even true. There wasn't much love lost between Savita and her bhabhi. It was only two years ago that Savita had sworn she was never going to visit her brother's house. Where could she have gone? Who was she with? Was she fooling people? Jamna was lost in a whirlpool of thoughts.

It was two o'clock on a Saturday afternoon. Savita had returned home that morning and hence was busy with household chores. When Vimlaben went to see her, she was mopping the kitchen floor. The sight of Vimlaben made Savita's heart lurch, 'Oh my God, she's going to start an enquiry regarding my absence.'

Savita: Come, Vimlaben. I was thinking of coming to your place after finishing this work. She said to herself: *How am I answerable to you, standing there like some policeman?*

Vimla: In fact, I also just finished my household chores, and your bhai would have left for office, so I thought I'd drop by and see you. It's been so long since I saw your face.

Savita: What is so interesting about my mug now? *Don't I know you have come to carry out investigations?* I was also so keen to meet you.

Vimla: Yeah sure. *Liar. Where were you for past two days? That's what I want to know.* So how are your bhai and bhabhi?

Savita: *I've been gone for two days and that's giving you a belly ache.* Well, you have to go to your natal home when there are ups and down, no? Bhabhi had not been feeling well, so I went.

Vimla: Women never have it easy. How's she now? *Rascal, whom were you having a dalliance with for two days?*

Savita: If I don't hear from them within a fortnight, I may need to go again.

Vimla: *Nicely done, everything has been fixed for the next visit.* I used to check after my brother, your husband, every day while you were gone.

Savita: *Of course. You love to do that, don't you? Play all coy with other people's husbands.* I know, he was so grateful, he went on and on about how much you looked after him. By the way, Jamna had come to see me.

Vimla: *She just changed the topic, bitch.* So I hear she has lost her vaadki.

Savita: Does she think I have stolen her vaadki? I returned her vaadki three days ago. She comes swaying her big bum every now and then, asking about her vaadki. As though we are all paupers, and she's the only wealthy person here.

Vimla: You know how she is.

Savita: So what can I do? I am not obliged to spend a lifetime with her.

Vimla: She's paranoid. The moment you speak with Jamnadas, she comes and stands like a shield, guarding him.

Savita: *Well, who can blame her for doing that when you're around?* She came twice to check the kitchen, and again this morning.

Vimla: Your 'just-like-home' relations with her have survived, thanks to your maturity.

Savita: Nobody in the building bothers to acknowledge her existence, you know.

Vimla: Jamna was always a petty person. She has lost one vaadki and makes all of Bhadrikashram fuss over it.

Savita: *Like you didn't do that when you lost your tongs. You made enquiries every single day.* I remember you asking around for your tongs a couple of times.

Vimla: I say, if it's destined to be yours, it won't go anywhere.

Savita: *Well, how will it go anywhere! Don't we know it was found at Shivla's home? You used to take hot almond milk for him every day.* So where were the tongs, finally?

Vimla: Why are you pretending to be ignorant? *You were the one who proclaimed from the rooftops that I was visiting Shivla with milk and jalebi every day.*

Savita: No, I really forgot, it's been a while.

Vimla: Oh, I am chatting away here, but I must rush to prepare something for Jaglo. He'll need his afternoon snack. *You have definitely had an affair with someone; I need to find out who it is.*

Jamna sat up. She opened a drawer and took out a piece of paper and a pencil. She sharpened the pencil with a penknife. She sat down on a chair and began to write:

20/3, Monday: I went to give Savita poha in the afternoon. At that time, Savita was sitting on a swing and mending a pair of pyjamas.

22/3, Wednesday: At 9 a.m. I had begun preparations for making vedmi and had put the toor dal to boil. Just then Banku masi came for a vaadki full of gram flour. She must have been in a hurry. She returned the vaadki through Tapuda in the evening.

23/3, Thursday: Jaglo came to borrow my silver vaadki and aachmani on behalf of Vimlaben. They had organized a Satyanarayan puja in the evening. At 9 p.m. they returned the vaadki with prasad in it.

25/3, Saturday: Vimlaben came to borrow a spoonful of curd to set her own. She returned the spoon the following morning.

26/3, Sunday: Savita returned the vaadki with urad dal in it. According to her, that was my vaadki. When the vaadki was returned, Banku masi was around. She remembers the arrival of the vaadki, but does not remember what kind it was. I don't use vaadki with flat rims.

29/3, Wednesday: The hostile Vimla pounced on me because I went to ask her about the vaadki, 'You think I am going to become a millionaire by collecting your vaadkis?' How conveniently she forgot that two years ago she had borrowed a basket from me, and when she was reminded to return it, she simply pretended she hadn't heard. It was a Herculean task to get the basket back from her. Such a liar, she wants to hide everything under her big bum.

1/4, Saturday: I have come to a decision. I will give Vimlaben's Jagla sweets and have him look for vaadki in every house. And if that mission is not successful, I will myself go to every kitchen and carry out an inspection.

Jamna tied up the paper in the knot of her saree, and lay down on the bed. Just then there was a knock on the door.

With a spinning top in one hand and dressed in gaudy clothes, the devil himself appeared at her door.

Jamna: Who is it?

Jaglo: It's me, Jaglo.

Jamna: I was just thinking of you.

Jaglo (running a string around the spinning top and holding a basket under his arm): You would want to get some work done then.

Jamna: Jagla, do you want peppermint sweets?

Jaglo: You offer those to me when you want me to do something. Hamein kabool nahin hai, manzoor nahin hai. (It is not acceptable to me.) What is being asked of me? The rate of carrying Savita's letter is a rupee; gone are the days of five peppermint sweets.

Jamna: Twenty-five paise.

Jaglo: I am not a beggar, your majesty. Don't even mention anything less than fifty paise.

Jamna: Who did you give Savita's letter to?

Jaglo: One rupee for revealing the name. State the task.

Jamna (walking towards the almirah): I am giving you a rupee, but you will have to tell me everything. And I will give you fifty paise once you are done with my assignment.

Jaglo (putting the rupee in his pocket): A week ago, I was sent with a letter to Vithalsadan to give it to Shantilal. I haven't mentioned this to anybody else. Now tell me what you want me to do.

Jamna: See, I am writing down five names from our building. Go to their kitchens and read the names engraved on their vaadkis. If the vaadki says Jamnadas Bapalal, then tell me at whose house you found it.

Jalgo: That's a lot of work. I will have to first deal with the children to check vaadkis at people's houses. You will have to pay me more for this.

Jamna: I will pay you for your efforts, but I must know by the second of next month.

⁂

Hmm, so Savitaben has begun to exchange letters with Shantilal. It will hardly be a surprise if she had been with him for the two days that she was missing. Shantilal's wife has gone to her parents' home for childbirth, and Savita has clearly made use of the opportunity. Human beings are unpredictable; you never know when they fall in and out of love.

Every Thursday, Jamna would light incense and joss sticks and place them in all the corners of the house. She would decorate her hair with flowers. Dinner usually consisted of dal dhokli and the bedroom lights would go off early that evening. On Saturdays and Wednesdays, Jamnadas would not sit outside at the otla of his house, chatting with the neighbours.

Today, as usual, Jamnadas sat down for his supper. Jamna had not made dal dhokli. It was customary to make dal dhokli every Saturday and vedmi every Wednesday. The dhokli was made with softly kneaded puris, moist with a considerable amount of ghee. Jamna would insist on adding spoonfuls of ghee to the vedmi while feeding him on Wednesdays. Today, there was neither insistence nor enthusiasm or love—nothing. Jamnadas gulped down the food with his head bowed. He washed his hands and while chewing on betel nut, asked, 'Why are you so sulky today?'

Jamna didn't say a word, just quietly picked up the dishes to put them into the sink outside the kitchen.

Jamnadas: Hello, why are you so angry with me today? Have you forgotten that it's Saturday?

Jamna: Who said I am angry at you?

Janadas: Then why did you decide to torture me with dudhi bataka today? It was a dal dhokli day today.

Jamna: I know.

Jamnadas: You know that I don't eat this kind of sick people's food.

Jamna: When I put away the dishes I noticed that you had hardly touched the vegetable.

Jamnadas: What is bothering you?

Jamna: Go ask your neighbours here at Bhadrikashram. They have not left a stone unturned in making my life miserable.

Jamnadas: What has happened?

Jamna: What has not happened, you should ask.

Jamnadas: Consider that question asked.

Jamna: Do you remember five years ago we had bought a set of stainless steel vaadkis on Dhanteras?

Jamnadas: What? When?

Jamna: Arre, when Neetu was born at Motabhai's. That same year you had a fracture in your arm during Navratri. That year, we had bought a set of eight vaadkis for eighty rupees.

Jamnadas: So what of it?

Jamna: One of them is missing.

Jamnadas: Never mind, we will get a new one.

Jamna: That type is not available any more.

Jamnadas: A better one may be available. Don't spill tears over this.

Jamna: Someone steals our vaadki and we go buy a new set like children? I want the very same vaadki, and let me be damned if I don't find out who took it.

Jamnadas: You can continue breaking your head over this, but I refuse to do so. Let me know when you want a new set.

Jamnadas made himself a paan. He put it in his mouth and went out to sit at the otla. That night the two of them slept with their backs to each other. Jamna began to think that a woman capable of stealing a husband was surely capable of stealing a vaadki.

On the evening of the second, Jaglo came as a bearer of bad tidings. He had investigated all five families mentioned in the note. Not one of them had a vaadki with Jamnadas Bapalal's name engraved on it. He charged a rupee and fifty paise as his fees. He had had to bribe children in four houses to get information. He had only incurred losses in this assignment. If Jamna would not pay him, he threatened to scribble 'Savita vaadki-thief' on all the walls of the building and make Jamna notorious. Jamna played with the money in her hand and said, 'Of course you have to be paid for your labour. But you must tell me, where do Savita and Shantilal meet?'

Jaglo's eye was on the money. He immediately said, 'In the Madhavbaag garden, on their way back from darshan in the evenings.'

He pocketed the money and fled.

Jamna began thinking. She remembered that when she had gone to Savita's place with a vaadki full of poha, Savita was fixing the buttons on a pair of pyjamas. Savita's husband wears dhotis, whereas her children wore half-pants. Surely those were Shantilal's pyjamas.

She remembered her conversation with Savita the same evening when they met again:

Savita: I simply cannot make such soft poha.

Jamna: *You are so miserly that you hardly put any oil.* So what? Everyone makes poha like this, don't you flatter me!

Savita: Flatter? Don't be silly. Why would Shantilal lie?

Jamna: Shantilal? Who's that?

Savita: The one who lives in the posh house across at Vithalsadan.

Jamna realized that if her vaadki was at Shantilal's, she was never going to get it back.

Jamna then thought of the twenty-second of the previous month. Banku masi had come to borrow flour and her eyes were moist then. She had refused to stay even for two minutes that day. Poor thing, she was so miserable. Her husband humiliates her for no fault of hers. In the evening her son came by with a vaadki full of gram flour. He looked despondent and did not stay to eat puran poli.

On the twenty-fifth, Vimlaben had come to borrow some yoghurt to make her own. She talked a lot:

Vimla: Your vaadki must be with Savita.

Jamna: I went twice but her house was locked.

Vimla: She was saying that her brother and bhabhi have called her.

Jamna: She and her bhabhi can hardly see eye to eye.

Vimla: So, where could she have gone?

Jamna: She'll look in one direction and aim elsewhere; you think you and I will ever know?

Vimla: We are still such simpletons. We just take people at face value.

Jamna: As they say, grief is not about the passing away of the old woman, but the fear that the lord of death saw the house.

Vimla: How much I had to go through when my tongs were lost! I had to hold all the hot utensils which had milk, vegetables, and rice with a rag. After ten days or so, it was discovered at Shivlalbhai's house.

Jamna: *Everyone knows that you would let your own house burn in your lust for Shivlal.* Really, it was found at Shivlalbhai's house? I don't seem to remember.

Vimla: *You are a match for Savita herself.* Of course, it's been two years so you are likely to forget. He had borrowed my silver vaadki and aachmani for the Satyanarayan puja.

Jamna: You remembered to send those things along with the prasad, as well as the yoghurt spoon.

Vimla: Savita is careless.

Jamna: She is devious. I had a tough time getting my bag back from her. I had sent poha in a vaadki. Now if that has gone to Shantilal's place, that's the end of it.

Vimla: Who is Shantilal?

Jamna: I don't know him. Savita was saying that he has a posh apartment in Vithalsadan.

Vimla: I have seen him. Savita is too much! She can make a flying bird fall whereas you and I may not even notice the bird.

Jamna: I don't know much about Shantilal. But, I must say, she becomes all coy when your bhai is around.

In the morning of 2 April, which happened to be Sunday, Jamna watched Ramayana on the television like a devoted wife waiting to be inspired, but Jamnadas noticed that her eyes fluttered towards the door every now and then.

When Ram had assembled his army on the island of Lanka and was ready to wage a war against its king, Vimlaben arrived. She gestured that Jamnadas was not to be disturbed, and she and Jamna quietly left the room.

Vimla: She just came home to give me the house key.

Jamna: Did she say anything?

Vimla: No. Madam looked very spiffy in a chiffon saree, lipstick, and a bucketful of perfume.

Jamna: Where has she gone? When will she be back?

Vimla: To watch Ramayana on Shantilal's colour TV, she said, and she will be back by quarter past ten.

Jamna: So dressed up to go to a neighbour's house?

Vimla: She has gone to seduce Shantilal.

Jamna: Anyway, let's get on with our task.

Vimla: I will wait outside and keep an eye out. If someone turns up suddenly, I will cough three times.

Jamna: Right and I will come out immediately.

Vimla: Yes, but be careful that no one sees you.

Jamna opened the lock to Savita's house and went inside. She began to inspect the kitchen—paniyaaru, platforms, shelves, washing area, utensils, bottles, boxes, ghee container, grains container, up and down, sideways—for a vaadki with the name Jamnadas Bapalal, but to no avail. She looked in the drawing room under chairs and tables, files and papers, clocks, carpets, double beds, fans...everywhere. But in vain. She looked in the toilet, the bathing area, storeroom, etc. After an hour she came out looking like an ash-smeared sadhu. Vimla then stood up from her surveillance post outside.

Vimla: Who's that?

Jamna: Alee, it's me.

Vimla: Why have you smeared your face?

Jamna: The house is full of dust. Lazy woman visits everybody in town, but doesn't clean her own house.

Vimla: Did you find it?

Jamna: Na re.

Vimla: She must have hidden it away somewhere.

Jamna: I have checked every corner. It's certainly not in this house.

Vimla: Chalo, it's time we left, she may appear like Yama himself.

Sunday evening was also marked by gloom. Jamna continued to stare at the white ceiling as she lay on the bed. Jamnadas could not bear to see her so unhappy. He sat next to her, and placed her head in his lap.

Jamnadas: Why are you torturing yourself like this? One vaadki is gone but it's not the end of the world. Another one will come. You are jeopardizing your peace of mind for a mere vaadki, and making me unhappy too.

Jamna: She ate our soft poha, do I mind that? I can't tolerate her usurping my vaadki. I don't want to stay in Bhadrikashram any more. Please look for a two-bedroom flat.

Jamnadas: You will feel lonely in an apartment.

Jamnadas stood up from the bed to bring a glass of water for his wife. Jamna refused to drink it. It was time for the Sunday movie, and she switched on the TV.

It was an Ashok Kumar film. Had it been a normal day, they would be eating dinner while watching the film. But today, Jamna's suffering marred that pleasure as well. Jamnadas watched the film half-heartedly.

A dancer swayed to a song on the screen. Acting like a drunkard, Ashok Kumar came close to her. The next moment, the dancer slipped something imperceptibly into his hands, whispering in his ear. He stumbled his way out of her chamber and straightened himself up in no time. He went and knocked on somebody's door and slipped in the object that the dancer had given him.

Jamnadas was startled as he watched the scene. He looked as though he had suddenly been bitten by a scorpion. He wore his chappals and sped out of the room at lightning speed. He went to the ground floor and knocked on Shivlal's door. Wearing the clip he usually had in his hair, Shivlal opened the door:

Shivlal: Welcome. How is it that you have abandoned a film to come here?

Jamnadas: Such are the circumstances, Shivlal. Should I watch the film or Jamna's dead body?

Shivlal: Oh my god, what are you saying?

Jamnadas: She has gone without food for the past two days.

Shivlal: Nothing's going to happen for ten days at least. She will lose some fat.

Jamnadas: Is that even funny? Can't you see the state of despair I am in?

Shivlal: Well, you need to be clear about what you want or else how would I know?

Jamnadas: Do you remember that a week ago you wanted cooking oil?

Shivlal: Yes, so what of it?

Jamnadas: I had brought it for you.

Shivlal: That's right, Jamna had gone for garba that night.

Jamnadas: That vaadki is missing.

Shivlal: It must be here somewhere. Let me look.

Shivlal turned the kitchen upside down as he looked for the vaadki.

Jamnadas: Did you find it?

Shivlal: I'm looking.

Jamnadas: If you can't find it, I may need to commit suicide.

Shivlal: It has to be at Vimla's place. I will ask her to send it to your house tomorrow morning.

When Jamnadas returned to his house upstairs, the TV was on, but Jamna was fast asleep.

On Monday, 3 April, Jamnadas sipped buttermilk during his lunch and asked, 'So what happened to that vaadki, hanh? Did you find it?'

Jamna: Yes, Vimla gave it to me this morning.

Jamnadas: Hope you are relieved now?

Jamna: Forget it.

Jamadas: Why?

Jamna: It would have been better not to have found it.

Jamnadas: Now what's biting you?

Jamna: The vaadki was at Shivlal's place.

Jamnadas: How come?

Jamna: God knows how! I can't bear the sight of him. With that clip in his hair, the way he speaks stressing each and every syllable,

I feel like slapping him!

Jamnadas: He's quite all right, really.

Jamna: You are such a simpleton. Vimla would give her life for him; doesn't that tell you something?

Jamnadas: What?

Jamna: Vimla will think I am close to Shivlal. Had the vaadki not been found, I would have been spared unfounded suspicions, no?

Jamnadas: But I haven't said anything to you, have I?

Jamna: I will have to find out how that vaadki landed there.

Jamnadas: Forget it, will you? We found the vaadki on account of our good karma.

Jamna: Your wish is my command.

Jamnadas sighed with relief.

PYRE

RAGHUVEER CHAUDHARY

Ash had formed on the embers. The night shuddered in the severe cold—severe enough to cool the ashes. Jeevan was sitting with his head resting on his knees. An owlet's screech from the west stirred him to wakefulness. He gazed indifferently towards the west and thought he shouldn't let the fire go out. He blew on it. Ash rose. He blew again. Fire. He blew once again and sparks flew. As the sparks flew, Jeevan was lost in thought....

Today, a young woman had died. Her pyre was still burning. Half an hour ago, Jeevan had gone to look once again. All the logs had burnt up. Nothing remained to be done. The logs of wood had broken down into embers. The cremation ground was warm. But now, ash will form gradually and in the morning only the earth below will remain warm. Some embers will survive, and be transformed into coals. There might be some bones among them. For a few days Jeevan's gaze will involuntarily fall on that heap of ash. Then the ash from the heap will mingle with the rest and there will be no way of differentiating the one who died last from the ones before. It will lose itself in the collective mass of several bodies. Jeevan will look at all this and reflect.

Jeevan's field is large, much larger than the cremation ground, which must be barely twenty bighas. The northern side is a thicket of babul. Towards the east are ravines and to the south is Jeevan's field. The southern end of the cremation ground intersects Jeevan's field, like a triangle intersecting a large rectangle. This intersection is the entrance to his field. The highway connecting the two villages passes through the ground. So Jeevan has to cross half of the cremation ground to enter his field. Sometimes, he halts before entering. He looks over his shoulder. He struggles to look across the ground at the other end. Late one night, he had dreamt that the other end was covered with peepul and jamun trees. The trees were not moving. The wind passed by the ancient trunks and whirled around in the centre of the pit. The roots of the peepul's stump on the western side of the pit lay exposed. On the roots was a roofless hut; Jeevan noticed a lonely child there. Golden locks fell over his eyes and his face was streaked with tears. The child was holding the middle finger of his right hand. He never looked up. What should Jeevan do? He felt like calling out, but something held him back. It was a dream, yet his eyes sought the place that he had seen. Finally, he persuaded himself to step into the field.

Yes, his field was larger than the cremation ground. The field was fertile and yielded a good harvest but one couldn't tell this from looking at his clothes and careless lifestyle. Yet it was a fact that his income from the fields was pretty good.

Jeevan's daughter is called Rai. She is five years old and very pretty, so pretty that one is reminded of Heti. It's been seven years since he was married. Jeevan has been cooking his own meals for five years now. When will Rai grow up and share the burden? And for how long can a grown-up Rai stay in her father's house? Jeevan doesn't think of these things; other people talk about them.

The village folk believe that Jeevan is not right in the head because he lives a reckless life. He doesn't *live*; he merely survives that way. Going by appearances alone, many people believe it. The Jeevan of today is a pale shadow compared to the Jeevan of four or five years ago when he shone like a bronze statue. Some people have fathomed the root of this transformation and don't contradict those who believe that he is mad. Jeevan himself does not oppose this; he knows what has happened to him. He knows.

Last summer, after a very long time, the people of the village heard Jeevan's strong and resonant voice. Of course, there was some hollowness in that voice. It was familiar, yet it lacked strength. That is why it might be an exaggeration to say that his voice was resonant. It might be better to say that this was the same voice that was once resonant. After all, how could the voice that resounded over the fields and the temple while singing the garba suddenly be reduced to nothing? That's why everybody was stunned. The gossipmongers of the village couldn't meet his eyes when they came to offer their sage advice. He told everyone off. What are you talking about? What do you take me for? They all retreated with their heads hung low. Jeevan stood alone on the threshold. For the first time in his life, he had turned someone away from his house. His house had always been known for its hospitality.

He stood up from the fire and went to fetch some hay from the cattle shed. He threw a handful into the fire. The flames rose to his eyebrows. But why was there no warmth in them? He thought it might get chilly. When he drew his hands away from the fire, his fingertips went numb. This was a sign of an oncoming chill.

Now there won't be enough time to sleep. He shrugged his laziness off and stood up to go to bed. The oxen jingled their bells in recognition. He tossed a few stalks of jowar into the cattle shed and climbed onto the roof, spread out a piece of cloth, and put a blanket over himself. Since the tobacco was over, he had to suppress the urge to smoke the chillum. The moon was setting. It was the eleventh day of the month of Paush.

He tossed in bed sleeplessly and finally sat up. Now what? He lay down again. Burying himself in the blanket, he tried to sleep.

Time passed quickly. Gradually, his body seemed to be weighed down. He tried to arrive at an understanding of his condition and his failure to do so exasperated him. From his right came the jingle of silver bangles which rang against his eardrums. A second sharp sound drilled through his left ear. After a while he could hear a third sound, the clink of jewellery. The three sounds merged and Jeevan felt a hand on his chest. The touch was not aggressive. It was alluring, like a garland around his neck. Could it have frozen out of inhibition? Skilfully, he pressed the hand. He caught hold of the 'body' that was attached to the hand. But there was no weight on the roof. The mystery cleared up. The other hand held the sickle...there was no doubt now. Jeevan grabbed the sickle and flung it away. It went up into the air and then fell. Its sharp edge penetrated the wet earth.

'People are right then.'

'What do you mean?'

'That you are….'

'Do you really believe it? Would I turn into a ghost?'

'Yes, of course. Human misery assumes the form of a shadow and wanders about.'

'No, no. That is your misconception. I have not become a ghost or anything.'

'Stop talking nonsense. Here, let me hold you in my arms. Now tell me.'

'Oh! You are a butcher.'

'Butcher? You too believe that, Heti, don't you? I don't care what the whole village says, but you say that too? How was I to know that a point of a sickle would give you tetanus and you'd leave me hapless?'

'The fault was mine, but now what? I was so piqued I drank the milk and sugar and hid the fact from others. It's not your fault.'

'But the whole village calls me a murderer.'

'That's not true. People must have forgotten everything. It's been years!'

'No, only yesterday Rai was asking me.'

'What?'

'Whether I had killed you since people have been saying that.'

'And what did you say?'

'I said it was true, child, I killed your mother.'

'Don't say that please. Oh God, how do I come back now? How do I become my old self and carry Rai? Or massage your legs? What do I do? What do I do?'

Heti sat up and put her head on Jeevan's feet and began to weep, 'Forgive me, it was all my doing. You should remarry now. Don't remain unhappy.'

'What are you saying? That will never happen.'

'I will not go today till you give me your word.'

'No, that's not possible. It will never happen. Never, ever.'

Jeevan woke up to the sound of his own voice. A jackal's howl from far away was suddenly stilled. A dog barked at the other end of the cremation ground.

He stood up and noticed that it was already dawn. Jeevan's eyes felt heavy with sleep. He tied a piece of cloth on his head and lit the fire. The darkened earth of the fallow field across from him began to glow in the light. Before the flames could rise, he saw the rajko grow. A woman walked across the field, her feet hardly touching the tips of the grass. The little white flowers of the rajko caressed the soles of her feet. The woman was tempted—she hitched up her pallu and sat down. She began to cut the rajko.

'Who asked you to do this?'

'I'll do as I like.'

'Get up now...trust you to do the wrong things.'

'And you must be Mr Right!'

'Get up, or I'll drag you away.'

'As if you would.... Coward.'

The sickle that had been grabbed now rose, and oh, it was almost as if it hit Jeevan himself on the head! He quickly shut his eyes. When he looked up again a few stains of blood had assumed different shapes and moved about before him. They acquired speed and soon formed a circle. The circle shrank in size and was filled up with the moon. The moon became stained.

The pink morning light burst out in the east. The picture became hazy. It kept receding and finally sank and disappeared in the west. The sky was rose-tinted and ready for the sun to rise.

Jeevan picked up a dry lump of dung near the shed. He placed it in the fire, put on his shoes that lay under the roof, and headed for home.

He walked along the edge of the field next to the path. He saw a fire beneath the mahua tree in a field near the village. A family of minstrels had camped there. Two children and their father—must be the father. The little boy had a sarangi. The father was perhaps teaching the song:

> *In the times long ago, O queen,*
> *We were the parrots of Lord Ram.*
> *In that northern land when the mango tree ripened,*
> *The male parrot pecked me....*

Jeevan had often heard that song as a child. The lyrics of the song had helped him when playing antakadi in school. Today, when he heard the lines, he remembered his childhood and the passage of time till that fateful day of Paush. On reaching his house, he stood on the veranda.

Rai woke up to Jeevan's footsteps. She came to her house from her aunt's. Jeevan milked the buffalo while Rai lit the chulah. Jeevan put on some water for tea and they both had some.

'You are.... You are weeping, Bapu?'

'No, child, it is only the smoke,' he answered, trying to make his voice sound normal. 'I have work in the field. Meanwhile, keep the fire alive till the food is cooked. I'll be back.'

He set off for the field.

The sun was up.

The fire in the cremation ground had gone out. Glancing once again at the extinguished pyre, Jeevan stepped into his field and looked again. He'll stay in the field till noon.

INDUBHAI GAAYAB

ANJALI KHANDWALLA

He was an ordinary human being. Intelligence: ordinary. Appearance: ordinary. Values: ordinary. Name: Indubhai. But his eyes set him apart. Craftiness lurked in their depths. His eyes were the reason behind him occupying the central spot; having once gained a toehold, he took great care to see that he was never dislodged.

Indubhai had a spotlight fixed behind him, like the sun. No one could tell though. This made him cast a very long shadow. The size of his shadow made everyone marvel at him. The sun-like brilliance of the spotlight overshadowed Indubhai's actual form and size. Blinded by the intense light, all that one could see was Indubhai's long shadow. Everyone worshipped him.

Photographs of this shadow regularly peered out from all the leading newspapers. And so the glory of Indubhai's shadow stayed fresh in people's minds. In fact, Indubhai himself sent these pictures to newspaper editors to publish. By placing them on the front page, they kept him happy. The reason for keeping him happy was the length of this shadow.

Everybody thought the shadow was Indubhai himself! Visitors stood far away when they came to meet him and talked to the shadow. Nobody visited him without a purpose. Of course, you could not even get through the gates if you did not have a prior appointment. But even after getting an appointment, it was Indubhai's prerogative to choose whom he wanted to grant the darshan of his shadow. Overwhelmed, visitors offered endless salaams. Nothing in the world was dearer to Indubhai than the salaams. Pleased, he would let his visitors ask for a boon at times. The visitors would ask for a son's admission, promotion for themselves or someone they knew, bank loans, a job, and so on. Nothing was impossible for Indubhai. He held the reins of virtually everything in town. He could pull at the reins and make anyone do what he wished. No one could afford to displease Indubhai—the reason was, of course, his long shadow. Undoubtedly, Indubhai was a human being; unlike any other, but a human being nonetheless. Ordinary, but he had never looked at himself in the mirror. By constantly watching his long shadow, he had also come to believe that 'Indubhai' was the colossal shadow.

He often told his visitors 'Describe my form!' Most visitors replied, 'The sutradhar of the entire city; you are boundless. We are the dust at your feet.' The description might vary slightly from person to person but the gist was the same: Indubhai equalled enormity and enormity equalled Indubhai. In the past, one or two people gave a different version, but Indubhai's powerful shadow devoured them in seconds.

⌡

One day, Indubhai was sitting in his chair in his office and rummaging through the length of his shadow. His mind was fully focused on this act. Suddenly, without seeking permission, a healthy-looking cockroach with a long moustache entered. Its gait was Napoleonic as it headed swiftly towards Indubhai's chair. On finding a Shudra shadow falling on his own, Indubhai raised his head and looked disdainfully in the direction of the cockroach. He let out a roar loud enough to tear anyone's courage to shreds.

The cockroach was either deaf or a true Rajput because it continued its march in the direction of the chair, unperturbed. It then climbed onto one of the legs of the chair. Indubhai yelled out for his guard—once, twice, thrice. His shouts ineffectively dashed against the wall and ricocheted. Then silence rang through the air.

The cockroach was exactly a yard away from Indubhai. Indubhai warned it for the last time and ordered it to retreat. The cockroach ignored the warning. It jumped over the arms of the chair and leapt straight onto Indubhai's kurta. For a cockroach of that size, this was indeed a record-breaking jump. Indubhai shrugged it off his kurta and sent it crashing head first out of the door.

It could be seen outside the door for a long time. Indubhai laughed at its insignificance and returned to his shadow.

The cockroach changed its strategy. Invisible to Indubhai's eyes, the cockroach now entered from the window behind him. Climbing up the kurta, the cockroach reached the stump-like neck jutting out from the kurta. Indubhai remained immersed in his shadow. He felt something crawling on his neck and tried to identify it. Indubhai was from a village; he was more than familiar with the touch of a baval. But this was something thorny, and yet it didn't prick. If only he could feel this in his ears, how nice that would be! A gentle scratching in the ear without the harshness of an ear-pick! As Indubhai relished this sweet fantasy, the cockroach's thread-like moustache brushed against his right cheek. With a sidelong glance, Indubhai saw its blackness. The chakra of Indubhai's wrath was set in motion. He wanted to crush the cockroach into chutney with his fingers. But the very thought filled him with disgust. Staining his fingers with this unclean insect's blood would only pollute his dignity. He decided against it and, instead, held the cockroach in his snot-smeared handkerchief.

The cockroach babbled and rambled something in its language. To Indubhai, it sounded like the rumbling of thousands of marching soldiers. The handkerchief with the cockroach fell from his hand.

On the ground, the cockroach's wings began to flutter. Then they flapped and it took off like an aeroplane. It flew around and landed on Indubhai's table, exactly at the central point of Indubhai's vision. Its eyes, like a pair of tongs, seemed to hold Indubhai's vision. Constructed carefully over many years, the edifice of Indubhai's self-confidence began to crumble slowly.

The cockroach's eyes were gradually widening. They seemed to be glowing until they shone with a spectacular radiance. One after another, several suns melted and slid into them and intensified the glow. Indubhai saw many men being carried into the radiance. Clutching at his remaining confidence, Indubhai tightened his grip on the arms of his throne-like chair.

The cockroach's jaw began to move. Slowly it opened its mouth wide and rushed towards Indubhai's shadow. It began to nibble at the shadow and then chewed through the edges. Waves of terror passed through Indubhai's entire being.

The cockroach gorged as though it hadn't eaten in ages. Pressing the last bit of Indubhai's shadow under its feet, the cockroach ate all of it. That's it...over.... Indubhai's shadow was gone.

A miracle! In the sixty years of his life, Indubhai had never felt such a flowery lightness of being. Once the shadow was peeled off, it also cleared the dirt from his pores. Coolness percolated for the first time through his skin.

Indubhai looked around. He realized how ordinary everything looked—office-table-chair. He saw Bapuji's photograph framed in age-old cobwebs hanging on the wall. It had been hidden all this time by Indubhai's long shadow.

Suddenly, Indubhai's eyes fell on his chair. It looked empty. He looked at his own body, now reduced to the size of the smallest lump of sugar. Indubhai held out a hand and spread his palm. His fingertips and nails—everything was intact. He looked down and checked his toes. He checked his ears, nose, cheeks, and face. Everything was in its respective place. His eyes once again darted to the chair. He pictured himself seated on the gigantic chair; he looked so tiny that he was almost non-existent. Curiously, he began to touch every part of his chair as if he had never seen it before. Then, Indubhai's gaze fixed itself on the cockroach now standing on the table. It stood still like a statue. The sun shone behind it. Light emanated from each pore of its body. Finding this illuminated cockroach unbearably dazzling, Indubhai tried hard to hide himself and looked for a crack in the chair. He hid in a crack and continued to stare at the cockroach.

He could see huge mountains. Oceans, jungles, countless cities, and urban and historical monuments. Indubhai recognized the tall torch-bearing statue. It had two feet planted in a river. He could not remember the Hindi film in which he had seen it. A number of steamers passed between its two huge feet. Dragged along by a steamer, Indubhai's eyes rested for a moment on his own city. He saw his mohalla. Then came his office...a drop hidden in the crack of a chair...everything was in the cockroach's body.

Indubhai shuddered as he watched this scene. He shut his eyes. Suddenly, the wind howled. Indubhai's eyes flew open. The colossal cockroach had begun to shrink. A storm arose from the void rising in its wake, large angry cyclones that fumed and frothed. The ground beneath the office began to quiver and the entire office shook and swayed. It seemed as if a churning giant had been let loose in his office. Papers lying on the desk began to flutter in the wind. The cupboard, table, and chair began to collide and crash against each other, now against the ground, and now against the wall. Indubhai was thrown onto a piece of paper. The storm, brewing within the four walls, went berserk and rushed out. It kicked open the windows on its way out. Glued to a piece of paper, Indubhai melted into the void.

The following day, the gates to Indubhai's office were wide open. The guard was nowhere to be seen. Indubhai's shadow, which typically reached over the gate and touched the road, had also disappeared. People crossed the open gates and crowded inside Indubhai's office. Indubhai was nowhere to be seen. They felt certain that Indubhai was no more. They shouted: 'Miracle! Glory be!'

Everyone went into frenzy. The fight which followed to claim Indubhai's chair was intense and bloody. In the end, the one with the longest shadow was crowned and 'chaired'. He came to be known as Indubhai II.

THE INVASION
DALPAT CHAUHAN

'The link to the soil was an ancient one. It had not begun today, yesterday, or the day before.... When the Pulayan turned the soil, the scent that rose from it would mingle with the air around, reach his nostrils, and intoxicate him.

He inhaled the scent of the fresh soil deeply, like a rare intoxicating perfume...

An experience that knew no satiety!'

—Paul Chirakkarode, *Pulayathara*,
1962, translated by Catherine Thankamma
from the Malayalam in 2019.

'It's time the millets grew cob heads,' Natho muttered, his eyes glued to his field swaying with a waist-high crop of pearl millet. In the long line of his ancestry, unrecorded of course, only he had the distinction of owning land in his name. So what if it was no more than a slim patch of government wasteland, a 'shred' as they called it? In another first, he had shrewdly inveigled none but the village head into renting him his pair of milk-white bullocks to plough the shred and even sow it without any trouble. And, truly, he was in luck, for it had rained adequately that year. He ran an appreciative glance over the lush green meadow all around him. Pleased with himself and his luck, Natho began to walk carefully along the narrow soil ridge that demarcated his shred. In no time, the scorching September sun would shine over his field and the seeds in the florets would ripen.

'They say, goddamn the merciless September sun. Under its

singeing blaze, many a Kanabi* turned tail and became monks, never to return.' Natho chuckled to himself.

But Natho was not to be deterred. And why should he when he had withstood it for as long as thirty years? Since his childhood, he had toiled like a bull in the sprawling farms of the upper-caste landlords as a bonded farmhand. Tiny rivulets of sweat would course their way down his body to his calves and feet and disappear into the dry soil underneath. Scalding, dazzling heat would pour down relentlessly and the standing millet crop would reel before the eyes of even the sturdiest of farmhands; one after the other, they would faint and drop off like slashed millet stalks. But Natho would be in his element and slave away, with undiminished zest. Generally, an ordinary serf couldn't cut more than two millet stalks in one sickle swipe but Natho would grab at least three at a time by their necks and decapitate them in a single lethal strike. Once the cob heads were chopped off, the remaining thumb-thick stalks, sweet as honey, would soon collapse like feeble, headless torsos.

Natho enjoyed the reputation of being a shrewd, bull-headed maverick in the village. Tall and heavy, he looked just like a wrestler. Amongst the handful of untouchables living in the village outskirts, he was the only one with a hot head and a brave heart. Due to his bullish ways, everybody in the village preferred to give him a wide berth; who would confront the proverbial scoundrel even a nasty wraith would fear? But his notoriety notwithstanding, the village was undivided in their opinion regarding a trait in Natho's character—that he slaved away in farms unrelentingly for hours together. He

---

*Kanabi, also known as Patidar, is an agrarian community that migrated in the second half of nineteenth century from mainland Gujarat to the princely state of Saurashtra to work as tenants in the fields owned by local Rajputs. Land reforms in the 1950s transferred vast stretches of land to these tenants, making them landlords overnight. Cash crops like groundnut and cotton yielded rich dividends and thus they diversified their agricultural profit into oil mills and cotton ginning industries. Eventually, they began to deal in foundries, brass industries, textiles, pharmaceuticals, and even real estate. Still operating in close-knit caste councils, Patidars or Patels are one of the most powerful communities in Gujarat.

would care neither for breaks nor bread when he was absorbed in his work. And it may sound rather strange, but for him this back-breaking work was a labour of love. The sharp swish of his sickle was dearer to him than the jarring splats of handlooms that went on day and night in the houses of his neighbours.

Standing at the edge of his land, he lapsed into his pet reverie about reaping a record millet crop that year. He would have so much to do; reaping the crop, arranging the stalks in neat piles and so on. Sweat would stream down his face, his bare sinewy arms and ebony back would be drenched, but he wouldn't care. Just then, a small butterfly, a pinch of yellow, fluttered about his face. Distracted by the quick winks of movement, he ducked his head, lost his balance, and took a pratfall on a heap of dry clods. Bursting out in snorts of self-mocking laughter, he grumbled silently, 'You idiot! Rein in your fantasies. No signs of cob heads yet and you're bloody dreaming about piles of grains. Let the cob heads grow first, then the florets will be filled with seeds, then they will ripen....'

However, the brief self-censure couldn't stop him from slipping into his fond daydream once again. Harvesting a bigha of millets is just a matter of a day for me. Give me a razor-sharp sickle and I'll pile up the hay in neat stacks. The next day, I'll tie it up into bundles of equal size. Such a relief that I don't have to depend on others for labour. My wife and I are enough for all the work. If slaving throughout the day isn't good enough, we can toil at night as well. Who's going to stop us? And both of us are sturdy like timber planks, aren't we? Seasoned grains of pearl millet, you see. We survive on the strength of our hands, not on alms or worse still, kissing ass. As his thoughts dwindled from hope to a shade of despair, a flush of bitterness washed over his face, leaving it bright red.

Shuffling along the boundary, he came to the point in the western hedge of his field where he had cut a small clearing. Removing the thorny tumbleweed that plugged it, he crawled out onto the narrow dusty road and pulled the shrubbery back in place with the blade of his long-handled axe. There was a visible spring in his step as he headed home. But the warm smile in his eyes receded as soon as he saw the village head ambling down the road towards him. He stopped in his tracks and, as was customary, moved to the edge of the road to let him pass. Letting his axe rest against his chest, he folded his hands and greeted the village head.

'Victory to Lord Rama, bha! What brings you here, to this side of the village today?'

'Rama be victorious, Natho. I'm not as lucky as you are and certainly not so laid-back. I have to worry about the well-being of the entire village and run around day in, day out.' The blowhard's leisurely advance came to a halt along with his bragging. Natho smiled knowingly.

'You bet, bha! How can a person as curious as you stay home and have peace of mind too?'

Natho's clever dig wiped the cunning smile off the village head's face. Keeping his face deadpan, he went straight for the sting, 'All that is fine. But tell me one thing, what have you sown there, in that government wasteland?'

When Natho heard the words 'government wasteland', his temples began to throb and burn as though molten lead had been poured into his ears. Salty bitterness rose within him. For a fleeting second, he felt like telling his foe to his face to mind his own business. But the village head, for one, had considerable clout in the region and then there was no point courting trouble just for fun. So, he decided to keep his cool and give an astute performance. In a voice choked with an overdose of emotion, he said, 'Oh! How can you forget it so soon, bha? Agreed, noble men don't keep a track of the kindness they do for the wretched. But I'll never forget how you used your good offices to get these few bighas transferred to my name. Anyway, do remember now, this isn't government wasteland any more, okay?'

'Oh... I'm sorry if that hurt you.'

The village head made a gesture of remorse and then, unable to supress the wry smile that spilt his face, immediately turned away. Seething with rage, Natho gnashed his teeth, but then said in a low voice, 'Why not? It'd hurt, for sure.'

'Only a fool would take to heart the words of an elder. The tongue is a boneless creature and slipping is its character, you see. But let me tell you, everybody in the village knows this shred to be a part of government wasteland....'

Such double-edged wordplay was getting on Natho's nerves. But he tried to put on a show of incomprehension, if not indifference. He didn't see much reason, at least now, to challenge the village head, though what he was getting at, he knew, could hurt him in the long run. It had been four years since his name was registered as the rightful owner of the land in the registry of the irrigation department. Further, his swaying pearl millets were there for everyone to see, a mint-fresh certificate that it was he who owned and cultivated the land. Of course, he wouldn't have got the land without the village head's intervention; let's give the devil his due. But does that mean he'd have to grovel for the rest of his life as the head threw his weight around and treated him like dirt? At once, he felt a churning in his stomach and an unusual heaviness in his chest. Streams of sweat rolled down his temples. Why would the devil have buzzed into this part of the village today of all days, something he'd be loath to do generally? His own farms, all of them, were sprawled on the eastern frontier of the village. Yes, he had a strip here too, but then much of it was under government encroachment and he had never bothered to cultivate it. The village head's sudden, ominous appearance made Natho furious. Lest he rant in rage and things go out of hand, he thought it wise to leave.

'Okay, bha, see you then.'

'Why are you in such a hurry? At least tell me what you have sown in your shred.'

'Nothing much, bha. Just a handful of pearl millets,' mumbled Natho as he hung his axe on his shoulder and hastened to leave. But the village head was not to be snubbed so easily. He asked in a cold-blooded voice, 'Is the crop ready for harvesting?'

Natho felt the lethal stab of the question in his back, but he kept walking, without bothering to turn around or respond.

Natho had chosen not to take the bull by the horns but the village head's dark, threatening words began to echo in his mind like an ill omen. Why on earth would he have asked about the readiness of the crop? Was it just out of curiosity? Or was there something more to it? A pox on him! Truth be told, from the day the land had been allotted to him, it had become a major sore point with the village authorities; nay, a veritable thorn in the flesh of the entire village. Conventionally, an untouchable couldn't own land in his name anywhere in the village. Arre, they could not lay their hands on the handle of a plough, let alone a piece of land. And that convention had remained intact till date. A storm raged in his head.

With the enforcement of new legislation, the fortunes of so many Kanabis had changed overnight. From lowly tenants to legitimate land-owning farmers, their climb was steep and stark, but nobody in the village seemed to really mind it. But the idea of an outcaste staking claim to land, even a shred of government wasteland, was still anathema to everybody, whatever their religion and caste. That Natho had not only taken possession of land but had cultivated it had rubbed salt into the festering boil on their bum. The land meant for the grazing of Mother Cow had been shredded and transferred to an untouchable? How terrible a sacrilege! What an obscene act of blasphemy! That Mother Cow would go hungry now just because of a dhe...* was a loss of face for the entire village. Stung by humiliation and goaded by a sense of vengeance, the village hadn't allowed Natho to plough the land for three years. This year, Natho had to appease the village head by hiring his bullocks, never mind the exorbitant rates, to be able to plough his field. But still, he knew deep down that they would not leave him alone, oh no.

---

*Dhedh: A conventional pejorative, a casteist slur, originally used for a person from the weaver community but later extended to all Dalit castes in Gujarat to suggest the polluting work of dragging and stripping carcasses, their caste-based occupation.

On the other hand, the village head was caught in a double bind. No doubt it was out of greed rather than anything else that he had ended up giving his pair of sturdy bullocks to Natho on rent. But now, people openly scoffed at him and very nastily at that.

'Look, our headman has turned into a dhe…. First, he used his good offices to get him land. Then he helped plough it as well. It'll be no wonder if he decides tomorrow to personally harvest it for that fool.'

After his chance meeting with Natho that day, the village head's visits to the western frontier became worryingly frequent. On the way to his strip when his black, vicious gaze travelled in the direction of Natho's undulating pearl millets, his heart would go up in flames. He would turn frantic with worry as to how to break the hex that the damned shred had put on his life. On a particularly hot day, he'd wish Natho's crop would burn down in the baking sun. On a chilly, overcast night, he would pray for a giant thunderbolt to strike it so hard that the whole standing crop was razed to the ground. But, alas, nothing of the sort happened. Despite being the village head and quite powerful, he didn't have the courage to set Natho's field alight in broad daylight. And surely, Natho wasn't one who'd take it lying down. Of late, he had become familiar with the nitty-gritties of litigations; in fact, he had been inciting others in his street to approach the law courts against oppression and injustice. On the other hand, the headman had garnered the ill-will of the entire village for helping Natho in this whole bloody mess. His opponents would put the blame squarely on him, saying, 'Bloody… there should be a limit to shamelessness. First, he helped him get the pasture. And now he says its government land. Why doesn't he bequeath his own farms to Natho? And if that doesn't suffice, let him ask and we'll transfer ours too.'

Searing taunts and venomous attacks sank into his heart like poisoned daggers. Restless and overwrought, he would spend every waking moment devising plans to reclaim his lost honour. One day, his nephew came over and raged against the way he had been sleeping peacefully on the matter.

'Uncle, I can't bear to look at the bumper millet crop in Natho's field. The line dividing a landlord and a dhe… is being smudged and you're looking away? Aren't you ashamed of yourself? Do something—and if you can't, give us a free hand.'

'What are you saying? Be clear, will you?' asked the village head in irritation.

'Then listen carefully. Ask that Liliyo, the cowherd, to let his cattle loose in Natho's field in the dead of night if not in broad daylight. If he comes complaining, you should cry foul. For God's sake, I don't have to teach you imperial ways.'

His nephew's clever ploy resonated with the desperate old man. And that night, Mother Cow had a field day.

୶

The ravages committed by the cows on the first night went largely unnoticed, though Natho couldn't dispel the lingering suspicion that something was amiss. It could be because he was obsessing over his field and millet crops a bit too much of late, he thought. But the next day when he saw a herd of five to seven cows destroying the crops under the bright morning sun, he was beside himself with rage. Heaving his long-handled axe in the air, he ran towards the rampaging herd, roaring like a lion. 'You bloody marauders, get out…may your bulls bite the dust.'

The sudden raucous din, booming like a battle cry, startled the cows and sent them scampering towards the clearing in the hedge from where they had come. Natho saw that a wide passage had been cut into the hedge and it didn't take him a moment to figure out who was behind it. 'Who else but that adversary of mine for my past seven lives? That blasted village head,' he muttered.

As he ran his gaze around in search of evidence, his eyes fell on Liliyo lurking behind the hedge on the roadside. The moment Liliyo saw the herd galloping towards the clearing, he instinctively dashed in, raising his heavy wooden staff to hit and drive the cows back to the field, completely unaware that Natho was charging right behind the herd.

Natho made up his mind to teach Liliyo a lesson he would remember for the rest of his life. But the very next moment, he saw the village head and his henchman tottering down the boundary of the adjoining field. In a flash, he figured out the whole game. He was lucky that he had come to his field a bit early that day, otherwise the entire crop would have been levelled. He thanked his lucky stars. The sight of the devilish threesome blew his fuse and he mentally prepared himself for a fight to the finish. Clutching the blade of his axe, he started thrashing the cows left and right. Shocked by the sudden downpour of stinging blows, the cows made a dash for the clearing without caring for Liliyo's attacks and bolted along the narrow dusty road. Seeing the village head approach, Liliyo plucked up his courage and began to yell furiously, 'Hey, bloody Natho, how dare you touch my cows? Have you lost it, damn you? Lashing at Mother Cow like that!'

Natho turned to face Liliyo, his face burning and eyes glowing like embers, 'Fucker of your sister! Can't you see how your cows have flattened my millets? The entire crop is wiped out.'

An expletive from an untouchable was too much for Liliyo to handle.

'Bloody dhe…, you have the guts to hurl filthy abuses at me? Rotting fucker, a good thrashing will bring you back to your senses. You've been asking for it of late.'

Liliyo darted threateningly towards Natho but as Natho heaved his axe in defence, Liliyo's heart sank. As such, Natho was a bull under the hide of a man and this episode had visibly made him wild with rage. As if that was not bad enough, he was wielding a murderous axe now. Liliyo froze, but the steady stream of abuses continued to flow.

'Yes, fuck, fuck, fuck you. Don't think I keep this axe just for show. It won't seek your permission before landing on your head. Bastard, does this field belong to your father that you let your cows in? I know your plans, okay?'

Liliyo didn't budge an inch from where he was; his entire body shook badly and his trembling legs, like those of his botulism-ridden cow, threatened to give way. As far as he could remember, whenever bickering came to blows, Natho paid his assaulter back generously, most of the time more than what was due; if he received a couple of punches, his aggressor wouldn't get to leave without a couple of broken bones. When Natho blew his top, he would fight with anything he could lay his hands on. And today, it was a deadly, freshly sharpened, long-handled axe. He might have hit the cow with the wooden handle of the axe but if it came to it, he wouldn't think twice before hitting with the blade. At once, Liliyo broke out in sweat.

The cows had already disappeared from sight. However, the dust kicked up by their frenzied stampede still hung in the air over the narrow dusty road. Liliyo stood nonplussed during the time it took the village head and his henchman to reach the spot. Without losing a moment, Natho launched into a raucous complaining mode, 'See bha…this Liliyo let…his cattle…in my field….and ruined…'

Panting heavily like a dog, he couldn't finish the sentence but began to point his axe accusingly at Liliyo. In order not to dignify him with attention, the village head began to look pointedly in the direction of the field, then bent over to peer at the bottom of the hedge and straightened up to ask in mock seriousness, 'Where are the cows, you mention, hanh? I can't see any of them here.'

Immediately, he turned to Liliyo and cocked his thick eyebrows at him, 'Oye Liliyo, where the hell are your cows? Are you people having delusions or have I gone blind?'

Unable to contain himself, he burst out laughing; the other two joined in with their hearty guffaws. Natho seethed with anger but couldn't decide on his next step. He was pitted against a gang of bulky, stout men. But there was no going back now, he realized. An all-out war it was either way. He tightened his grip on the handle of the axe and steeled himself for any eventuality. Liliyo found his opportunity during the brief lull and began to plead with the village head, 'Bha, I didn't let the cattle loose in this wasteland on purpose. The herd was passing by and seeing that the government pasture was hedged in, the poor things were literally in tears. I took pity on them and allowed them to graze around the hedge. Some of their horns probably got tangled in the hedge and hence this clearing. Where is the question of an invasion in all this? You tell me, bha... do justice in the matter.'

Liliyo ranted away animatedly and winked at the village head as he finished. Natho realized that the stage had been set to make a scapegoat of him. But unfazed, he looked at them fiercely, hung the axe on his shoulder, undid the knot of the kerchief, and began to tie it firmly round his head once again. Seeing that Natho was preparing for a fight, the village head's heart sank. At a loss as to figure out how to diffuse the mounting tension, he blurted out what piqued him the most. 'Oye Liliyo, tell me one thing. Isn't this shred a part of government wasteland? What's wrong even if you put your cows to graze in it? Why, the poor animals too have a share in the wasteland, don't they?'

The others began to snigger as the village head turned to Natho, 'You sowed the millet here and the cows grazed it. That's how things balance out in this world. Get this straight in your fat head and buzz off.'

Natho felt as if bubbling lava would erupt from every single pore on his body. His bloodshot eyes began to spew flames. Shaking his head in maddening rage and disgust, he asked, 'So, that's your tune, bha, isn't it?' His voice cracked as if ground under his gnashed teeth.

'You heard it, Natho. Now take off before I give you a good bashing.'

For a moment, Natho felt like heaving his axe across the old man's frail frame and cutting him in two. He even lifted the axe from his shoulder. The village head immediately moved back and signalled the other men to give him cover. But before they could take a step forward, Natho landed a violent blow on the ground near their feet and spat out in a voice that boomed like thunder, 'Damn you, my shred is government land, isn't it? Okay, I am going. But remember, the village well is also on government land. You want to have fun? Let's have it then.'

He lifted the axe and swaggered off, swinging it from side to side. His ferocious eyes dug into the trio who looked on, their mouths agape and hearts aflutter. After what seemed a long while, the village head stirred, waking as though from a nightmare, wondering what Natho would do now. Surely, he was not one to keep quiet. Helpless and feeble, he gaped at his heavy, broad back receding into the distance.

'Okay then…I'll take your leave, bha,' Liliyo interrupted the village head's dark reverie and hurriedly set out in the direction of his cows. Heaving a weary sigh, the village head trudged on to follow Natho's trail, his sidekick in tow. The dusty road ahead sloped up to a small hillock and from that junction onwards forked into two narrow pathways, one meandering through a neat row of farms leading up to the village and the other slithering straight to the taluk office. The village head saw Natho mounting the hillock. Reaching the top, he stood reflectively for a while, turning his gaze in the direction of the village, taking in with measured eyes the outskirts dotted with trees, wild shrubbery, and the village well, and then climbed down the long serpentine road, disappearing like the setting sun.

⁘

Well past high noon, Natho returned home, panting and sweating. He had got into a real tizzy, it seemed. He downed a potful of water in one draught and set out again. 'What calamity has come upon the village that you are rushing out without caring for lunch?' his wife huffed.

'Let me inform everyone first…keep the rotla and curry ready… I'll be back in a minute.'

One after another, Natho visited all the houses in the untouchables' lane and briefed people about what had happened. A massive wave of fear washed through the lane, but no one so much as uttered a word, for they didn't have the courage to oppose Natho, and even if somebody did, Natho was not going to pay any heed. From the day Natho snatched away two bighas of land from the jaws of the authorities, people in the lane had lived in fear of serious trouble. Everyone knew that the village would not take this affront lying down and due retaliation would come, sooner or later. And time had proved them right. In their hearts, they resented Natho's adventures but in public they had to pledge support.

Natho polished off a pile of rotlas and came out of his house. Twisting his massive frame languidly, he lumbered to the sagging string cot laid out in the courtyard and plonked himself down. Peering keenly into the distance, he began to wait for his cousin whom he had sent to the hillock for a quick inspection. The sun seemed to shine extra bright that day as if to charge Natho with golden heat and raw energy for the daredevilry that was uppermost in his mind, an invasion of a different kind.

After a long while, he saw his cousin hastening towards the street. He jumped up as his cousin came up to him and whispered in his ears. At once, he rushed into his house and came out clutching a pitcher and a coiled rope in his left hand and the long-handled axe in his right. A pall of terrifying silence stretched over the entire street as Natho stomped his way out, a veritable omen of death walked past them, but none had the courage to stop him.

Hanging the loose loops of rope on his left shoulder and pounding the earth with the handle of his axe, Natho strutted right through the village, cautioning the upper-caste villagers of the catastrophe he was about to unleash on them. The news was delivered to the village head by his spies.

'That Natho, a pitcher and rope in hand, has set foot on the village main road. Just like that…no kerchief on head…no sounds of caution…'

At once, Nathos' warning 'the village well is also on government land' rang out in his head. He adjusted his turban and roared, 'Goddamn it. He's out to pollute the village well.'

He hurried to the village square and asked a group of four or five young men to grab their sticks and scythes and follow him. 'Come along! To the village well…and bump off that dhe….'

Natho reached the village well. It wore a deserted look except for a couple of women who hurriedly sneaked away when the apparition called Natho showed up. He saw a huddle of people from his street peering at him from behind the giant trunk of a banyan tree in the distance. Putting his axe down, he coolly slipped the noose of the rope around the neck of the pitcher and tightened it. Then he swaggered up to the waist-high wall of the well and sent the pitcher tumbling inside. As the pitcher sank, he pulled it out, and without bothering to take his clothes off, poured it over himself. He must have performed the ritual about three times over when he saw the village head in the distance charging like a mad ox, hurling filthy abuses at him, a crowd of about thirty villagers in tow. Nobody knew why but all of them stopped at a comfortable distance from the well.

The old man let out a bellow, 'You bloody dhe..., you have the audacity to pollute the village well, heh? Bastard, you'll pay for this with your life. Hey, what are you waiting for? Knock this scoundrel down.'

The resounding holler of the village head jolted the young men out of their stupefaction. They broke into a sprint, waving their sticks and scythes in the air, followed by the village head. Natho was ready; in fact, he was waiting for this moment. He dropped the pitcher and rope to the ground, picked up his long-handled axe, circled it over his head thrice and went tearing down the dusty road towards the village head, roaring and swearing all the while. Seeing an axe-brandishing Natho charging towards them like a tornado, the gang stopped in their tracks and, without a second thought, turned tail. The village head too took to his heels. Scuttling to a safe distance, the pack of retreaters relaxed their astonished sphincters and turned around to see where their tormentor was. Natho had called off the chase and, standing like a towering palm tree, he beckoned them with an insolent wave of his hand, 'Come on, you buggers. Today you'll have it from Natho....'

The village head's face flushed with rage at this public insult.

The group of villagers behind him began to hoot and holler. That Natho would be bumped off was certain, but not before sending a couple of them to their graves. So, they just barked away, digging their heels into the burning sand. Finally, unable to take this flagrant exhibition of cowardice any more, the village head thundered, 'Give me the bill hook, you cowards....'

Trembling from head to toe, he flew into a mad rage, snatched the stick from the hands of a callow boy, and hared off. This act of bravery animated the crowd behind him, and they began to root for him with shouts of 'Kill him, knock him down'.

A great hue and cry rose. Natho was ready, raring to strike his nemesis down in one fell swoop. But before the duel began, a commanding voice rang out.

'Freeze!' A gunshot rended the sky. 'Anybody who makes a move goes down. Hands up!'

A police inspector on horseback cantered in from the direction of the hillock, the pistol in his hand pointing at the sky. Two constables on foot flanked him, their rifles danced on their backs as they struggled to keep pace.

At the sight of the inspector, the village head froze; he stood like a contorted statue. The crowd of villagers fell silent too. The inspector reached the well and growled, 'What's going on here? Don't you know the law?'

The village head dropped the stick and began to plead with the inspector who raised his eyebrows at the constables. Quick to execute the order, they trained their guns on the crowd and everyone ran for their lives. The inspector looked sternly at the village head to suggest that he leave. Getting the silent message, the village head gave Natho a final filthy look and set off, grumbling under his breath, 'Bloody dhe.... Never mind, all he could do was wash himself, that too outside the well. He didn't fetch water home or drink it, and the well can't be polluted just by an untouchable bathing, oh no.'

Translated by Hemang Desai

NAME: NAYANA RASIK MEHTA

VARSHA ADALJA

'Name?'
'N...a...y...a...n...a.'
'Full name?'
'Nayana Rasik Mehta.'
'Hmm. Sarnamu?'
'What?'
'Address...where you stay, kuthe rehvanu?'
'Jay Mahal, Marine Drive.'
'Wow, near the sea, dariya samovar?'
'Yes, sahib. Near the sea, dariya saame.' She matched his Marathi with her Gujarati.

'Savant! This is that building, remember, where we had gone for a theft case...what was its name now, kaay naaunv?'
'Seabird.'
'Yes. First-class building.'
'Sahib...my complaint.'
'One minute. Don't do ghai, shanti theva. What's the rush?'
'Ji.'

The inspector stood up and went inside. She clutched the edge of her pallu like it was a source of support, and waited. The inspector had told her not to make haste, to keep calm. That's what she had done for so many years. Bas, now she only had to wait for a little longer.

Timidly, she looked around. She was the only woman in the police station. It was a large room with three desks and ramshackle wooden benches that faced the desks. She sat in front of the desk belonging to the one the inspector called 'Savant'. The inspector himself was at the second desk. The third desk was stacked with papers. Perhaps someone had left it that way and gone out of the room a short while ago. The dirty, faded walls of the station endured the weight of all kinds of documents. A corridor cut across the room. Beyond it were other rooms and cabins, and then, another corridor with a gigantic iron cupboard. There was a constant bustle of people coming and going in the corridor. The telephone kept ringing. In the chowk outside, three or four men sat cramped together on wooden benches, their shoulders touching. One had unkempt hair, another soiled clothes, yet another had unsteady eyes. A stray mongrel lay sprawled on the ground. A constable rubbed tobacco on his palm and opened his mouth to chew. A plant withered under the blazing sun. The wind screeched like a prisoner in pain, and poked her body.

She stood up, suddenly afraid. Everyone stared at her, as if she had horns coming out of her head. Her courage burst like a bag of water. This very moment, I should be leaving, fleeing, she thought. She was the daughter-in-law of a respectable khandaani family. What was she doing in a police station?

Khandaan? Family, lineage. She wanted to laugh. Rasik's wrathful face flashed before her eyes, his hand raised, ready to hit her, a vein about to burst in his furious eyes. And there, telling the beads of her rosary with not a care in the world, was his mother, her mother-in-law—Nirmala. With cold, steely eyes, she had watched Nayana, making her feel as though a heavy boulder had been unleashed upon her. The visual unfolded before her eyes.

No, she was not going back. It had taken her five years to traverse the distance from her in-laws' home to the police station.

The police officer returned to his desk. He yawned loudly as he sat down, and then cracked his knuckles. Nayana read the name on his badge: S. P. Jadhav. She licked her lips and stood up, erect. Jadhav opened the complaint book, ruffled its pages, and grabbed a pen.

'All right, madam, at what time did the theft take place?'

'Sahib....'

'Haven't you read the warnings in the newspapers—don't hire servants without doing a background check, haan? You should find out, na, if they have any criminal record. Ask us, for instance....'

'Sahib, listen to me—'

'Do you have a photo and tencha gaanvacha address? His village address? There's no need to worry. How much money did you lose? Did you bring a list of the items stolen? Wonderful. What, do you not want to tell me? Look, I am quite busy.'

She stammered, 'Sahib, there's been no theft.'

'So why aren't you telling me what happened, madam? Did you lose your mangalsutra in a local train? Is your dog missing? Some roadside Romeo must've teased you. I am a terror to those kinds, I'm telling you.'

'Sahib, my husband hits me, and my mother-in-law also...with....' Her voice choked. She had meant to fall into Rasik's arms and lose herself in fantasies of companionship—how did she end up in this situation?

Jadhav put his pen down. His lips curled. Savant came and stood beside Jadhav.

'Jadhav, what is madam's complaint?' Savant asked.

'Domestic violence,' he replied in English.

'Oh I see...I thought....

'Savant, you know how it is, this so-called "domestic violence". The husband must have been peeved about something, must've yelled, and madam made a dash for the police station.'

She looked at both men with petrified eyes. Would they refuse to write down her complaint? She immediately said, 'No, no, sahib, that's not how it is. You must listen to me.'

'Of course I am listening to you, I am,' he repeated in Marathi. 'How long have you been married?'

'Seven years. But—'

Savant was incredulous, 'Seven years! That's a long time. And you suddenly rushed to file a complaint today? Did he suddenly become cruel?'

'See, madam, you seem to be from a respectable family. Khandaani ani sanskari ghar. You must be educated too, right? By doing this you are jeopardizing your family's honour, do you understand?' Jadhav continued.

'But...but will you at least hear me out?'

'Woman, you listen to me. Have you informed your family that you are coming to a police station?'

'No, no....'

'Bas then. It's not too late. Go. Go home. Married life madhe saghda hote, all kinds of things happen in a marriage.'

'Utensils will make some noise or develop small dents when they're kept together, do you understand?'

The other day, Rasik had slapped her—suddenly, out of the blue, for no particular reason. The sabzi was not made well, apparently. She was stupefied. He had hit me? Rasik had struck me? What's worse was that, this time, everyone was watching: the driver had come in to pick up the car keys, the maid to serve water, and sasuji was watching, as usual, her fingers moving over the rosary beads. Her eyes had dripped venom. Those eyes followed Nayana everywhere, piercing, wounding, and branding her.

That poison had gradually become a part of Nayana's life.

You have no accomplishments. See how poorly you drape a saree. The moment you set foot in this house, we were raided by the Income Tax department. See, there she is, reading books all day. You want to become a book-queen or what? You don't have any respect for our customs and traditions. Hai, hai!

It had become impossible to live, eat, and sleep. Her mother-in-law was a machine that worked relentlessly all hours of the day, throughout the year. Nayana had become neurotic just listening to her complaints, but sasuji showed no sign of exhaustion. She continued her litany, and plotted against her.

Initially, she would confide in Rasik, but he would make light of the matter, and say that she was being delusional. She raised me after Papa was gone. She took care of the business until I was ready. She is now trying to train you. Can't you see? This is really her way of showing love; she's involving you in our family. She made golpapdi sweets for you, and fed you in front of me, didn't she? Everything will be fine.

But nothing was fine. Whatever the mother-in-law had done for her son was now being extracted from Nayana, with interest. One man between two women—God, what a clichéd, ancient quarrel!

Had she been told by an acclaimed astrologer that this was how her life would have turned out, she would have laughed in his face. She had told her parents; I refuse to marry someone from our caste, with matching horoscopes. I don't want an arranged marriage. She had the privilege of saying these things to Mummy and Papa. She wanted to marry Rasik. He was from another caste, an attractive young man who had made her dream of freedom, of living life on her own terms. She had insisted on marrying him. But Rasik was completely under his mother's influence. At times, Nayana even wondered if his mother was using tantric magic to influence him. Sasuji went to Shastriji's school for Vedic lessons. She had earned a name for herself through her knowledge of the Bhagavad Gita. She reminded Nayana to ensure that the family honour was never compromised; outsiders shouldn't know what happened within the four walls of their house. She had learned from Shastriji that women's endurance alone would bring India back to the era of Aryan perfection.

At times, Nayana was tempted to go to Shastriji's school and scream at him in the presence of a roomful of devotees. She wanted to ask him, 'Shastriji, what does it mean to be sahansheel, full of endurance?' What do those who sit in air-conditioned rooms and pontificate know about the flaming environment of her day-to-day life, how she was scorched by humiliation daily? And what heaven should she expect after this? The one that belongs to divine men? But she couldn't bring herself to say any of this. Rasik could not understand her problems. He hit her now without any inhibition, not caring even about what other people would think. Her parents had told her, it's your life; you take care of it, and had begun to spend more and more time with their son in the US. They had a green card now, so they came and went as they pleased. She wasn't able to tell them anything except whine vaguely about her cantankerous mother-in-law. By all appearances, Nayana had everything that was required for a happy life. Rasik was the only son, his mother was spiritually inclined; they had a house, a Mercedes—what else could she want?

Her life revolved around Rasik. He would wake up at such-and-such hour; he'd have such-and-such for breakfast, served in such-and-such plate. His lunch had to be packed in different boxes on different days, and the dishes had to be different each day. He had to be served lime juice upon his return, followed by dinner and dessert. After this, Rasik sat with his mother for an hour, chatting about everything in his life. At the end of an exhausting day, Nayana would finally get some rest. She got a few crumbs at night as her share of the day. Just two days ago....

'Bring gulab jamun for Rasik. In that Bangkok plate, okay? Not some random dish,' her mother-in-law told her. 'Middle-class mentality she has,' she said to her son.

Nayana brought the gulab jamun quietly. He has barely finished his dinner, and now he was having mithai. She couldn't help speaking up, especially since Rasik had begun to develop a paunch, 'Mummy, let it be, please. How many people have had heart attacks in your family! Papa also....'

'How inauspicious! Are you listening to her?'

But she had stood firm, 'It's true, isn't it? Rasik, why aren't you saying anything? You have high blood pressure and all this sugar, every day....'

Sasuji had gotten up then and, with tears in her eyes, had retreated to her bedroom. Rasik had stood up promptly.

'Nayana. What did you just do? You hurt Mummy.'

Nayana had held his hand. 'What wrong did I do? Let her be alone for a while, she should realize that her proximity is affecting your health.'

Sataak. Rasik had slapped her hard. Nayana had had enough. Some day she would have to say it. 'You hit me, do what you like. I will speak the truth. Do you have no value for my love, my concern?'

Rasik pushed her away, 'I do value it, but is this the time to talk of all that?'

He had fled towards his mother's room. Nayana was tired of watching the television, waiting for him to come out. She noticed that it was past 2 o'clock. What were the mother and son doing behind a locked door this late at night? The night felt desolate and frightening. If they didn't want a third person, perhaps the mother and son should have....

Yuck. She felt disgusted with herself. Her attempt to inject life into a lifeless relationship was amounting to nothing. Enough.

'Listen, Inspector sahib, you listen to what I am saying.'

'Madam, what do you mean by that, haan? There's a lot I notice, thanks to my job. This is how life is everywhere. Assaj hote.'

Savant pulled up a chair and sat down. 'Okay, so we will write your complaint. What, then? What will you do? Where will you go? If you go back to the same house, the police will have to keep an eye on you, or else those people will torture you even more. Do you want to go to a women's organization? Or to your parents? What do you want to do, karaicha kai?'

'My advice to you is, go home, and forget about everything. If you leave home, you will have to take up a job, and roam around. Instead of working under a strange man, you might as well adjust to your own man, right?' Jadhav added.

The two men exchanged a meaningful glance and laughed. She felt that, perhaps, the inspector had taught his wife a lesson or two today.

Savant yawned, 'Arre, we have such experiences. We have seen instances when the daughter-in-law could be dying of burns but she won't mention the in-laws. You seem to be lucky in comparison.'

She was infuriated. Does she have to die for justice to happen? What of the slow death she was heading towards already?

She cleared her throat and stood up.

'Listen, Mr Jadhav and Mr Savant. I want to file a complaint.

I will bear the consequences—that's my responsibility. I have done my homework. You make a complaint under Article 498 of the Indian Penal Code. It will lead to an arrest and, eventually, a court hearing. Now tell me, will you write it down or should I go to your superiors?'

On that late afternoon, she came out of the police station. The heat scorched her body. The road was dug up, and the tar was hot as lava. She paused for a moment, wiped the sweat off her face, and began walking down the jagged path.

DOORS

HIMANSHI SHELAT

'Silly girl, you'll kill yourself this way. It's been four days, isn't your stomach aching? Don't you see how blissfully those girls go and squat? You are such a fussy little thing.'

Savli reluctantly got up to go to the ditch. The thought of the ditch made her shiver. Two days ago, it had rained heavily. Slippery, mucky lanes, full of puddles of dirty water, had to be crossed to reach the bushes. Then one had to find a relatively decent spot and squat on the dirty wet grass, flattened by God knows how many feet. If a frog leapt onto her foot, or an earthworm brushed against her, she would scream. Heart racing and eyes watchful, one had to somehow finish off the 'task', but none of this seemed to bother Sevanti or Devu. They could defecate anywhere.

Amidst giggles Sevanti would remark, 'No need to splash through the mud and go all the way there.... Come, let's squat here, no one has the time to look at us.' She was incorrigible!

In the dim light of dawn, one could see shadows gliding like ghosts along the road that led to the ditch. The whole scene would have seemed quite eerie had it not been such a dreary routine. After all, people living in and around the slums had always used open land to relieve themselves. It did not seem to bother anybody. Timid and painfully shy, Savli was the only one frightened to be in the open fields.

'Savli's mother wants us to take her along, but God, Savli is so picky. No, here, not there, you keep walking endlessly, and finally she may agree on a spot.'

'Alee, listen! Where do you think you are going? You'll have some insect clinging to your feet if you go that far....'

Then Savli would have to stop. Hiding behind the bushes and staying close to her companions, she would squat. But at the slightest sound of approaching footsteps, she would stand up. The open sky would hang over her and even a tiny hole appeared cave-like.

While they lived in the village, Baapa, her father, would make her and Budhiya sleep outside on a string cot. In the middle of the night, her eyes would fly open and Baapa would be missing. The door of the house would be shut. She would hear jackals howling from far away, or hear the wind rustling among the dry leaves and brush off the top branches of trees. Something seemed to move in the grass of the yard next door. At such times it seemed the darkness would swallow her whole and, even on a cold night, she would be soaked in sweat. Once she was so scared that she had pounded on the front door violently. When he saw that nothing was really wrong, Baapa had slapped her, though not very hard. After all, he had been rather groggy.

After that, she had always felt too scared to knock on the door and wake up either Baapa or Ma. But having to spend an entire dark, desolate night outside with her eyes wide open made her knees go weak with fear. Budhiya was very young. He snored away without a care in the world.

Things are different in the city. The crowds surge and simmer through the days and nights. Everyone carries tins of water into the open. Nani kaki had once taken her to an enclosed toilet. There was a queue, of course, but at least one could shut the door. But after going inside, she realized that it wasn't much of a door. The latch was broken. She had specifically reminded Nani kaki and Pani several times to make sure that no one pushed open the door. But both of them had got busy chatting and laughing, and soon forgot about her. A huge man with a big moustache had thrown the door open with a dhad...aa...ak. She had frozen. When she tried to rise, her legs trembled. The rascal stood laughing outside and even winked at her. Since then Savli avoided his gaze if she ever bumped into him anywhere.

On the festive night of Aatham, there was a film screening at Dayaljinagar. She slept through most of it, but the memory of a pink tiled washroom and a fairly-like girl engulfed by bubbles of soap remained etched in her mind. Sevanti had said that bungalows had such bathrooms. Perhaps that was why she worked in a bungalow. As for Savli, the tattered gunnysacks draped around four bamboo poles that made up her bathroom were so worn out that she dared not remove all her clothes to bathe. She was afraid people would be able to see her. The road behind the bathroom led to a factory and cycles and two wheelers whizzed by. Good-for-nothing boys loitered around, whistling. Even though she was shielded by the gunnysacks, it felt like she was bathing in the open. Sevanti and Mumtaz had started their menstruation cycles five or six months ago. They said, 'It's so difficult to "go" on such days. You have to keep everything suppressed.' They, of course, took care of all this when they went to work in the bungalows.

Pani had said that she too would have 'this'—meaning, filth, every month.... Ma would simply not stop blabbering then. Even now she went on and on: 'Our princess wants soap every day. She hasn't yet brought a single paisa home, but her demands exceed everybody else's. The way she scrubs, the soap is down to a sliver within a week.'

There is a mela at the maidan today. People from the locality are running back and forth from the mela. For the last couple of days, Pani and Sevanti have been persuading her to accompany them, but her mother wouldn't agree. She probably thought that Savli would spend five or ten rupees there, and so, it was better not to let her go. Sevanti didn't have to ask anyone to go to the mela because she worked and earned her own money.

Finally, Ma relented and allowed Savli to go. She combed her hair with oil until it was slick and plastered her face with talcum. Ma had reminded them to hold hands tightly because if they got lost, they would end up looking for one another all night. 'Make sure,' she had said, 'you come back before it gets dark and don't stop for too long at any one place.'

At the fair, crowds swelled near the long rows of bangle sellers. Suddenly, there was pandemonium. It was difficult to figure out what was happening. In the confusion, Savli was separated from Sevanti. She shouted but nothing could be heard in the noise. Standing alone, she was about to cry when a kind-looking woman grabbed her hand and carefully pulled her out of the crowd.

The woman asked her, 'Dayaljinagar? Come, child, I'll take you there, don't be afraid.' She wiped her misty eyes on her frock sleeves and began to walk with the woman. The woman hailed a rickshaw.

'First, let us go to my house and inform my family. Then we'll go over to your house. You are not in a hurry, are you?'

She shook her head. The rickshaw went swiftly though narrow lanes and resplendent shops. Some doors were open, some closed. Everything was so unfamiliar, but she was not afraid. Bai appeared to be kind. The rickshaw stopped in a corner, in front of a huge house with a big veranda, and gigantic strong doors.

There was a courtyard in the middle with rooms on the upper floor. A few faces peeped out of small windows, but the windows were immediately pulled shut. There must be many people staying in such a big house, Savli thought, as she looked around her.

Muffled sounds of song and laughter seemed to come from somewhere. But she could not see what was going on upstairs. The doors of the rooms appeared firmly shut and even the ones that were open had pink floral curtains hiding everything inside.

'Aati hun abhi, I will be back soon. We will go to your house and I will drop you,' Bai said before disappearing inside.

Sevanti must be looking for her in the crowd. Everyone must have gone back home and Ma would have brought the house down. 'This is why I had said no. How do we now look for Savli in the crowd, my grain-sized girl in such a mad rush?' Ma always called her 'grain-sized'.

Suddenly, her stomach ached. She was hungry and thirsty and now she had cramps. The cramps were hardly surprising. After all, she had avoided 'going' for three days. Once Bai comes back, she would ask her. Surely, this house has all sorts of amenities. It was better to finish it off today; then there would be no cause for worry the next day.

Something moved and churned inside her; she became impatient and confused. As soon as Bai came she would quickly ask her—why would anyone refuse something like this?

She immediately asked permission when Bai reappeared.

'Sure, sure. Arre, Munni, take her.'

There were two big bathrooms on either side of the courtyard, with pretty, smooth, pink-and-blue tiles. She thought of the bathroom in the movie she had watched. Next to the bath was a clean toilet with doors that shut and strong walls...did one go in there? Did they all go in there?

Wide-eyed, she stared at the door and the latch. Once the door closes, everything outside gets shut out. She is safe inside; no one can open the door nor peep in. There's no need to rush.

'Go inside,' Munni ordered.

She floated through the air with joy. Dazed, as if in a dream, she went in and the door shut behind her—tightly.

THE UNBLEMISHED ONE
MOHAN PARMAR

His eyelids began to droop, but he continued to sit, looking like an invincible warrior. His daughter Rama was playing noisily, interrupting Radha as she sat winding the bobbin. Radha was well and truly frustrated. She tried drawing Kanti's attention by gesturing at Rama, but Kanti was unmoved, lost in his own thoughts. He wound the cloth onto the cloth roller and resumed weaving. In the course of weaving, one of the threads of the yarn got entangled in the heddle and the shuttle went flying, hitting the mud-baked wall. It made a visible dent on the wall. 'Bloody....' Muttering, Kanti stood up and wrapped a towel around his waist.

Radha came rushing to him. She looked at Kanti and asked, 'What's going on with you today?'

'That's just the way it's going to be now,' Kanti replied tersely.

He picked up the shuttle and sat down at the loom once again. He put the broken thread on the bar and began to weave. The broken warp-yarn had left a mark on the woven cloth. The heddles going up and down the reed that was striking the cloth bothered Kanti today. His foot stomped vigorously on the treadle. The twine passing through the heddle snapped, and the heddles hung loosely from the weaving frame. He lost his grip on the beater. With the other hand, he had held the gilloli handle, which had been imprinted with his fingerprints now. He almost slapped his forehead. He missed Ahmedabad. He would probably fail at settling at the loom. He looked up. The eaves on the roof above had come off, and sunlight seeped in through the cracks, falling limply into the room. The light created sun-patterns on the floor. He looked at them and was reminded of his childhood. Those patterns used to unveil, to his childlike mind, the mysteries of the skies above. He had seen the alternating shades of the sun and clouds sweep through them.

The wall that now stood damaged by the shuttle would serve for him as the background against which Kanti would throw light and the patterns were reflected back into the room. Thinking of all this made him want to be a child again. His gaze slid to the bar, he saw the lease-stick on the warp-beam which was tilted. He manoeuvred it angrily, and a couple of warp-threads snapped. He yelled at the wailing Rama. She was frightened out of her wits.

Kanti got up from the loom and went towards the earthen pot of water, the paniyaru, and filled a glass with water. He looked steadily at the water. He thought of Ahmedabad. Radha was sitting at the loom, struggling to fasten the bobbin on the bar. His eyes moved from the roof and fell upon Radha's back. A sigh escaped his lips, 'Poor thing, she has gone pale.' His eyes swept over the dishevelled loom, where threads hung down listlessly. He felt terribly irritated. In a flash, he set out of the house. He punched Rama, who was annoying her mother, on her back. Radha was perplexed. A yelping Rama ran to the neem tree and stood underneath. She began to cry loudly. Kanti glared at her, 'Shut up, you....'

'What are you doing? Do you even realize? You keep suffering inside; open your heart to us so that we know,' Radha said.

'Spare me your wisdom and mind your business.' Saying this, Kanti put on his chappals. Glaring at Rama, he began to head out.

'But listen to me at least....'

'I will be back, the thread has snapped, you complete the warp.'

Dogs were barking in the small lane outside. A snake charmer was walking towards the neem tree, playing his flute all the while. He came to the neem tree and began his performance. Rama was now busy watching him at work. Kanti stood watching for a few minutes. Children had gathered around the neem tree by now. A rascal of a boy held a brick in his hand, waiting to hurl it at the snake charmer at the right moment. Kanti's eyes met his, and the boy quietly threw away the brick. Had Kanti been in a cheerful frame of mind, he would have found this amusing. He walked away instead. He passed Puri ma's home on the way. His feet halted. Puri ma was in the veranda singing lullabies for Dala's child as she gently pushed the whimpering child inside the cloth-cradle.

'This wretched boy refuses to sleep. My hands are so tired.' Puri ma took the baby from the cradle and held him in her arms. On seeing Kanti, she placed the baby back in the cradle, and invited him in, 'Come, come, bhai. Alya Dala, your friend is here.'

Dala was inside the house singing the bhajan 'Come soon Nakalank, the unblemished one'. The bhajan described the perfect saviour who would come from the East and marry the untouchable Meghli.

'Enough, enough, you seeker of Nakalank!' Saying this, Kanti made himself comfortable on the heap of cotton.

'What, bhai, out for a stroll?'

'My heart is not in weaving. The wretched cotton is also a mixed one. The threads keep breaking.'

'So don't use brutal force on them.' Dala's eyes twinkled with amusement as he looked at Kanti.

'Ma, light the fire.'

'Stop sucking your mother's blood, where is that wife of yours?' Puri ma snapped.

'She has gone to shit.'

'So let her come back. Your prince refuses to sleep. The moment I move from here, he starts wailing. God, release me from this nuisance of a life now.'

'So die then.'

'I will, and see what that does to your reputation.' Puri ma stood up and went to the kitchen. She lit the fire and, after putting the water for the tea to boil, she came back to the cloth-cradle and resumed the lullabies. Dala offered a bidi to Kanti and said, 'You are comfortable doing the towels, right? See, I am slogging over the bed sheets.'

'I don't enjoy weaving any more. I can't get the mill out of my mind.'

'Foolish man, do you think it's wise to rely on others and ignore this? Why is it so bad?'

Kanti blew on the bidi. His gaze shifted when he heard the clanging noise of the toilet-can. Dala's wife, Beni, had returned and was fastening the toilet-can on the peg. Kanti greeted her, 'There you are.'

'So your majesty is finding it difficult to work and offloading all the anger onto a child, hanh? Poor Radha, how much she wept,' Beni replied.

'Let her weep. As it is I am upset, and there's ruckus in the house.'

They could hear the snake charmer's theatrical voice. It sounded like he was putting on a grand performance. Kanti's eyes met Beni's and he laughed.

Beni mocked him, saying, 'How can this place be compared with Ahmedabad? You were the hero there. This is back-breaking work. Threads will break and harnesses will snap. Everything has to be done manually. If you lose courage like this, you will not earn a paisa.'

Kanti was reminded of the time when the mill closed down. He had felt then that it was just a matter of a few days. But fifteen days went by. There was no sign of the mill reopening. He kept making attempts to go back to the mill, but returned, his face despondent. He had waited patiently for a month or two in Ahmedabad. Many others like him had packed up their belongings and returned to their native villages. When he first brought up the subject of going back to the village to Radha, she had merely said, 'As you wish.' When he returned to the village, with Radha in tow, everyone had looked at him with surprise. Those moments were the hardest for Kanti. In his earlier visits to the village, he could show off. His ironed clothes and city look impressed everyone. Radha's urban language and the jewellery she was wearing drew all and sundry to her. But when the two of them returned to the village after the closure of the mill, people were shocked. Kanti went into the house. He sat in a corner and broke down. When he emerged after a while, he looked as if he had woken from a deep sleep, lost and disoriented. Dala had comforted him, 'I am around, why are you so worried?

You know how to weave. I will help you in any way I can.'

Dala's support had made Kanti feel better. He had brought a loom to his house and had begun to weave. In fact, he did enjoy weaving. He was independent. He was not a labourer or slave to anyone. He looked at Dala with tenderness in his eyes. Dala was blowing the smoke away and thinking. Suddenly, he stood up and began to rummage through the pockets of his shirt that hung on a peg. He started looking through some papers. Kanti asked, 'What are you searching for?'

'Nothing. It's a private matter.'

'What is private for people like us!' Kanti said. 'So tell me.'

'It's the bill for the cotton bales I was looking for. This time the yield is not going to be good; the bed sheets will cost more.'

'Now stop fussing over it, sit down.'

Kanti held Dala by the hand and made him sit down. Beni brought tea. She put the kettle and teacups on the floor and headed back to the kitchen. Dala offered tea to Kanti. They were both sipping tea when old man Jetha's son, Natu, arrived.

'Come, Natu, drink some tea with us.'

'I am in a hurry. The two of you can come along. We have guests for my sister's aanu ceremony.'

'Has Revanda come? All right let's go. But why don't you have tea first?' Dala offered Natu a cup. Natu left after drinking tea, and a little later Dala and Kanti stood up to leave.

People were sitting in Jetha dosa's veranda. 'Ram, Ram,' Kanti and Dala greeted everybody.

Revanda said to Dala, 'Bhai, you haven't bothered to visit our village of late.'

'Who has the time with all this weaving...you have it easy, with so much land, you can go around the village visiting people!' Dala laughed. The two of them found a place to sit amongst the others.

The sunlight shone through the neem tree, waking up a sleeping dog. The dog ran away, then came promptly back to sit in the same place.

Jetha dosa handed out bidis to everyone, and called out to Natu, 'Alya, why haven't Motiram and Talshi come?'

'Talshi kaka has gone to sell his wares. Motiram was busy straightening the cotton knots when Karsan rabari's cow came rushing and ruined it all. He has said that he will come if he can.'

'All right.'

After drinking tea, Kanti was eager to leave. He looked at Dala, but Dala was busy talking. He had not done any work and that bothered Kanti. Radha must have mended the broken thread and woven it. He was itching to do his share. He wrapped his striped towel around his waist and tied it up with a drawstring. He stood up to leave, but Dala said, 'Come on, sit down.'

Kanti sat down.

Revanda took a deep puff from the hookah. He swirled the smoke in his mouth and said, 'That fight is over, by the way, Har da.'

'Which one?'

'The one about Gova Sompara's daughter.'

'Arre bhai, put that to rest now. That fight ruined the entire pargana, the communities of both villages.'

'But that was the boy's fault, Kala's son, isn't it?'

'Of course it was the boy's fault, but he has lost his nerve now. He will pick up the girl if she is ready to be sent,' Isha quipped.

'Wasn't the boy being difficult?'

'True. He stayed in Surat with someone for some days, they say. Now he is on track. These people of 26 parganas have their noses up in the air.'

The moment 26 was mentioned, Kanti could not control himself. 'Now leave behind this 26 and 44 pargana business.'

'You will not understand. Alya, do you even know what a pargana is, or even your father's origins and gotra? When such good gossip takes place, these young ones jump right in without knowing anything,' Narsi kaka said in jest.

'Look at this Narsi!' Jetha dosa said.

Kanti was about to respond when Dala signalled him to remain quiet. There's a lot Kanti wanted to say about the village council: 'You have divided the pargana into two. You are not even interested in solving problems. When elders break the laws of the pargana, it's acceptable. When others do it, you make a mountain out of a molehill. If you have any spine, why don't you combine the parganas? Why are you sitting around looking at each other's faces? Does anyone dare? Leave it to young people like us. And see how we will unify the parganas in no time. In Ahmedabad, we co-existed happily. If someone from 26 parganas passed away, we even went for the cremation. These people in the village have refused to participate in each other's pargana. They have stopped attending each other's festivities and funerals. This has only increased the distance between them. It will only make it more difficult to unify. We young men don't feel any such distance. It is a seventy-village pargana. Forty-four on one side and twenty-six on the other. See how difficult it is for the women as well. This Dala's wife, Beni, for instance. Her cousin died at his natal home, but because he is in 26 pargana, nobody even went to comfort the family. What do they think of themselves, these turbaned leaders of the community? They fatten themselves and thrive, but there's nothing good for the rest of us. They have only sown further seeds of difference between the villages. What does one say? Whom does one say it to?' He felt like making a public announcement. But he didn't. The hookah was circulated among everybody, and it was now Jetha dosa who puffed on the hubble-bubble and narrowed his eyes, saying, 'Whose son is he, the one who just spoke?'

'You didn't recognize the fellow? He's Varu dosa's son.'

'I did, I did. Which village was it where he went to sell the the woven pachhedis and had Narsi's legs broken by the Patel? The same Varu dosa, no?'

'Yes, yes, the same,' Hari kaka laughed.

'What was that?' Dala asked.

'Arre, it's worth listening to, I tell you. Jetha, why don't you tell him?' Hari kaka said.

'No, Hari, you do it.'

'So it was like this. Varu and Narsi had gone to sell their wares in a village. They had entered different vaas quarters. Varu must have been in the Patel vaas and was showing the woven sheets to a Patel woman. The Patel woman liked them. Varu got carried away, and said, "I especially brought them for you." The Patel woman was irked. Varu ran for his life. Meanwhile, Narsi entered, calling out, "Woven pachhedis for you, buy them for nothing," and entered, for all his sins, the same vass. The Patel husband smashed his bones instead.'

Everyone laughed. Even Kanti rolled with laughter. Revanda said to Narsi loudly, 'So, didn't you clarify?'

'The moment I would open my mouth, smash, another blow on my body,' he also laughed, baring his teeth. 'Those times were different. Varu was an audacious fellow. In one particular village, two Muslim men sat with a coin before them. They racked their brains trying to decide which emperor it belonged to. When the two of us passed them by, one of the men said, "Mehtar, you tell us to which king's reign this coin belongs." Varu took the coin and turned it this way and that. Then he said, "This is that king who reigned for two days in Delhi. Do you know the name?"

"No," the miyan said.

"That emperor was called Varu the emperor."'

Everyone broke into laughter.

Conversation flowed like this aimlessly, and the dogs of the lane began to bark. The dog sleeping under the neem burst into action and joined the other barking dogs. Everyone looked in that direction. Mangaldas mukhi was entering with a stick in his hand and walking in their direction. On seeing the mukhi, Jetha dosa deferentially brought a chair from inside the house. The mukhi sat down saying, 'How nice, Kanti is right here. You are the man I wanted to meet.'

'What is it?' Kanti asked. Dala stared at Mangaldas's face. What did the headman want with Kanti that it had brought him all the way here? He was intrigued.

'Bhai Kanti, you know that I have a road contract. While Somo was around, I wasn't bothered. All our Patels have gone to do work for others. I don't have an educated person left with me. I thought instead of bringing an outsider, it was better to have Kanti. You are educated, and you have lived in Ahmedabad, so you know everything. That's the reason, bhai. And also, I trust you. This is a good time for me to hand over the task to you. I will have nothing to worry about then.'

'That's true. And Kanti is not sloppy. He knows how to work,' Dala added.

Dala knew that Kanti was not enjoying weaving. The kind of offer Mangaldas was making would let Kanti earn some money. Mangaldas mukhi appeared like a god to Dala. Kanti was overjoyed to hear this. Today, when the thread had snapped, he was severely tempted to give up that work. Mangaldas's presence was providential. But he was not going to bare his soul to Mangaldas. He remained quiet, and let everyone see that Mukhi was doing this because he needed Kanti.

'Tell me, Kanti, will you come?'

'I will come, but I should be able to make sense of it.'

'You need to see if it brings me profit. I trust you, that's why I have come all the way here. Ever since you have come back, I have been meaning to give you some work. By God's grace, the contract has come through, and luckily you are also here. You come early morning tomorrow and don't forget.'

'That's fine, Mangal da. You would remember from our days of studying together that I am short-tempered. I don't tolerate wrong things.'

'I know, I know,' Mangaldas laughed and said, 'You come to my farm tomorrow. I will explain everything to you. I will give you much more than what you get out of weaving. And the food will come from my home, bas.'

'Sure, I'll be there.'

'All right then, I will leave. I need to go to the sarpanch's home.' Mukhi was about to get up.

Jetha dosa requested, 'There's tea being made. Do have some.'

'No, Kaka, no. I had tea just before I left.' Mukhi got up and began to walk away. Kanti laughed. But the Mukhi did not turn back and simply crossed the vaas.

Dala spoke up, 'Just see, Revanda! How kind our mukhi is, do you see even a trace of arrogance? And he also gave Kanti work.'

'Absolutely. The darbars in our village would never visit us. In fact, when we go out, they think we are showing off and have forgotten our place in society.'

'Bhai, it is entirely due to this mukhi that things are calm in this village. You all know about this anti-reservation campaign that's going on. We don't have any problem here. The mukhi told us not to worry about anything. And why should we think of fighting? These rascals went to become leaders and that's why they are waging a war.'

'That's good to know.'

Jetha dosa brought tea. Dala and Kanti gulped down the tea and left. On the way back, Dala playfully punched Kanti, 'There you go, see how well it turned out for you. You don't have to fret about threads snapping now.'

'You're right, I am sick of weaving. I got what I was looking for. And the work will last for at least six months. And, God willing, the government will take over the mills and resume. For all you know, the mills may start very soon.'

Kanti came home and told Radha about the new development. An overjoyed Radha said, 'That's great. You were so tired of this that it broke my heart to see you like that.'

'Have you finished the weaving?'

'Yes.'

'Come on then, let me fasten the waft and, if time allows, I can complete it today.' Kanti entered with thread combs. The heddle still looked dishevelled. Kanti fastened the waft and was thinking of sitting down at the loom. Just then Radha asked, 'Mind if I do it?'

'Will you be fine with it?'

'Teach me.'

'And what if you don't pick it up?'
'Everyone learns on the job.'
'All right, then sit.'

Radha sat down at the loom. Rama, who had made herself comfortable in a little alcove, was amused to see her mother at the loom. Kanti sat down beside her and said, 'You will be able to manage the two-treadle cloth, but this is more difficult and you will have to be careful. Keep your left foot on the first treadle, and right foot on the third one. Press the first treadle and put the shuttle; then the shuttle again. Then you need to shift your feet quickly—the left foot on the second treadle and the right on the fourth treadle. Press the second, insert the shuttle, press the fourth and insert the shuttle. Now keep alternating the treadles, first one and three, then two and four. Do you understand?'

'This sounds difficult, but I will try.'

Radha struggled as she tried. She sometimes pressed the fourth treadle after the first and the third after the second. This lasted for a few minutes, 'This design has changed.'

'Of course it will change. Your footwork is faulty.'

'It goes like this, na?' Radha briskly shuffled her feet. With one hand on the gilloli, she did it with such grace that Rama clapped her hands and laughed.

'Good for you, Radha Rani! I have been sitting at the loom for ten years, and I have still not learnt how to weave. Look at you!' Beni said as she entered the house.

Kanti laughed, 'Go on, you leave that to me.'

Radha got up, and she and Beni sat down to chat in the verandah. Kanti cut away the threads that had changed the design. He got back to weaving with renewed enthusiasm. By the evening, he had finished, and felt light as air.

The following morning, Kanti went early to the mukhi's farm. The mukhi had built a pucca house on his farm. The farm was very close to the village, so he had decided to stay nearby. On earlier occasions when Kanti visited the village, he had made it a point to meet Mangaldas. Kanti and Mangaldas had studied together through primary school. After the seventh grade, Mangaldas stopped going to school. Kanti went on to middle school, which was three miles away. Their friendship deepened when Mangaldas married Deeva, who was also their classmate. Mangaldas knew Deeva respected Kanti a great deal.

As such, Mangaldas was wise and intelligent. He had made quite a mark in the village despite being young. Even the elders in the village respected him. He had sought Kanti's advice on certain important matters. If he happened to visit Ahmedabad, he would visit Kanti in the chawl. When the textile mill closed down, he comforted Kanti, saying he would inform Kanti if he found a job suitable for him. Mangaldas had been true to his promise, and therefore Kanti was excited to start working with him.

'Come, Kanti, sit down.'

Kanti sat down on the charpoy. The mukhi gave him a cup of tea and went inside the house to get ready. Deeva was feeding the cattle. Kanti's gaze steadied upon Deeva's back. Deeva had not yet noticed his presence. The two of them had been classmates during primary school, and many memories of that period came back to Kanti. He laughed to himself as he thought of those days. Suddenly, Deeva turned around. She was startled when she saw him. She quickly wrapped up her work and came towards Kanti. Their eyes met. An overjoyed Deeva came close to Kanti and said, 'When did you come?'

'Just now.'

'You've lost weight.'

'I know, but it's all right, I guess.'

'How long have you been in the village? Do you feel like coming to meet us or not?'

'How do I come for no reason?'

'You've forgotten everything, right?'

'Only what needed to be forgotten.'

'My memories have not gone.'

'Especially the memory of Jayanti Prajapati, na!'

'That rascal is best forgotten,' Deeva pouted. Her eyes shifted to the door of her house. The mukhi had not yet come out. She wanted to chat with Kanti without worrying. Kanti had taught Jayanti Prajapati a lesson, and she was amused by that memory.

'What gall he had, the scoundrel!'

'But what a coward he was at the end! Had I not given him a whack that day, he would have always harassed you.'

'So true, had you not appeared, it'd have been a disaster for me. I didn't even know the man, but he was after my life. He came into the classroom thinking I was alone. I had no idea that you were standing in the lobby. But he had not seen you either. And he held my hand with such confidence, like he had known me forever.'

'And how his confidence had been smashed to smithereens! I wanted to crush him into pulp, but I let that temptation go.' Kanti had straightened up now. Deeva looked at Kanti with great attention. Kanti felt that had it not been for the advances Jayanti Prajapati had made, he would not have known Deeva.

He started to mumble something as he looked at Deeva. There was a lot he wanted to say. But he didn't. How much Deeva had looked up to him since that incident! The two of them would leave school together every day after that day. They would chat for hours at the fork from where their respective lanes started. Once, Kanti remembered, Deeva had insisted on visiting his house. There was such romance in those days.

Then it was time for the secondary school examinations to be over and done with. They met during the SSC exams. Deeva was accompanied by her brother. They couldn't talk much. But Kanti felt happy when Deeva married someone in his village. Not that he could meet her, considering he was mostly working in Ahmedabad. Moreover, he did not want to build on their adolescent feelings.

On seeing that Kanti had grown quiet, Deeva went inside the house. The mukhi was ready to leave. He and Kanti headed towards the site of the road construction. The mukhi familiarized Kanti with all the important matters. Kanti was somewhat familiar with the road construction business, so he did not have to make an effort to understand. From the first day itself the mukhi handed over all the responsibilities to Kanti. It was important to keep an eye on the fields, so it was not possible for him to pay any attention to the construction. Leaving everything to Kanti's judgement, he left. Kanti established a rapport with the labourers and began the work. His easy-going manner inspired the labourers to work. The mukhi felt relieved to see the amount of work that had been completed by the evening. The two of them wrapped up some chores and came to the field. The harvest was in full bloom. The field workers were returning home. Deeva came running. Her tall bony frame seemed to sway with the breeze.

'You are back?' she greeted.

The way she looked at Kanti almost made him forget himself.

The mukhi went inside the house to remove his kurta. In that minute or two, Deeva had managed to ask Kanti, 'You must be tired, no?'

'Of course.'

'The village sun is harsher too, you know. People from the city find it difficult.'

'I am used to this sun now.'

'Make sure it doesn't scorch you.'

'It belongs to my birthplace; let it scorch if it has to. It's much better than the shallow warmth of the city, right?' Kanti laughed. So did Deeva. Her laughter had a honey-like sweetness, Kanti felt.

Having changed, the mukhi came out of the house. He looked at the two of them and said, 'Look at this pair of brother and sister-in-law, laughing away! What's so funny?'

'Nothing funny, Kanti bhai says he's made his peace with the village sun, that's all.'

'Kanti is Kanti of course. He's one of a kind from his caste in this country, I tell you.'

The mukhi waxed eloquent about Kanti. Deeva asked him, 'Is

Kanti bhai eating with us?'

'Yes.'

'No, no. I must go home today. I have not informed Radha. She must be waiting for me,' Kanti said.

'Sorry, Kanti, you must eat both meals at my house. I had already told you this.'

'No, Mukhi, please. I will go home,' and Kanti began to walk away.

Deeva turned to the mukhi, ready to chastise him, 'You are not even insisting, why would he stay then?'

'I am more than happy to, but I can't physically force him to sit down and eat, can I?'

'Let me see how he refuses…' Deeva went and stood before Kanti. 'We must seem like ordinary people to you, no? We insist so much, but that doesn't mean you have to be puffed up with such attitude.'

'That's not true, Bhabhi! I had told Radha that I would eat at home in the evening. If you pamper me like this, I will be spoilt. I promise I will eat both meals at your place tomorrow.' Kanti managed to wriggle out of the situation with great difficulty.

However, from the next day, Deeva had staked a claim on Kanti. She fussed over him about every small thing. Kanti found her behaviour incomprehensible. She was Mukhi's wife, and on those grounds, her fussing over Kanti was uncomfortable for him. He had tried impressing this upon her, but as days went by, Kanti found his own behaviour towards her also changing. Deeva's chiselled body and voluptuous breasts caused him to abandon his senses. He found the Deeva of today more attractive than the sixteen-year-old classmate. An invisible wall that stood between them seemed bothersome to both. Deeva was like a pungent pepper. When Mukhi's brother, Sendha, visited their home and spoke casually with Deeva, she put him in place with such brutality that Kanti felt sorry for him. When Sendha saw Deeva talking to Kanti with all her charm, he felt jealous and began to make plans to poison the mukhi's ears so that Kanti would be asked to leave. Deeva understood his intentions, so she prohibited Sendha from coming to her house.

Sendha stopped coming and Deeva heaved a sigh of relief. Even in the midst of work, Kanti would go over to the house for a bit. If Kanti did not, Deeva would sulk and go over to meet him in the field or she would refuse to talk to him for two days. Finally, Kanti would indulge her. She would wait near the wicket gate for him in the evening if he was delayed.

One day, the mukhi had gone out of town. Kanti had come early and was sitting on the haystack. Deeva was washing clothes at the well. On seeing Kanti, she hastily finished washing the clothes and prepared to come and meet him. On spotting a snake behind Kanti, Deeva lost her mind. Throwing her bucket aside, she ran towards him like a maniac. She pulled him away from the haystack, then made as if to hide him under her sari. Kanti's heartbeat went up. It was a good thing that the crop hung low and hid them from the labourers working in the field. Nobody noticed. That day Deeva and Kanti simply exchanged looks and didn't say much to each other. Kanti understood that Deeva was very attracted to him. Now, they would brush against each other. So, if the mukhi had gone directly to the sarpanch's home and Kanti found himself alone, sitting on the charpoy at the mukhi's house, Deeva would give him water and nudge him. It's not that Kanti did not like this. But he would think of the mukhi and hesitate. He strove hard to save himself from an awkward position. He knew that if the mukhi were to find out, he would not be able to tolerate the betrayal. Kanti reduced his visits to the mukhi's house in the middle of the day. He was beginning to lose himself in work and the mukhi was very content with the way things were progressing with the road construction. He felt his faith in Kanti was well-placed. And the fact that he and Deeva laughed together over things did not seem unusual to him. He was familiar with Deeva's easy-going manner. One day, Sendha had said to him, 'You should have found another person, this one will drive a wedge in your home.' The mukhi had retorted, 'Mind your own business, and if you are going to take care of the work, I can throw Kanti out this minute.' Sendha had to shut his mouth. He knew his limitations. His problem was Kanti's closeness to Deeva, not with Kanti working for his brother.

One day, when the mukhi was out of town, Sendha lurked near Deeva's house. He kept an eye on her every move. Sendha needed to check if Kanti was ignoring his work to come to her house. On finding out that the mukhi and the sarpanch were both going to be out of the village, he had rushed to the mukhi's field. Deeva had just finished cleaning the cattle shed and was letting her feet cool. On seeing Sendha, she felt dread in the pit of her stomach. She got up and went inside. Sendha turned in the direction of the labourers. He went and lit up a bidi next to Chaturji. With a bidi in his mouth, he headed towards the patch of fallow land near the field. Deeva came out of the house and wondered what would happen if Kanti turned up while Sendha was still around. She was petrified of Sendha, who refused to budge. On seeing Deeva outside the house, he turned in her direction.

A shudder ran through Deeva's body, 'Why is the scoundrel bent upon being here?' she muttered to herself. Sendha came and stood right beside her.

'How are you, Bhabhi?' Sendha laughed.

Without saying a word, Deeva began to the sweep the floor. As she bent down, Sendha's eyes feasted upon her back. Deeva was not aware of this. She wanted to get rid of him by ignoring him.

'Kanti works quite well, isn't that so, Bhabhi?'

'I don't know.'

'I have heard that you can't praise him enough.'

'Perhaps.'

'Of course, of course, I am the only enemy in your eyes, while a stranger....'

'I beg you, just leave me alone.'

'I must appear bitter as poison to you, no? No worry, if you don't like people like us, here I go.'

Sendha left, feigning exasperation. The moment he left, Kanti arrived. Deeva was worked up. Kanti stared at her. With tears in her eyes Deeva said, 'How come you are here early?'

'I couldn't focus on my work. My heart was here.'

Deeva felt comforted by Kanti's words. Wiping her tears she said, 'Keep your heart with you then.'

'I tried, but it wouldn't stay with me, so I rushed here.'

'How long can this go on?'

Kanti sat down, somewhat despondently. Deeva looked at him from the corner of her eye, 'Do you want to sit outside now?'

Although she had said that, she was suddenly reminded of Sendha. He had just left, and if he returned, there would be utter disaster.

'You can't come inside. To be honest, I am very scared of Sendha. He has begun to hover around all too frequently now.'

'If I am not scared, why are you so worried?'

'We have to observe some limits, don't we?'

'Should I make tea?'

'No.'

'So you want to just sit and mope?'

'Yes.'

'Should I bring a rosary for you then?

'You want me to turn into a sadhu?'

'What is the alternative?'

'When is the mukhi returning from his visit?'

'Probably tomorrow evening or day after.'

Deeva went to collect the clothes that had dried on the clothesline. She was lost in her thoughts. She had dropped the mukhi's jacket twice. Her mind was whirling. She folded the clothes and went inside. When she came back and stood before Kanti, her lips fluttered with nervousness. Kanti looked at her lips straining to say something. He said, 'You want to say something?'

'Yes...but,' Deeva smiled nervously. Then, 'I don't think so.'

'Please do. Upon my life, you have to tell me.'

She turned to look at the field with sadness in her eyes. Suddenly, she turned to Kanti and said, 'I want you to come here at early dawn tomorrow.'

'What for?'

'There's a reason. Chatur will take the chillies and leave this evening. He will return only tomorrow afternoon. The mukhi is not here. There's not a single soul in the morning. What are you looking at me for? You will come, won't you?'

Kanti kept quiet. His foot scraped the floor. Deeva walked up to him, and said, 'You will come tomorrow, won't you?'

With his toes still scraping the floor, he ended up saying, 'Yes.' The neem tree they were sitting under rang out with the melody of many birds.

That night there was a bhajan gathering at Khoda's place. The invitation to join had come in the evening. Kanti finished the day's work and was about to lie down on the charpoy when Radha remarked, 'Are you planning to sleep already? Don't you want to come for the bhajan?'

'No.'

'Arre, how is that possible? What will people say if you don't come? They would think I am to be blamed for it.'

'Come on, why would they do that? I need to leave early tomorrow morning, and if I am not able to wake up....'

'I will wake you up.'

'All right, after a while then.'

As he lay down on the charpoy, Kanti began to think: Mangaldas Mukhi is out of the village. Deeva has called me early in the morning. If I go to the bhajan gathering, it will be at least three in the morning by the time I return. If I am delayed, it will ruin the entire plan. Deeva has called me early so that nobody will see us. Can't I just miss the bhajan? he asked himself. But the next moment he thought that if he were not to go to the bhajan gathering, people would think he was a non-believer, and Khoda would surely reprimand him the next day. What would he tell him then? Kanti turned on his side. As such, he liked to go to bhajan gatherings. While he was in a chawl in Ahmedabad, he did not miss a single such occasion. He did not sing bhajans, but he liked listening to them, and he also enjoyed the bhakti element.

His mind kept alternating between the desire to go and Deeva's face. He couldn't decide what he wanted to do. His body felt a surge of desire. For the first time, he was going to enjoy himself with someone else's wife. He had never imagined that he could have such relations with someone other than Radha. Deeva had poured such affection on him. Despite trying to restrain himself, he was irresistibly drawn to her. Now there was no solution to this knotty situation. He recalled his conversation with her today, and his heart began to pound with excitement.

Kanti lay on his back. Radha had finished bathing at the vada behind the house. Dust clung to her feet. Stamping her feet, she came up to Kanti's charpoy. She saw Kanti with his gaze fixed upon the sky. She asked, 'What do you see in the sky?'

'What?' Kanti was jolted out of his reverie and he looked at Radha. She laughed.

'Where did you get lost? I thought you were able to see something other than the moon and the stars.' Kanti wondered if Radha had suspected something, but she was looking amused and he was relieved.

He said, 'I feel tired working in the heat all day. So it feels nice to just lie down like this.'

'So how long is this road thing going to last?'

'Two or three months more.'

'Any news about the mill reopening?'

'I have a feeling that the moment this job is over, the mills will resume.'

'That would be good.' Radha began to look at the stars in the sky, and suddenly she recalled something, 'Oh by the way, I have managed to finish one bale with the warp you loaded on the loom. When you have a moment, help me with the next round of weaving. I'll be able to do it myself by and by.'

Kanti looked at Radha with affection. Radha's gaze had shifted to Rama, who was playing with the other children. Kanti rubbed his eyes as flashes from the past came up before him: he was married before he had even started working at the mill. His parents had been alive then. Since they were both old, they had to be looked after, and he had to do the weaving during the day, and at night another longish piece—how much Radha had helped with all this. When he had worked in the mill, his shifts were few and far between. On some occasions, he was away for twenty days or more. Radha laboured at home and looked after his parents, while he barely managed the rent of the house. His parents passed away. They had to concede to the pressures of the extended family and conduct the death rituals. He had run into debt at that time. He had brought Radha to Ahmedabad then. Until he found a permanent job, the poor woman had to slog.

He felt like saying to her, 'How long will you keep stitching up torn pieces, Radha?'

Kanti turned again. His eyes fell upon the bare wall, its paint peeling. He was looking at the hazy shapes when someone punched him in the back. He was startled. He saw a laughing Dala behind him.

'Come on, let's go to the bhajan gathering. Look at you lying down like an old man. We break our backs weaving all day, but we're nowhere near the bed until at least eleven.'

Kanti sat up. He held Dala by the hand and sat him down. Radha stood at the otla with her head covered. Kanti said to her, 'Let's have some tea.'

'No, forget it. I don't want chai-vai,' Dala said.

Radha stood for a few moments and then went over to where Rama was playing. Kanti and Dala were busy chatting. Dala mentioned to him that the anti-reservation riots had begun in Ahmedabad. Kanti was interested, but before they could continue the discussion, the tablas and dholaks at Khoda's house interrupted them. They stood up to leave.

By the time they reached, the bhajans had started. After about five or six bhajans, people stayed to have some tea. The anti-reservation topic came up again over tea. Ratilal master had returned from Ahmedabad the day before. He related the nature of the scuffles in

Ahmedabad. The subject shifted to the villages. Ratilal said, 'I'm so glad we don't have anything like that in our village. In the other village they have set Harijan houses on fire.'

Kanti wondered: Will my actions put the entire village at risk? Yesterday, when I had stood next to Deeva, there were some Patel women looking at me suspiciously. And Sendha is thirsting for my blood. God forbid, if Sendha announces to the world about Deeva and me, it would be the end of peace here.

Harji Bhagat picked up the tambura after tea. The bhajans started again. The first one, 'Oh Lakhaji bring us the key and open the locks of our souls', made Kanti's heart dance with joy. Kanti said to Dala, 'Why don't you sing as well?'

Dala had a good voice. 'But Harji Bhagat has to give me a chance first,' an amused Dala replied.

Narsi kaka, who sat next to Dala, said, 'Harji, give the tambura to Dala now, let him sing a few bhajans.'

Dala strummed the tambura. Kanti looked at him. Dala followed the saakhi couplet with an invocation to Ganesh. Starting a new bhajan, he sang, '*Look how high is the climb to the mountain, dear one, why do it....*' Everyone was riveted. Dala's voice was melodious and clear. They all watched him with rapt attention. Kanti was enchanted. He saw a garland of mountains before his eyes. It had precipices. Kanti felt giddy. He felt as if he had tumbled into a ravine while climbing the mountain. Dala was in his element. His words reverberated from one corner of the house to another. With one hand on the manjira, and another on the tambura, Dala continued to cast a spell, with one bhajan after the other. Kanti was lost in the rhythm. It was two o'clock, and then three. People stopped singing and began to talk of the spirituality of the bhajans—about Brahma, the mystery of divine power, the true meaning of bhakti, and so on. From the way people talked it seemed like God was almost within reach and amongst them. Kanti became more and more lost in this world. Sleep was miles away. One by one people began to leave, but the more devoted ones stayed back. Kanti looked outside. It was dawn. He thought of Deeva and his heart missed a beat. He immediately got up, without drawing anyone's attention. He reached home, almost panting for breath. Radha was awake. The sky had begun to clear. Radha looked at Kanti and said, 'You sat there all night. Do you even remember that you were supposed to go to work early morning? Go, have a bath. I have kept tea ready. I'll go to the toilet and be back soon.' Kanti bathed, got ready, drank his tea, and came out of the house. Radha had tied up the woven bale and put it in a corner. He lifted the heddle and came and sat beside the loom. He arranged the heddle, shuttle, and all the parts properly. He shifted the thread combs away and sat down at the loom. Radha put away the toilet-can and washed her hands and entered the house. On seeing Kanti at the loom she asked, 'You didn't go to the mukhi's house? Why are you at the loom?'

'I didn't feel like it. I don't want to go anywhere. I will go back to weaving now.' Saying this, Kanti began to sing: *'Sakhi, who knows the sixteenth and seventeenth art...'* in a full-throated voice as he threw the gilloli in the air. He wove as if he was competing with the warp and weft. Radha looked at Kanti; she was puzzled but was arrested by his movements. Just then, Beni came running.

'Alee Radha, did you hear?'

'What?'

'Early this morning, Sendha bhai raped the mukhi's wife.'

'What?' It was Kanti who exclaimed, instead of Radha. He pressed his foot on the treadle. The heddle-cord snapped, and the heddles hung loosely from the bar.

THE STAIRS

CHANDRA SHRIMALI

As she sped down the stairs, the entire floor shook. The derelict staircase seemed ready to fall apart. Watching her descending the stairs with such breathless speed, the old women, crouched near the public taps waiting for water, turned up their noses in disapproval. Amba could not help chiding her, 'Alee, Surya's vahu, careful…careful. Do you hear? Slowly, slowly, these are useless stairs. You will smash your knees if you are not careful.' The newly-arrived Chandan could not understand what was going on. With her face half-covered by a veil, one end of which she held between her two fingers, Chandan looked at Amba and asked innocently, 'What, Ambama?'

Amba laughed, 'Silly woman, "what Ambama" she asks! You are the one I am talking about. I must say, you are, no doubt, educated but not particularly wise. See, this staircase here is not even fixed properly. Next time, don't come down so fast. God forbid, if something happens to you, poor Valima will be in trouble. She will be angry, poor thing. You must come down slowly, like this.' Chandan replied, 'Fine, Ambama, thank you for reminding me.'

She began to walk slowly now, swinging merrily on her way to the toilet, a lota filled with water in her hand. Once again, Amba caught up with her and nudged her gently. She took her to one side, 'Stand aside, will you!' Amba had turned from a mere neighbour into a friend within a few days of Chandan's arrival. 'What had suddenly come over her now?' Chandan wondered. While Amba was pushing her aside, she noticed a middle-aged man in a white khadi cap, holding an umbrella in his hand, walk by. Once he was out of sight, Amba remarked, 'Alee! Has your mother-in-law not taught you anything?'

Chandan looked at her quizzically, 'Who was that man?'

Amba replied, 'Hasn't your mother-in-law told you about the

big and small people in the chawl? I'll ask Valima to tell you when I meet her. The man who just passed by is a Somo member. He is a member of the Dadra mill and also of the...God knows...some important thing.' Amba scratched her head; she knew for certain that a Somo member was important. She had heard that the chawl was provided with taps and toilets owing to Somo members' influence. Chandan looked at Amba with wonder in her eyes. Amba didn't know what else to say, so she continued to babble, 'This Valima is the limit. Now that she has brought this educated daughter-in-law, she has stopped bothering about anything else. You are a child, after all, but how could she forget? When a "big" man from the chawl is passing by, you should keep to one side, understood?'

Chandan nodded, 'Understood, Ambama.' Chandan turned to leave, but once again, Amba ran behind her and pulled Chandan's pallu to cover her lota. Then, gently tapping Chandan's cheek, she said, 'Now go, bahurani!' Readjusting her pallu and veil, Chandan began walking in the direction of the common toilet.

A delicate seventeen-year-old, Chandan got married to Bhola Maharaj's son, Suryakant, last year and her annu was arranged this year. For the first time, Chandan had to do household work. She hadn't had much responsibility at her own home because she had two older sisters. In any case, Chandan was a smart and capable person. In no time at all, she took on all the chores in her in-laws' house. She did everything willingly and enthusiastically, but the moment anyone called her 'Surya ni vahu' she would be upset. She couldn't understand what pleasure the chawl people derived from distorting names! Not only were young people's names distorted, but even older and respected people were not spared. Somabhai Chauhan was a municipal Corporator, a man of standing. Even the youngest child in the chawl referred to him as a Somo member. Chandan's neighbour Amba was a mother of seven, yet everyone called her 'Amli' instead of Amba. Shyamalbhai was a clerk in a bank, but the moment anyone called him 'Shyamaliyo', he dropped everything and came. It seemed people had got used to such rudeness. Initially, Chandan did not like this. Her husband had such a nice name—Suryakant. Everybody, including the women and children, called him 'Surya' and so Chandan became 'Surya ni vahu'.'

Chandan liked Amba's gentle reproach. As she was reflecting on this, she noticed that all four toilets were occupied. All they needed was a board announcing 'Houseful'. With her, two other women also stood with their bottles of water, shifting this way and that out of discomfort. One of them asked the other, 'Mani, this is Valima's son Surya's wife, right?' The other nodded, 'Yes, she is the wife of Bhola Maharaj's son Suryo who lives on the upper floor. She had the first annu this year.'

Finally, the toilet was free. An old woman came out unhurriedly. There was such filth around the toilet that it was impossible to set foot anywhere. But, everybody was used to filth. And where else could they go? Chandan hesitated to go into the unoccupied toilet; after all, the other two women had been waiting longer. As she hesitated, the two women exchanged a look and whispered, 'Let her go. If she gets delayed, Valima will jump up and down.' Then they said to Chandan, 'Go, vahu, you go first.' Chandan gingerly placed her foot in the toilet. Once she was settled, she removed her sari from her head and rolled up her pallu into a ball to cover her nose. The stench was nauseating. Her father had a house in a colony and they had a toilet in the courtyard. This place, on the other hand, had one room and a kitchen, a chowk of 4 feet by 3 feet for bathing. But Chandan was a happy person. Her husband, Suryakant, loved her dearly, and wouldn't let her out of his sight. Whenever it was necessary to visit relatives and pay their respects, he told his mother clearly, 'You go, if you want to. I am not sending this one to pay respects or massage their legs.' Thinking of one such heated conversation between the mother and the son brought a smile to Chandan's lips. The bunched up sari slipped from her nose and an explosion of foul smell assaulted her senses. Chandan quickly took some 'haathpani' and stood up. She walked out thinking of the incident at her wedding annu. The thought made her smile as she climbed the stairs.

Chandan's father-in-law, Bhola Maharaj, was a practicing Brahmin for both the Vankars as well as the Chamars. The maharaj's presence was considered essential for all kinds of rituals—weddings, engagements, re-marriages. After the annu ceremony, the bride could stay for a maximum of five days at her in-laws' house. But Suryakant was so stubborn that he extended that period to seven days. Chandan's eldest uncle came to fetch her with the intention of staying for the afternoon meal and returning with Chandan in the evening. But Vali vevan turned out to be an insistent hostess. She made all kinds of delicious food and virtually killed him with her kindness! Alongside the food was Bhola Maharaj's unending and interesting conversation. He gossiped about everything under the sun—the new ways of the community, the panchayat, and so on and so forth. Six days went by in this manner. Then came Sunday, but it is considered inauspicious to send a daughter-in-law away on a Sunday. So, they quickly finished off the ritual of 'pastanu', pretending to send off the daughter-in-law by getting her dressed and making her sit in the neighbour's house for a while, then bringing her right back! Evening drew on and Suryakant's face began to look glum. He announced to Valima, 'Chandan and I have been invited to my friend Kanti's house for a meal. So she can't be sent today.'

Valima asked, 'Which Kanti is this now? You have three friends by that name. Which one do you mean? I will go to his house and tell him that it's not possible.' What could Suryakant say? Dinner at a friend's place was only a ruse. In fact, he had picked up two tickets for a late-night show of the film *Junglee* at Alankar talkies. He had planned to have dinner with his wife at Moti Mahal, followed by the movie. But Valima's inquisition made him nervous. Now which Kantilal should he mention? Were he to mention the two Kantilals from his chawl, Valima may actually go to their house. That would expose Suryakant. It wasn't appropriate to take your wife out late in the evening for a meal, let alone a movie, when the annu period was on. Valima was a very superstitious person, so she would never have granted them permission. That is why Suryakant had to think of an excuse. Suddenly, Suryakant thought of his friend Kanti who lived in the Jeevram Bhatt chawl. Kantilal of Jeevram Bhatt chawl called Valima 'foi'. His father and Suryakant's nana were good friends. The two of them had worked together in a mill and used to visit each other often. Some years ago, however, Valima's father Halji Maharaj had passed away and Pitambar Maharaj's health had also begun to fail. When they retired from the mill, the interaction between the two families reduced to a large extent. But Suryakant and Kantilal had studied together in college and so their relationship continued as before. Suryakant knew that his mother was not likely to go and make enquiries at this Kanti's house. It would not be possible for her to do so with guests at home. So, using his presence of mind, he mentioned Pitambar Maharaj's son Kanti. Exasperated, Valima said, 'All right, ask your father. He will be good at handling Chaturdas vevahi.' With this, she signalled to Bhola Maharaj to come to the kitchen. Chandan's mota baapa surmised that there were plans being made for delaying Chandan's departure further. He could see that Suryakant had seated himself in the kitchen and Chaturdas could hear his voice. Chaturdas was also quite clever and worldly. He was aware of the current trend among young people. Vali vevan called her husband into the kitchen; a sign for Chaturdas to guess what was coming. Bhola Maharaj found an excuse to go into the kitchen. Taking the hookah from Chaturdas's hands, he said, 'Give me the hookah, vevahi. The fire needs rekindling. Let me put some fresh tobacco and relight it. Meanwhile, you lie down.' Chaturdas lay down next to Nandlal.

Nandlal was barely seven years old. He was the youngest brother of four sisters. As Chandan's 'anwar', he had come with her to her in-laws' house. Suryakant was very fond of his young brother-in-law. After lunch, Suryakant had taken him out. Sitting by Kankaria Lake, they had eaten ice cream. Then he had taken Nandlal to the zoo and brought him back, tired and sleepy. Nandlal was fast asleep now, quite in keeping with Suryakant's plan.

Bhola Maharaj placed the hookah next to the chulah. Valima filled it up with fresh tobacco and relit it. Handing it over to him she said, 'Here, give this to vevahi and persuade him to let vahu stay back today. After all, Surya's friend has invited both of them to a meal, so they will have to go. We will send Chandan vahu in the morning. Ask him to relax tonight.' Bhola Maharaj looked at Suryakant who immediately looked down. As for Chandan, she clung to the wall for dear life to make herself invisible. On his way out of the kitchen, Bhola Maharaj threw a triumphant glance in Valima's direction with his hookah held proudly like a shining sword. On seeing Bhola Maharaj's enigmatic smile, Valima concluded that Abhimanyu had overcome the eighth hurdle. And that's what happened finally. Chandan's annu was arranged on the eighth day and that was that.

Exactly a year after her marriage, Chandan came to her in-laws' home again. Bhola Maharaj's small family had been living in one of the rooms on the top storey of the necklace-shaped chawl for the last twenty-five years. The 'room' was rented at ten rupees per month and it was divided into two sections. The front portion was used as a 'drawing-cum-dining room' as well as a bedroom for Chandan's in-laws and her younger brother-in-law. To the left was a 4 feet by 3 feet washing-place-cum-bathroom. Normally used for bathing and washing, on some occasions, it also served as a urinal, especially when nobody else was at home. Valima herself had whispered this information into Chandan's ears.

When Chandan went for a bath, the other members of the house moved away for a while. Chandan had learnt to turn the washing space into an instant bathroom by propping up a string cot as a door and throwing a sari over it. Her father-in-law worked the night shift. He left for the mill at around eleven o'clock every night. The sasu and the vahu took turns to bathe before he returned from work. They also did the housework together. Chandan found it very difficult to fill water from the common tap and climb the stairs—she had to carry one pot of water at her waist and another on her head. Apart from Amba, the other young girls from the chawl helped her out and looked forward to hearing her say 'thank you'.

Chandan had passed her matriculation examination with a first class the previous year, and she had a 'distinction' in English. Everyone looked forward to hearing her say 'thank you' in her sweet voice. Chandan's slim and delicate body, her long, dark eyelashes over a pair of playful eyes attracted the young girls of the chawl and they constantly surrounded her. Among them, she, too, became a little girl. Her veil, which came down all the way to her chest, sometimes fell off when she was chatting with the girls. When this happened, Chandan trembled like a leaf. She looked frightened as if she had been caught committing a crime. The girls couldn't stop giggling then and even the old women of the chawl showed their toothless grins.

The social system was so rigid that you had to keep your head covered even in the presence of the mother-in-law. The womenfolk felt a great sense of guilt if there was any suggestion of change. Chandan was the first one to initiate the revolution. She and Valima were the only two women at home. Bhola Maharaj slept the entire day, while Suryakant worked. The young brother-in-law Bhanukant alias Bhanko went to school. Chandan was not supposed to show her face in Valima's presence. In fact, not only had she to keep her face covered but she was also supposed to keep her mouth shut. If something had to be said, it was to be conveyed through gestures. Chandan found this very difficult, and Valima didn't like it either. Finally, the daughter-in-law and mother-in-law made a sort of arrangement by which it was decided that Chandan would cover her face in public and remain silent, but not at home. It didn't take people long to realize that Valima had made Chandan drop the veil and that the two of them talked unabashedly with each other! Gradually, they only veiled when the men were around and eventually all the women in the chawl followed the example of 'Surya ni vahu'.

With Chandan's help, new additions were made to the collective tasks the chawl women engaged in. Apart from embroidery and stitching, this also included spinning and weaving and reading the Ramayana and the Mahabharata together. Chandan also got the filth around the public tap cleaned regularly. When the Seth's 'men' visited the chawl to collect the monthly rent, Chandan spoke to them. The houses needed fresh plaster and paint, while the stairs needed to be repaired. But the Seth's fellow paid little heed to Chandan's request. She said to Amba, 'Ambama, how can this go on? If they don't get the stairs repaired, we should stop paying the rent from next month.' Amba shared her worry about the stairs and said, 'What can you and I do by ourselves? You talk to Surya and see. A few men and women have to get together and force him. The rascal will not budge otherwise. If no one agrees, then you and I will handle him next time. Let's see how they get away with it again.' Amba's face radiated confidence and strength. The thirty-five-year-old Amba was known for her courage in the chawl. She had had seven pregnancies of which two were miscarriages, but Amba still stood strong like a brick wall. She would begin to sweep and mop and cook two hours after she had given birth. Her sturdiness and strong will invited comments even from the men who said, 'Is she a woman or a witch? So many children and still going strong....' Amba cared little about what people said. Once she set her mind to something, she did it, regardless of what anyone said. She had trained Chandan well, who now had become accustomed to the ways of the chawl. When exasperated, Chandan would swear and abuse freely. She had come a long way from the one who had endearingly said 'thank you' each time someone helped her. Once, when the man who collected rent had stared at her as she washed her hands and feet at the common tap, she had almost hit him with the dhoka and had cursed him loudly. Chandan now had a reputation as one not to be trifled with. She and Amba had got together a few other women who were prepared to be aggressive on the issue of repairing the chawl staircase.

But the following month, a terrible accident took place before the Seth's 'man' came for the rent. After the seemant ceremony in the seventh month of pregnancy, Chandan was to leave for her mother's house for her delivery. Unfortunately, Valima fell sick after the ceremony, so Chandan could not go. Feeding and entertaining guests and relatives had taken a heavy toll on Valima. Chandan's father made earnest requests to take his daughter back with him, but this time too, Suryakant succeeded in getting his way. Valima was sick, so Chandan would go after a few days. What could the father do? He gently stroked his daugher's head and left. By the evening, when all the guests had left, Valima had a high temperature. Suryakant immediately called for Dr Trivedi, a very nice man who practised just around the corner. The doctor examined Valima and gave her medicines and an injection. Bhola Maharaj paid the doctor his fees.

People from the chawl milled around Chandan's house to see why the doctor had been called. It had to be a very serious illness, they thought. Suryakant saw the doctor off. Dr Trivedi was an old man and slightly overweight. He had climbed the stairs with great difficulty and on his way down, he almost slipped on the last step. Fortunately, Suryakant was right behind him and prevented the fall. People gathered around to see the doctor and they couldn't stop sniggering. Amba lost her head when she saw them giggling, 'Stop doing khee…khee…now. You can't even let out a fart when the Seth's fellow comes for the rent, can you? Does it occur to any of you to get this staircase repaired?' Meekly, all those who had gathered turned away. It was essential to mend the stairs, but who could go and say this to the Seth? If they did any dadagiri, the Seth may turn them out of their homes and where would they go then? They had left their villages and come to work as menial labourers in the mills of Ahmedabad to make ends meet. They lived in fear of the seths and the sahukars.

Valima's temperature came down at night. Chandan applied balm on her head and limbs and went to lie down. The last three days had been tough on her, what with her advanced pregnancy and increasing housework. Chandan and Suryakant occupied one half of the partitioned room, while Chandan's in-laws and young brother-in-law occupied the other half of the room. Chandan's little bedroom also included a tiny kitchen, not to mention a trunk for mattresses.

Adjacent to the wooden trunk was Chandan's string cot that turned this space into a bedroom at night. And yet, Chandan was happy; showered with Suryakant's love, she desired little else. However, setting foot on the rickety stairs every morning sent tremors through her body. Even today, she complained to Suryakant, 'Do something about these stairs, please. I feel dizzy when I climb the stairs with a pot of water on my head.' Suryakant drew her close and assured her, 'I will not pay the rent this time, and if the bastard makes a fuss, I will break his legs.' Chandan was relieved to see her husband's anger. She went to sleep without a care in the world.

The chawl women 'booked' their place near the public tap by keeping their pots in a queue. In order to avoid a rush, they would start doing this at six o'clock every morning. Every day, Chandan would also wake up by half past five. She would swiftly descend the stairs and put her pots in the queue. Since the doctor had been called to tend to Valima the previous night, it was late by the time Chandan went to bed. The next morning, she woke up a little later than usual. After brushing her teeth with the datum stick and finishing her other chores quickly, she picked up a bucket, placed a pot at her waist, adjusted her sari, and covered her face.

The moment she placed her foot on the second step, she slipped. This particular step was the nastiest; Chandan fell and so did her pot, which tumbled all the way down to the filthy spot near the public tap. Women gathered around the common tap shouting in panic, 'Surya's vahu fell...Surya's vahu fell.' Amba yelled out to Valima from below, 'Valima! Come down immediately!' Chandan quickly got up and dusted her clothes, 'Ambama, I am not badly hurt. But look at my poor pot!' Taking the mud-smeared pot in her hands, Chandan checked it on all sides. There was a huge dent on the bottom. Amba said to Chandan, 'You go up, I will bring your pot and also fill water for you.' Chandan sat down on her hunches near the tap and said, 'Never mind, I am not hurt at all.' What Chandan couldn't understand was why her chaniyo felt so wet. Frightened, she immediately stood up. Standing next to her, Amba saw her face become white with fear. She hugged Chandan and said, 'Alee, what happened?' Chandan did not answer and her head began to spin. Amba noticed that Chandan's chaniyo was soaked in blood. She was petrified. She called out to the women around, 'Hurry up, get an auto quickly. This girl is having a premature delivery.' Meanwhile, Suryakant, Valima, and Bhola Maharaj had also come down. Someone got an auto from the corner. Amba almost lifted Chandan into the auto. She sat pressing her clothes between her legs. Suryakant was thoroughly bewildered. Putting decorum aside, he hugged Chandan. Valima panicked. Amba said to her, 'Don't worry, we will all come with you to the hospital.' Chandan was immediately admitted to a hospital. The doctor examined her and announced, 'She has bled a lot. We need to give her blood. The baby has also shifted its position.'

Despite all their efforts to save the baby, Chandan had a miscarriage three days later. A fair little daughter died even before being born. There have been no new stairs in the chawl so far.

CREAMY LAYER
NEERAV PATEL

It's no joke to manage a wedding single-handedly in this *cosmopolitan* city of Mumbai, away from your all loved ones. And, honestly, things like shopping for clothes and jewellery, party plot, finalizing caterers, beauticians, decorations, and music for the party, and accommodation for guests, and myriad such things get done in a wink, fatafat, as you keep tearing leaves from a cheque book, one after the other. That's all it takes. But it was the so-called minor formality of scripting the kankotri or the wedding invitation that left the Vaghela couple most confused. After a lot of back and forth, they finally decided on two kankotris, with different designs and different texts—one in Gujarati, the other in English; one for the people from their caste, another for rest of the world. Haansh, they felt relieved!

Shalini looked smart and sweet in her air hostess uniform. The kankotri received much appreciation from her colleagues. Captain Chopra apparently said to her, 'Oh, such elegant language!' while the flight purser Swaman Deshpande said, 'What a nice work of abstract art you chose for Ganesha! And that saptapadi shloka in italics....' One would have thought the recipients of the kankotri considered themselves lucky—such was the magnitude of the pleasure they conveyed on receiving it. As for Shalini, she felt a surge of pride when she was told how cultured and tasteful her parents were. However, what made her most happy were the kisses the pilot, Kulin Joshi, showered upon her. It was comparable to nothing else. She, Miss Shalini Vaghela, would soon be known as Mrs Shalini Joshi! 'Arre, how can anything be missing from a wedding at Bapu's place, hanh?' one of the clerks, aware of Shalini's caste disguised behind the Rajput surname, remarked with sarcasm in his Kathiawadi accent. Shalini was too lost in a fantasy world to notice.

The Vaghela couple left, armed with a long guest list and joyous at the thought of delivering the kankotris in person. Their well-meant enthusiasm turned out to be short-lived. They took a taxi from the Ahmedabad airport to their native village. They were so unrecognizably well-dressed that they looked pardesi, a couple from another country, and the moment they arrived, their relatives descended on them. Taunts and reprimands were hurled from all directions, 'Oh ho, bhai, finally you remembered your ancestral land, hanh? Your old man joyfully came every new year and made an offering to our goddess during Navratri, and Ramapir's proud and colourful flag was unfurled thanks to his efforts.... But you are a big sahib, what with your studies-vudies and all. Bringing up your beloved daughter in Mumbai, you forgot all about your family. Does it even mean anything to you, tell us, this family of yours?'

Instead of the sweet words of welcome they had anticipated, the Vaghela couple were subjected to such taunts. It was embarrassing. Of course there was some truth in the accusations hurled at them: Can relations between bhai–bhabhi, sister–brother-in-law, kaka–kaki, mama–maasi, foi–fua be maintained without meeting often? Had they not left the village to go to the city, had they not abandoned their traditional occupation for white collar jobs, had they not left the cattle sheds to live in an apartment would they have been able to foster these relationships? Perhaps.

The paternal cousins had quite the same attitude. They were not very literate, but the youngest one had been tempted to go to school, lured by the prospect of a mid-day meal. He had haltingly learnt to put letters together. With arduous effort he managed to read out the kankotri to everyone. On hearing their own names among some two hundred hosts they felt pleased: Dhulabhai Punjabhai Vaghela, Kalidas Punjabhai Vaghela.... But then the Mota Bhabhi turned the kankotri over, and snapped: 'What, bhai, you forgot to put our kuldevi Chavanda Ma on it? It is through her blessings that our clan survives. Have you become such a savarna that you cast aside our own mother? You have included the picture of your kind of coat-pant wearing God, but abandoned our ever-present mother goddess.' With a broom over her shoulder, she muttered on her way to the village, 'Go get your daughter married into a rich family, our presence will not bring any glory to your aangan.'

Instead of the image of the kuldevi and a kankotri beginning with the invocation, 'With the grace of Chavanda Ma....' the Vaghela couple had chosen to put the image of Babasaheb Ambedkar, a sign of a new awakening. One would have thought they had committed a heinous crime! They didn't realize that such a gaping chasm had grown between them and their community.

They joined hands and beseeched everyone to forgive them. The youngest bhabhi, who stood with a veil drawn over her face, her eyes lowered, began to speak, 'We can barely manage two meals a day, how will we manage to pay the fare to come to Mumbai, tell us. Here, our children wear clothes sewn together from discarded rags and if we weren't begging for leftover food from other homes, we wouldn't have been able to feed them. Wouldn't we stand out among you big-big people? It's not so much about us, but you will feel ashamed of us.'

Precisely. That's why the Vaghela couple had planned two different kankotris, two different menus, and two different receptions. Appearing to think of a solution, Mr Vaghela slowly took out money from his wallet and said, 'Take this and please don't worry about anything. Buy good clothes for all and please attend the wedding. Be large-hearted, forgive us our mistakes and honour us by being there.'

The relatives were pacified, and it appeared things were back on track. The youngest daughter-in-law poured a glass of water from a cloth-covered pot placed next to the door for the couple. Mrs Vaghela saw this unhygienic water and blurted, 'No, no. We have brought water with us.' She took out a Bisleri bottle from her bag and gave it to her husband. Meanwhile, a young girl from the neighbourhood turned up. 'Here, have this tea. It's made entirely of milk. Especially made for your kind of people.' Mr Vaghela could not take his eyes off the creamy layer on the surface of his tea. Ever so quietly, veiling his discomfort, he picked up the cream with the tip of his finger and flicked it away.

Disappointed with the state of their community as well as the behaviour of their relatives, the Vaghela couple bade goodbye to their homeland with a heavy heart and sped away to the city. On the way, they wondered how the other side of the family would respond.

They halted at a grand building next to the banks of the Sabarmati River. The building befitted its grand name, 'Kailashdham'. The Vaghela couple went past its beautiful lawns till the end of the estate where the servant quarters were situated. Just then, pall bearers alighted from an ambulance, chanting 'Ram Bolo bhai Ram' and carrying a dead body. Instead of greeting his relatives, the Mama rushed off towards the electric crematorium. This was the Mama they had come to invite for his customary role of mameru during Shalini's wedding. The Vaghela couple had made this trip from Mumbai especially to persuade him to come. Considering the situation, they decided to be patient and wait.

'Look at this, bhai, the wretched fever has taken over the bloody city...I have not had a moment's rest. The munshipalty people are not granting me leave either. You chose to come at such a bad time....' Mr Vaghela tried to smoothen the awkwardness by changing tack, 'Where are your sons and their wives? I don't see anybody.'

'Bhai, to each his own dhandho. People have to fill their bellies, no? Can you do that without slogging? The eldest son's wife is a sweeper with the civil hospital. The eldest son works in a morgue. The little ones have spread a sheet to collect the few coins people toss after paying their respects to the dead. The younger son is not far away. He has proper employment. You can meet him while you wait for your mama to come back,' Mami suggested.

The Vaghela couple wished to escape the stifling modern crematorium, so they promptly accepted the proposal. They took directions from Mami and got back into the taxi. Everyone they asked for directions on the way was amused, 'You want to go to the mayor's bungalow?' Why would a mayor live in a poor basti of Dalits? They reached their destination and found a well-built structure that looked like a corporate building. It announced itself confidently with large letters: 'Sulabh International'. Below that, in smaller letters, it said, 'Pay and use Sulabh toilet'. Right at the centre of the posh foyer stood a young man preening as if he were the owner. The Vaghela couple went directly up to him. The young boy nonchalantly gave the rates, 'One rupee for urinating, two for the rest.' When he realized that the people in front of him were his relatives, he felt sheepish, but immediately recovered his confidence by ordering someone, 'Go and get two kadak-meethi cups of tea and two pouches of water as well.' The Vaghela couple used their kerchiefs to protect themselves from the assaulting stench around them. They declined the tea but the young manager of Sulabh Shauchalaya would not take no for an answer. The cups of tea were served at his table. Mrs Vaghela absolutely refused to drink the tea. But Mr Vaghela felt he did not have a choice in this matter. He stared at the tea cup. Haansh, this tea was missing the creamy layer....

From the Sulabh toilet, the Vaghela couple headed back to Kailashdham to seek the mama's consent, making a stop at a posh area of the city to meet the maasi. Originally built as quarters for MLAs, these houses had become deserted once Gandhinagar became the capital. They had now been given to employees of the Ahmedabad Municipality. They looked worse than slum quarters. Maasi's husband had gulped down two pouches of country liquor and was bragging, 'See, bhai, all of us have sarkari jobs.' Mrs Vaghela looked around with characteristic feminine candour, and noticed that quite a few objects in the house were 'imported'. Gleeful at her surprise, Maasi began throwing light on the matter: 'Our younger son's wife works at the international airport. People have to pay money to see airplanes. She manages to get inside airplanes and cleans them. Even the bathrooms on these planes have a sweet fragrance. She brings home everything passengers leave half-finished and unfinished from foreign liquor to chocolates. Your Shalini works on a plane, who knows they may end up meeting each other someday on the same plane in Ahmedabad....'

The very thought made the Vaghelas shudder! Mama continued,

'The elder son drives the garbage van for the slaughterhouse and the younger son drives the dog-catching van. We are all sarkari employees; kuldevi has been kind to us. How are our people doing in Mumbai, tell me? We hear that everyone, rich or poor, stays in a jhoppadpatti. All show from the outside but the work is still the same—clearing shit. When your father went from the village, that's what he used to do. Now you people have studies-vudies and have found clean upper-caste professions.'

Mama's whiplashes had to be endured. Eventually, the Vaghela couple managed to convince him to be part of the mameru ceremony at Shalini's wedding.

To bring an end to this insufferable situation, they began striking out names from their list. Mr Vaghela's father's friend lived in Saurashtra, a remote village. But his father had insisted that his friend must be given the kankotri. The old man was, after all, his childhood friend.

After offering double the usual fare, the taxiwallah began to speed through dusty roads. At the end of the village stood an isolated hut. The darbars of the village were confounded to see the taxi turn in that direction. The moment they reached, an old woman called out from within the hut, 'The old man has gone to another village to give kalotri, the death news.... Jerubha used to do that but he's gone now, so this bonded labour has fallen on my old man's shoulders. He will be walking from one village to another delivering the news, so who knows when he'll be back. It could be tomorrow or the day after.' The kankotri that bore the name of the old man who had gone to deliver kalotri was handed over quietly to his ageing wife. The Vaghela couple could not bring themselves to say, 'The two of you must come for our daughter Shalini's wedding.'

By this time, Mrs Vaghela was at the end of her tether. She snapped, 'Chalo, we can post the rest of the invitations. I don't want to spend a moment longer in this place. Let's take the next flight to Mumbai. I have so many preparations to do for our lovely daughter's wedding....'

On seeing her parents return by an earlier flight, Shalini was overjoyed. 'Mum, you handed over the kankotris to everyone, right? Our house is going to be full of so many people from the family!' Educated in a residential convent school, Shalini was going to meet her extended family for the first time. The Vaghela couple was in no mood to respond. Mr Vaghela was thinking to himself, 'Such a huge social and cultural gap!' It felt as though he had been thrown out, excommunicated by his own people. As he sat on the sofa, he called out to Shalini, 'Shalu, please get me a cup of tea. And listen, from now on, do not add cream to my tea. I feel bad for the creamy layer now....'

CONGRATULATIONS

BINDU BHATT

It was past five in the evening when I could leave office. By the time I cleared my table and came out, the elevator had gone down. It would have to go down five floors, and come back all the way up to where I was. Then it would have to go down five floors again for me to reach the ground floor. With one hand on the folds of my sari and another on the railing, I raced down the stairs. If someone had seen me then, they would have thought this woman was being chased by a ghost. When I reached the third floor, I heard Ahmed chacha calling loudly, 'Mehtaben, phone for you.' Who could that be? Prashant? But he would only return home between six-thirty and seven. It would be unusual for him to call at this time. Had something happened? I chided myself for thinking that way, like I had been doing for the past six months. What's the worst that could happen? In the last ten years, I had managed to remain unfazed by everyone—family, neighbours, office. What's left now? And let's just say that no decision has been made—so what? But Prashant—will he be able to prevail against his family? A dominating and combative daughter-in-law like Rucha on the one hand and the menopausal devoted wife, Ramaben, who grew more religious as each day passed, on the other?

After Nikhil's marriage, Ramaben had told me, 'I have told Nikhil's father that I have completed all my duties. I even have a daughter-in-law now. Now you take care of yourself!' I had felt like asking her to give Prashant to me at that moment. But then I thought, when has she ever refused me? In fact, she had honoured my opinion even while choosing Rucha as her daughter-in-law.

I climbed up two floors. When I picked up the phone, the operator gave me the side-eye. I held the receiver to my ear, but there was no response. The phone was neither connected nor disconnected.

Someone was listening with a sly smile to my panting voice as I repeated: hello, hello. I was exasperated. What kind of a joke was this? Before I could slam the receiver down, the operator quietly took it from me and put it back on the cradle. She offered me a chair and pressed the bell for water to be brought for me. But I promptly stood up. What if a voice used to commanding now sounded plaintive?

I nearly ran to catch the elevator. No sooner did I say 'ground floor' than I realized that the lift was going up. Oh dear. The liftman was staring at me. I took out a handkerchief from my purse and wiped his gaze away. Along with the kerchief, my hands had grabbed an invitation card from my purse. It was for the closing ceremony of a handloom workshop. I wanted to go, but without Prashant, it didn't seem much fun doing anything. He wasn't around today. These days, he looks torn and broken to me. Whenever I see him, I can't stop thinking about Ramaben. I fear that his guilt about me is weighing him down. I find it hard to even look at him—I have to muster up the courage to do that. Yesterday, he said to me on the phone, 'Yeah, everything's fine. After all this suffering, if you are able to accept our friendship, it's more than enough.' I cannot manage his kind of equanimity. I become anxious very easily these days. It could be a trivial matter, but I weave a web like a spider.

The lift went down. I felt like a pail that had broken free from its pulley and was now tumbling down into the well. Like an unanchored pail, I managed responsibilities without any support. It has made me a frazzled person. I came to the main road and, like every other day, I walked towards the Jhaveriwaad bus stop. I realized that it was already past five-thirty. I was late once again. Was the hearing of the court case over by now? Of course, these things don't take long when there are two consenting partners who wish to end a marriage. But it can get delayed if the lawyer or the judge is absent. Or say, Ramaben herself is absent. Or, God forbid, she raises an objection. Would she, really? Well, she hasn't uttered a word of protest so far. But what if she buckled under pressure from Rucha? I mean, I have always been beholden to her. What then....

Prashant often complains, 'The moment I step into the house, I feel hemmed in by the ugly atmosphere.' When this happens, I defend Ramaben. 'She looks after you so well though. Feeds you, takes care of you. And look at your home, it shines like a mirror. She keeps it so tidy.' He'd react violently, like he was banging his head against a wall. 'Oh please, even hotels do that much. It'd be all right if one didn't have all the conveniences in the world. But I can't understand why she wouldn't look beyond herself, at me, for instance. So self-absorbed.... At times her self-sufficiency really bothers me. You know, this situation is like a handwoven rug. It may disintegrate, but it won't give up its coarseness. What kind of life is this? An acclaimed expert on traditional Indian handicrafts at work, and mired in the universe of narrow community and family circles at home, like some blinkered animal in a farm. It's so stifling, really. Had you not been around....'

Arre! Before I could dwell more on these thoughts, I collided with a country bumpkin. He barely heard me apologize before asking, 'What eez time?' Five-forty-five, I told him, and hailed an autorickshaw. This was no time to brood. It was getting late. By six-fifteen, I should be home. My home is all the way in Pritam Nagar, and I have to thread through Relief Road and the Nehru Bridge traffic. Had I left fifteen minutes earlier I would've avoided the peak-hour traffic.

The clamour of menacingly close vehicles surrounded me. The autorickshaw made its way through everything, the driver employing part chicanery, part strategy. The auto brushed against something, and almost toppled over. My eyes closed, and my hands moved to my ears to block out the noise. I simply cannot and will not drive; how do you hold a steering wheel when you're so faint-hearted? Never mind your own, but you can't jeopardize other peoples' lives, can you? But I have thought about this before, why am I even thinking about this now? I felt like getting down from the auto and running home. What could have happened? If everything had gone well...

then what follows? What am I going to do? God knows. My chest sounded hollow, like I was an empty thermos flask. Just then I saw a hoarding: Gujarat Handicraft Haat. They had a sale going on. This was where I had first met Ramaben.

There had been a sale on that day as well. The previous day I had made plans to shop with Prashant. I waited for three whole hours, and finally went on my own. The moment I entered the haat, I noticed Prashant at the silk counter. I was going to burst like a pressure cooker. You, you...I was ready to scream. Before I could say anything, Prashant placed his hand on the shoulder of a woman standing next to him and said, 'Rama, look at that one.' Oh! So we are with shrimatiji today. I must turn back, I had thought. This was the woman about whom I knew everything. Every single thing. She specializes in making mohanthaal and khaman. She would not step outside her home until she had lit the diya. She hated the colour white. Arre, I even know that she does not like night lamps. But she does not even know my name.

'Rama, take this one.' I noticed that Prashant's hand was on a beautiful kosa fabric. I wanted to put my hand on his. Ramaben's jarring voice brought me back to reality, 'Oh no, I don't want to wear an old woman's sari.' Had she noticed how Prashant smiled when he found a colour he liked. You want to steal that smile away! Prashant was saying, 'Come on, take it. Even if you wear it only once, it's still worth it.'

'Look at you,' she said. 'Throwing away 800 rupees like that? Had it not been for me, your style, your attitude....' She kept talking but Prashant had turned away from her, towards me. 'Arre, Mehta? You are here. Rama, come here. Let me introduce you to Padmajaben. She's the purchase officer in our office. She also goes to all kinds of shops and does her shopping, just like you.' He had smiled wanly as he said this.

Ramaben had been joyous, like a blind person who could suddenly see. She said to me, 'I had to drag him here, he just wouldn't come.'

From that day on, Ramaben took me along whenever she went

shopping. The first time I went to their home, Ramaben talked about her son, Nikhil, and the snacks she had prepared. Nikhil must have been in the fifth standard then. He had looked at my light-coloured eyes, and decided to call me Bhoori aunty. Prashant would watch all three of us. He was like a solitary tree on the banks of a river. I stood apart, safe in his shade.

'Ya khuda!' Though he was a veteran of the roads, these words slipped out of the rickshawallah's mouth. A middle-aged woman riding a two-wheeler had a close shave with a bus. Thank God, she was saved—saved or saved up for something worse? I can't make up my mind any more about whether whatever happens is for the good, or if it's only in preparation for something worse to come. The traffic came to a standstill near Vijlighar. Two city buses waited side by side, almost rubbing shoulders with each other. When this happens and I find myself looking into the window of a bus, I wonder which of the two buses I am sitting in.

There was a time when I had decided I was going to have an entirely professional relationship with Prashant. Ramaben's affection and trust made me feel like I was doing something illegitimate, and the guilt I felt almost killed me. It was like being complimented on wearing somebody's hand-me-down sari: it left me feeling diminished. She did not even hint that she knew what was going on. If she received an invitation to an art or cultural exhibition she'd say, 'I hand this to you and him. You both are different. I don't like all this.'

Something similar had happened one day. Nikhil had cleared his twelfth standard with good grades. Prashant had made plans to take the family out for a movie, and dinner afterwards. Prashant and I had been sitting together during lunch when Ramaben phoned. She said to him, 'Now listen to me, I cannot come. I have to visit my aunt who has come from London. She has just lost someone close to her.' Prashant handed the receiver to me. She continued, 'Why don't you do one thing, take Padmajaben instead of me. You know I don't like all this. All right, I'm hanging up.' Ramaben hadn't even waited for Prashant to respond. Prashant sat across from me, with his palm open. I gently put my hand in his.

'Should I go via Nehru Bridge or Lakkadia Bridge?' The rickshawallah asked me.

'Nehru Bridge,' I replied.

I often say to Prashant, 'I don't care who designed the Ellis Bridge, it is so unstable and narrow. I feel like it'll collapse any moment and plop down like a camel in the middle of a desert.' The show at Roopalee Cinema was not yet over. Bridge Corner was also not open yet. It was our favourite place. We stroll along the Sabarmati at least twice a month and drink tea or coffee at Bridge Corner, before parting. Prashant would get emotional sometimes and say, 'Padma, we are like two banks of a river.' I'd stop him from saying anything further and say, 'Prashant, there's a strong bridge connecting us. Never mind if the waters rise.' You know, last year, I was transferred to the Ashram Road branch. The office people must have thought, at least this would keep them separate. But Ramaben would call every now and then, leading to shopping expeditions in Kalaniketan, Deepkala, or Asopalav. The office people didn't know where to hide their sheepish faces. With Nikhil's wedding, all wagging tongues came to a halt.

But what if the bridge breaks down today? What if the banks are able to meet each other now, unmediated? An empty expanse unfolded before my eyes. I feel like asking the rickshaw to turn back. But what if someone calls me at home? What if Prashant comes home? No, I can't abandon him like that. Whatever will be, will be. Was God watching all this? The God of Sanyaas Ashram on Ashram Road? Ramaben must have disrupted her routine today. Every morning Prashant would drop her on his two-wheeler at Sanyaas Ashram. Perhaps Rucha will take her today. But she must also be on leave today. My own niece, and yet she couldn't understand! I had assumed after going to a medical school, she must have ceased to be like her mother; she must have learned to understand not only human anatomy but also the human heart. I had thought an architect like Nikhil should have a doctor as his wife, and that would give Prashant's family a fresh beginning in society. But Rucha asked the question that Ramaben had not bothered asking: 'What will people say?'

'Ben,' the rickshawallah was saying to me. 'Ben, what is to be done? There is a traffic jam at Pritam Nagar. Looks like there has been an accident.' Was it Prashant? Oh my God, he must have been riding his scooter with all that anxiety. I ran towards the spot. I saw a bus and rickshaw in the distance, and felt relieved. But the next moment I felt ashamed of myself. The bus stood in the middle of the road, blocking the entire road. There was a body on the road: it was that of a middle-aged woman. I ran back to the rickshaw. I told the driver to go via the Lakkadiya Pul underpass. I almost forgot to breathe. My legs shook. I kept my eyes shut. A dead body had appeared before my rickshaw—spreadeagled, with half-open lips and wide-open eyes. A gold bangle on each wrist. Scattered beads of a tulsi mala next to the body. I was walking over this body. There were shifting dark shapes around it. Swarms of vultures and crows hovered over the corpse. I kept asking the rickshawallah to go faster. I took off my glass bangles and put them in my purse. A vehicle passing next to me blared its horn and startled me. A crowd of people chased me, chanting, catch her, catch her....

I wanted to get home as soon as possible. Before the dead body was wrapped in Ramaben's patola sari, I needed to be home.

'Ben, your house number?' the rickshawallah asked.

'Fifty-four. Yes, yes, fifty-four.' I wiped my spectacles with my kerchief and noticed my neighbour who was shifting houses arranging all her plants in a lorry. One of them was a tulsi plant. Someone stood at my gate. I paid the rickshawallah and made to open the gate to my house. The person standing at my gate placed his hand upon mine. It was Prashant. He said softly, 'Congratulations.'

I tried to remember who he was, and blurted out, 'For what?'

NIGHTMARE

MINAL DAVE

My fingers fly over the computer keys but my eyes are on the clock. I won't be able to catch the first MEMU train today. Mrs Rao drives me nuts! She has to think up this assignment at the very last minute, just when it's time to leave. Sure, she has a point when she says that the office has reopened after ten or twelve days. But, my dear woman, you merely have to ride pillion on your husband's bike and then you're home for a hot meal of idlis and sambhar. As for me? If I miss the train, I have to wait at the station for a good hour or so and then travel for another two hours to a different city, fearful and trembling, in what's probably going to be an empty compartment. But how can I expect you to understand that? There! Thank God it's over...ah! There's an auto here. Good.

Arre, bhai, hurry up please. The curfew's been lifted after so many days—no wonder people are rushing out of their homes as if they've been uncaged. They're a mindless lot, taking off in their cars and two-wheelers now, but if one firecracker bursts, they'll rush home to lock themselves up again. Good God, did this light have to turn red this very minute? But as they say, akarmi no padiyo kaano, the unfortunate one also has a broken bowl. I've got exactly seven rupees with me, so I won't waste time looking for change. All these people coming out of the station—please, would you make way for those who have trains to catch? And these railway people, they're just incorrigible. Trust them to put the staircase right at the end of this long platform. My train is from platform 4 and is just about to leave. Let me run...just the last two steps and....there! Damn! Missed it.

'Ben,' the chaiwalla says, 'now you'll have to wait for an hour.' Why is he looking at me in that strange way? There's not a single commuter on the platform. Two minutes ago it had been swarming with people. Now they seem to have taken off like a flock of birds when someone hurls a stone at them.

Perhaps I should go to Smita's house. I'm not likely to have company on the train, even if I spend a whole hour at the station. Fear still hangs in the air. When the chaiwalla looks at me, I'm afraid. Who knows, he might throw things at me. Who knows which caste he belongs to. People like us don't believe in caste, creed, or community, but he can't know that, can he? He's looking at my chandlo, my mangalsutra. No, no...everybody's not like that. I'm thirsty. Where's the bottle of water—I think I had put it in my bag...oh, there it is, but it's empty!

Maybe I should call home from this phone booth and also buy a bottle of water. And a magazine. Vikram answers the phone. He's upset that I couldn't catch the first train. But I hang up on him. I don't allow his annoyance, swinging through the phone, to reach me. The fellow manning the telephone booth dispenses advice, 'Ben, don't go home so late by train. Things were different earlier, but now you can't take any risks.' So what has changed in these last ten days, I ask myself. Do people not shed tears any more? Don't they love? Aren't babies born any more? Have flowers begun to wilt before they blossom? Nothing's really changed. But then what is the reason behind this fear, this suspicion everywhere?

Let me do some browsing at the bookstall. It's all the same: the newspapers are full of the play of numbers, the dance of death, the game of fire, the fury of bullets.... I pick up two magazines and settle down on a bench.

The platform is deserted. The fires have been put out at the tea stalls and the oil used for frying savoury snacks has gone cold. The boys who work at the stalls are half-asleep. Bottles of aerated drinks have been returned to their crates. The lame boy who polishes shoes is sleeping peacefully, using his shoe-stand as a pillow. But the dog lying near my bench is restless. He looks around, then gets up, looks around again, cranes his neck, pricks up his ears as if listening to something, and then curls up again.

Then he's up again. There are two dogs fighting on the platform across ours. Is he frightened of them?

I notice that there is a woman sitting next to me now. She wears a thick black burkha and only her hands are visible. She has a large cloth bag with her. The veil of the burkha hides her eyes, but I can feel her gaze upon me. Why did she have to come and sit next to me when there are so many unoccupied benches on the platform? What does she have in mind? Is she carrying a bomb in that bag of hers? What if she leaves the bag here and walks away and the bomb goes off, what will happen to me then? That would be disaster for my poor husband and children. But let me not think such things. Poor thing, she's just sitting quietly. But does that mean she's really harmless? Should I move away? Maybe go elsewhere? My tongue is stuck to the roof of my mouth, refusing to move. My fingers clutch my handbag. Despite the chill of the evening air, I am perspiring and a bead of sweat falls from my forehead onto my hand.

'Kem ben? Where are you off to?' Chiman, the daawada seller, descends like a saviour. I feel blood surging through my veins again. It is as though the curfew has been lifted once more. 'You're late, ben, the first train has left.' Smiling, I nod, afraid to open my mouth. What if I stutter?

'Why are you sitting here?' He signals me to get up. 'At such times, you shouldn't be sitting here.' But my feet will not move. Chiman smirks at my foolishness and walks away. He's right. I should get up from here. You never know what she might do, this woman. She could pull a knife out of her bag and stab me and no one would see. Arre, she only has to kick me and I will collapse. Look at her hands, how big and masculine they are! Is there a hardened criminal hiding behind that burkha? How do I get up? Why did I have to travel at this time? Lord Ram, please let me reach home safely. Should she try anything, I will tell her, listen, woman, take what you want but don't kill me. My throat is parched and hurts; my hands are frozen. I decide that the moment I see someone coming, I'll get up. I discreetly look around the platform for another person, moving my eyes from one side to the other. Not a soul. Where have all the people gone?

It seems like it was only yesterday that this platform was buzzing with life—trains coming and going all the time, people rushing from here to there; it was difficult to even find a spot to stand. And the ladies' compartment in which I travel every day—at every station women would pour in, like grains being threshed, and some would get off the train. Once they find a place to sit, handbags and baskets are opened and beans, peas, and garlic are taken out. They begin to peel, sort, and sometimes, chop. At times, needles and colourful yarns emerge and turn into flowers and petals on saris and kurtas and woollen jumpers. Packets of papad, pickles, chutney, and masala are bought and sold. The tears of women tortured by husbands and mothers-in-law are wiped, bittersweet office gossip is exchanged, sweets are distributed to celebrate engagements and weddings; occasionally, even blows and curses are traded, Ramrakshakavach verses and the Gayatri mantra are chanted, or room is made to offer namaz. As we cross more stations, the vacant seats fill up.... But where are all these faces today? Where are the bags of peas, beans, garlic, papad, and masala? They seem to have been replaced by terrified faces and bags full of suspicion. How can I get away from here?

Arre, the train has arrived. I didn't even notice it entering the station. Okay, I have to head straight into the ladies' compartment. Oh dear, the burkha-clad woman is climbing in after me. Why doesn't she leave me alone? The compartment's virtually empty—barely two or three women. A fisherwoman is fast asleep with her empty basket next to her. The basket stinks but at least there is the presence of another human being. The woman in the burkha sits facing me.

It is dark outside, black like the burkha she's wearing. There isn't a sliver of light for me to hold onto and sail through this dark ocean of the night. What shall I do? I shut my eyes, hoping the darkness will go away, hoping to escape those eyes which are fixed on me. What must she be thinking now? People say that you can't trust them. You never know when they might draw a knife and butcher you. I remember a classmate of mine from college, Hasina. Her brother had stabbed his wife. I couldn't help wondering if this woman might also do the same.

Oh God, someone's shaking me. I open my eyes—it's the woman in the burkha! Oh no, what will she do to me? Should I shout for help? The fisherwoman is fast asleep. She won't know if I get killed. Should I jump off the moving train? Oh God, please, please come to my rescue! I promise never to get on this train again. I'll even give up my job and stop commuting. It is better to starve than to suffer this nightmare.

'Benji, benji,' the woman says, 'I'm getting off here. I'm so grateful that you were around; imagine travelling alone at such a time. I was so scared, you know…it is so difficult…I can't believe it!'

She's frightened, like me! I burst out laughing.

'What's there to be scared of, ben? I do the "up-down" every day.' My voice suddenly acquires more force than the train's whistle.

She places her hand on mine and says, 'Khuda hafiz'. It's moist and sweaty and as she touches me, my sweat merges with hers. The train stops. I help her with her bag, which suddenly seems light and harmless. She melts away under the faint light of the station. The fisherwoman yawns. She stretches her limbs and takes a bag out of her basket. The greenness of beans spills out and infuses everything. The stars twinkle in the dark and brighten my way home.

THE BILGE WATER

NAZIR MANSURI

At daybreak, an impenetrable fog had settled everywhere. One could barely see what lay ahead in the docklands. Wrapped in a dirty blanket, Uko was smoking bidi after bidi, sitting on the wooden plank in the middle of his small fishing boat. The good midnight sleep deceived him like a mortal enemy. The dense fog bank had set in towards the end of the Posh month. Terrible biting cold winds were freezing him, and he sat shivering. Utterly dejected, he just did not feel like going home. The siren of the lighthouse on the high slope of Bhaatgaam village kept howling endlessly. On one side of the dock, on the sandy beach, lay the village with densely crowded huts. The huts were roofed with Mangalorean tiles and had walls built from a basket-weave woven from palm fronds. Bhaatgaam lay in front of the dock made from huge rafters and bamboo supports. The low-set huts lay in the midst of palm and local badam trees. The fences were made of dense thorny Bhungra cacti. These fences enclosed numerous small fields and vegetable patches. From the dock, Uko 'Kavusio'* glowered furiously at the village. As people thought he was extremely sharp, they called him by his pet name Uko 'Kavusio', or 'the cunning'.

'Damn it, why the hell has he come back? And just look at the way he talks, the bastard.... How I would love to butcher him, the bloody son of a bitch! Folks who disappear at sea do not come back and...and just see this fucking pest Bhikho Malam who has come back!' Bhikho Malam had disembarked from his ship the night

---

*Many Gujarati proper names change with the mode of address. For instance, Uko becomes Ukaa when addressed informally and Bhikho becomes Bhikha. Uko's pet name 'Kavusio' indicates his cunningness and 'Ghamat', which literally means 'bilge water', indicates that he is a nuisance in the village. Bhikha is 'Malam', which indicates that he is a reputed captain and sailor.

before. His was a rented cargo ship from Rajpara. It was a colossal hulk with two monstrous engines, and three huge masts, and its gigantic sail resembled the outspread wings of a monstrous crane. The previous night, when the tumultuous waters of the high tide were surging, the mammoth ship had entered the dock, throwing up large quantities of water on either side. It was loaded with the cargo of Mangalorean or European roof-tiles from the coastal region of Malabar and a great many stacks of enormously thick timber. Bhikha Malam had returned to the Diu coast after almost twelve or thirteen years. He was overjoyed when he saw the roofs and flickering lanterns of his village. 'O God, I had left my full-bodied woman behind....Who knows how she is now! She was like a huge cruiser when I left...has she turned into a Basrai crane by now? O let me go, she has been waiting for me for so many years!' Bhikha Malam's arrival reduced Uko to ashes. It was a bolt out of the blue, the return of Bhikho Malam who disappeared twelve years ago... 'Why the hell has this blackguard turned up now after all these years.... This fucking wet blanket...this whoremonger must have kept all sorts of women wherever he went: Africa, Mozambique, Lisbon, and God knows where....The seasoned sailors keep women wherever they go. Why didn't he remain wherever he had been...? He talks of making me a 'mama'...what does he take us for, bums? Idiots? Bastard!' His eyes fell on the rear of the dock. The monstrous ship could barely be seen due to its black colour. The fog caused the ship to vanish and reappear every now and then.

The opaque fog settled down in the deep and broad inlet. The marshland was forested with weeds. One could see the huge pillar-masts of the sails and the two smaller masts. The ship unfurled its sails, which were large enough to hidef almost half of the village from view. Large ropes, pulleys, and leather stripes hung from the ship. The sight of the wooden ebony-coloured cabin of Bhikha Malam at the bottom of the pillar-masts filled Uko with odium. The high tide settled down at midnight and the enormous beams of timber were offloaded using thick ropes and pulleys from the ship.

Some eight to ten petromax lanterns were hung by the people from the lumber mill. There was commotion and shouting on the wharf at midnight. There were annoying screeching sounds of the ship's pulleys and leather straps. The Valsadi timber logs falling into the sea made loud splashing sounds. It was as if the dockyard had woken up in the middle of the night and the clamour was simply unbearable for Uko. 'These scoundrels won't allow me to catch even a single wink....' Uko was at the end of his tether due to the unceasing shouting of the sailors. Their voices were coarse and booming. 'Do you think this shore belongs to your father? Bloody devils! Sister fuckers! Are you born of human beings or ghouls? You have found time to do this work at this time of the night!' Uko spat spitefully. His shouts were lost in the booming siren of the lighthouse. Fishing was closed due to the Agiyaras, or he would have liked to flee to the seas to fish at this very hour. Staying on the shore was intolerable. He felt a deep urge to run away into the deep sea. 'Where should I go and what should I do?' He got up to spit and nonchalantly looked into the bottom of his small boat, at the bilge water collected near the bottom of the sail. The boat was an age-old one with a broad plank and made of thick wood. Only once or twice a year would he mend it. However, he had not repaired it in the past year or two. He had opened its engine and fixed it some time back. Moreover, the last fishing season was very difficult, as the sea had become tumultuous and there were a couple of sea storms too; hence he was not able to repair his boat. He used to apply water-resistant paint to it to prevent bilge water, but it turned out that he was not very good at the job. Consequently, bilge water would creep into his boat often. Aunt Raji, who owned the boat, would admonish her nephew and others who would hire it: 'Scoundrels! You do not maintain your boats properly and you roll into the high seas! You rascals, you will drown and die and will have to press the feet of Old Man Sea! Who will come to look after your mother? Your uncles? Only if you leave aside your drinking orgies for a while will you find time to repair your boat! My sturdy boat is made from good strong wood...no one in this village has such a good boat! You rogues, look after it properly....' Raji would grumble but in vain. Uko and others would listen to what she said with crestfallen faces. Then things would continue as usual.

He saw the bilge water at the bottom of his boat. He threw away his blanket and started removing the foul-smelling water with his paddle. Even his paddle was dilapidated. It was a good metallic paddle. He had changed its lock washers often, but he had to go all the way to Kodinar to buy them. This time the washer was in a deplorable condition. There was plenty of bilge water in his boat, but his paddle chucked out the water, making gargling sounds. The bilge water reeked of oil and diesel. Uko started pumping out the water. He had not had a wink of sleep the whole night and his paddle was rusted and limp. He had to unbend its rod after a little pumping. It seemed ready to break. The heavy boat screeched and started ejecting the bilge water. The boat was so heavy that his thighs were cramped, and his feet ached. Uko started removing the water furiously.

Boats and shipping vessels of all types surrounded him in the harbour. The sailors, fishermen, and their mates were fast asleep and had planned on getting up late as fishing was closed. As the clamour of unloading logs of wood from Bhikha Malam's enormous ship anchored in the harbour went on until the first crow of the cock at dawn, they had not been able to get a wink of sleep. The sailors and mates flung the choicest and vilest of abuses at the colossal hulk. So what if Bhika Malam had returned after ages? They did not care for him.

Now a foul-mouthed fisherman would occasionally raise his head from under the dirty blanket, stare around, and bawl: 'Hey, you asshole, why the hell are you making that screeching noise at this time of the night? Your Aunt Raji is playing a pipe back there at your home or what? Stop that sound, you sister fucker or else I will smash you.... Uka, you bilge water, you will remain bilge water forever!' Someone else flung a leather bucket at him. It hit him on his ribs and fell on his thighs, spinning in circles. 'You son of a bitch, why don't you let us sleep for a while? We will fall at your feet if you want, we will drag our arse and beg of you if you want it that way.... Please stop this squeaking and screeching, for heaven's sake! If your auntie does not let you sleep back home, why the hell do you jack off in this boat here? You just come to the shore and see how I thrash you. You jerk, let the devil take your mother....' Uko the 'bilge water' continued removing the filthy water from his bumboat with his paddle. He could hardly think of anything else to do. Bhikho Malam had returned to his house and so he did not feel like going home. 'See the way the bitch talks, "O my Malam has come...ploughing the seven seas"...he has surely fucked around on his way.... Who the hell told him to go overseas in the first place? And how does she go around in the garments he has given her, yodelling on the beach dunes! It's so infuriating...why does the bastard have to turn up after a dozen years...and that wench in spite of him showing his face after fifteen years is all merry and joyous singing, "O, my Malam has come after fifteen years!" Go raise your skirts and chase him for all I care!' There was no one to hear him. He was chewing a datan shoot and was totally exhausted from paddling. He was sweating profusely and panting. A shooting pain coursed through his thigh—he had a cramp. His guts hurt. He abandoned paddling and lay down. He turned this way and that on his dirty mattress in his boat. The opacity of the fog and the screeching noise irritated the boatmen of various vessels. Due to the dense fog, they could not make out who was making such noise. They merely threw the foulest of curses at him. 'What the hell, who is this bloody scrounger at this hour? Drag him, batter that bastard...that fucking son of a bitch. He seems to be a motherfucking Portuguese rascal. And who is with him?' The wharf was filled with shouting and curses. Uko lay down, panting. He heard the foul abuses and was filled with rage. 'Let dogs take your mothers, why the hell are you screwballs cursing? Shut your bloody mouth or else I will have to come down and smash you...just let me meet you on the shore and I will thrash you...have you seen this ray-fish whip of mine? Who wants to mess with Uko Ghamat?' he shouted. Uka's name silenced the shouts on the wharf. He was only in his thirties but was so short-tempered that he got into fights often. He would not let anyone have the upper hand. The whole village would cringe on seeing him. 'A bare-assed bastard...' they would say. Women would mumble, 'Raji is too arrogant.' The fishermen would say, 'Bloody bilge water,' and grimace.

Smallpox had left Uko with pockmarks all over his face. One of his eyes had a squint. He was hefty, dark, and imposing—a hulk actually. He seemed domineering. Only Raji believed that he was a submissive man. His irascibility would land him in fights and brawls in the village or at the wharf. He would mercilessly thrash a fisherman, drag him to his home, and even lash his wife or sister with the ray-fish whip. 'Take care of this son of a bitch...why the hell did you send him to fight with me?' The day there were quarrels in the village, he would be the nemesis for his foes. Police constables had often taken him into custody. He had become so hardened that being beaten up hardly mattered to him. He was nicknamed 'ghamat' or bilge water.

The bilge water would often gather in his boat and ruin his fishing. He would return to the shores early. He was a master thief. The owners of the vessels would tolerate him when the boats were full. Otherwise, they all thought of him as a worthless fisherman who would ruin his fishing because of the bilge water and return early. He was an orphan. He had stealthily entered the village late one night with the people fleeing the Portuguese invasion of the lighthouse island. The people who had fled the invasion had left the village a long time back in trucks and six-seater vehicles. Uko had been broke. The drivers refused to take him with them. He had stayed in the village that night. The village was almost deserted. There was a desolate-looking orchard on the beach at the end of the village. It was Aunt Raji's orchard. It was abundantly green and overflowing with fowl and cattle. He slept outside it. Aunt Raji had actually locked up her home and fled, leaving her farm to the sleeping Uka due to the news of the invasion. There was thunder and bombing. There were fighter aircrafts and pitch-black armoured cars. Then, all of a sudden, they disappeared. Raji returned after a couple of days. Uka had looked after her cattle and fowl. He was a twelve- or fifteen-year-old sickly stripling. Raji was elated to see that he had taken good care of her cattle and fowl. She allowed the waif to live on her farm. Ever since his childhood, Uka had been a rogue. He would pick on the entire village. However, he was exceedingly docile with Raji. No one but Aunt Raji was dear to him. He loved to keep looking at her. 'What an attractive woman! Her gait…just like a Barsai crane!' Uka hardly knew anything about his parents. He used to live alone in the orchards of Diu. He would make ends meet by stealing from the farms. He would sell off people's fowl and goats. He would make merry whenever he made some money. At times, he would run errands for people. He would take down neera or toddy or set up their pots. Or he would sell them in the village. It would suffice for two meals. But he would rest by snuggling up in a filthy torn blanket as if he were a nobody. Raji would take care of him. He would slog like a beast on the farm and on the boat. He was exceptionally industrious. Raji would bake fresh and hot bajara rotla for him at daybreak. He would rub some jaggery, ghee, and oil on it and relish it. 'O why are you so worried about what villagers will say or do? Why do you bother about them? Are you a Patel of the village or what?' she would lovingly rebuke him and feed him.

It was daybreak and he was hungry. He got down from his boat near the shore. He thrashed around angrily in the dense fog and reached home. Thorny weeds were thriving and the fowl were pecking around in search of grains. The forest birds were creating a commotion.

Flocks of ravens had descended from the palm trees and forest on to the beach. Raji's house looked desolate and quiet. The windows were shut. Raji had spent a sleepless night. Bhikha Malam was unloading cargo from the ship. She had lit a lamp and was watching him ecstatically. Sleep was like a foe to her. Bhikho returned at the first crow of the cock in the morning. He took a shower in sweet water and slept like a log. Raji kept awake the whole night, smiling as if she were crazy. Her joy had drained her. She wanted to catch a little sleep and so she had lain down. Otherwise, she would be up at dawn preparing bajara rotlas for Uka. Both of them would gorge on them in the morning. When it was sunny, they would have tea. Uka was furious at the sight of the closed door. 'Is the bastard bedding her in the morning? He has just returned...and he has started....' He gave a sharp kick to a hen strolling around him and it fell some distance away. He snapped a branch off the old saag tree. Raji had planted it when Uko was made a part of her family many years ago. He tugged at the branch of a nearby thorny tree. The tree was full of dew and he was drenched when it fell. He went away to the farm. There were pots of toddy liquor that had been hanging on the trees since the previous evening. They were yet to be brought down. He kept thinking about what Aunt Raji and Bhikho were doing and was dejected. He would play mischievously with Raji at times and she would playfully hit him and start crying...she was like his queen. 'The sailor will be hungry after his journey...' she would say, and then weep and cry in her tall wooden bed!

Raji's farm was around five bighas. It was quite large and the vegetables grew year round. The cattle were thriving, and as the land was near the beach, the local bajara and jowar crops were in abundance. The local chillies also grew in plenty. Raji did not have to go out looking for a merchant to buy her chillies as the women from nearby villages would take them from her. She would earn a lot by selling in small quantities. The date and palm trees were also in abundance. She would make vinegar from the toddy. Uko would carry huge jars of vinegar all the way up to Kodinar and nearby villages of Chikhli-Kaj and Nanawada to sell them. Uko was like a sea-god to Raji. Thanks to Uko, the farm had been lush green, her boat had yielded good returns, and she was not lonely.

༺

Raji was reclining on a massive timber bed, which had an umbrella attached to a bedpost. She had finished her chores and her meals and was relaxing. She used to feel very forlorn in her huge mansion and sprawling orchard at such times. Once Uko had arrived, she did not long for her husband. The chilly plants were yet to be watered. The day was just about to break. Uko was punctilious with regard to his work. He busied himself with the task of taking down the toddy pots from the palms. He was wearing khakhi trousers and he scratched both his thighs as he hurriedly started climbing the trees. His thighs were burning and aching. Aunt Raji went on with her usual what-would-my-Bhikho-be-doing. Uko seethed and fumed at such talk. He brought down the toddy pots and arranged them in a circle under the tree. Raji would hang containers under the tree. He put all the pots in that container and carried them back assiduously on his head. Aunt Raji wasn't at home as he entered. Bhikho, fresh after his bath, was wearing white garments and sunning himself comfortably on a bulky mattress. He was munching away on sheera from a copper dish. Uka brought in the toddy pot container and shouted, 'Where's Aunt Raji?' Bhikho stared at him with a squint. He smiled cunningly. As Aunt Raji was not around, Uka had to unload the container from his head without anyone's help. Bhikho shouted, 'Hey you, you jerk—watch out! You will spill toddy all over the place. Your palm trees leaked the whole night like bilge water, it seems. Don't you understand it will turn sour? Don't you think of anything other than toddy first thing in the morning? Who the hell are you? You think this orchard belongs to your father? Off with you, you waif...go away to your leaking boat!' Uko glared at Bhikho furiously. He carried the container inside and emptied it. There were some pots of *mahua* liquor in the house. Raji would keep the fresh liquor ready and when Uko would return after a hard day's work, she would offer it to him gently and drink with him. 'Come have this, if it gives you some consolation after all that hard work, it will have served its purpose,' she would say. He picked up a couple of those pots on his way out.

He had the container in one hand and the pots in the other. 'Hey, you son of a bitch, where the fuck are you taking those pots?' Bhikho roared. Uko halted and glared at him. Bhikho was startled. Uko walked away. A hedge made of thorny shrubs surrounded the house. He kicked open the door of the hedge and went away smiling. 'Where are you taking those pots? What a shameless man! Brazen bastard! Just let him come back,' Bhikho shouted.

Uko returned with two huge containers of toddy, one on his head and another under his arm. He gathered some vegetables from the beach dunes and arrived at Aunt Raji's home. She was at home. He had hardly sat down on the veranda when he saw Aunt Raji and his mouth flew open at what he saw. She was dressed in a new satin ghagra and a tight short choli. The dress was the colour of kevadia flowers. She had just emerged from her bath and had left her hair loose. She took some sheera in a plate. There was something in the way she carried herself. She pretended not to notice Uko. Uko was crestfallen.

'Now that you have returned like a big shot, why can't you eat some more sheero?' she thrust all of it onto Bhikho's plate. 'Even kids like Uko can eat this much sheera. If you are the big leader now, you must look after your body,' she said and smiled flirtatiously. 'O he is not a kid any more,' Bhikho said bitterly, 'He is one hell of a grown-up bastard now.' Raji smiled as Uko continued to stare at her. She looked at him and said, 'Come on, why did you fetch two containers of toddy? One would have been sufficient. Now that this sailor has come, we would have had them later.' She had kept huge copper dishes full of dry fruits that Bhikho had brought on the bed. The dishes overflowed with cashew nuts, almonds, dates, and walnuts. Since the morning, she had been busy gifting these away to neighbours and friends. She got up to give away those gifts and on her way she covered the dishes with her garments and said, 'Hey Uka, there is a plate of sheera for you.' She left in a hurry and her satin garments rustled as she left. Uko was transfixed by his aunt's appearance. He was also greatly infuriated. He got up and slipped away from the back of the orchard. He heard Bhikho clearing his throat. He was enraged. He stomped around on the beach and stopped under a huge Ravantadia palm tree. He threw himself on the sand. 'That woman has gone mad! So what if the sailor has returned—is he a big Portuguese lord or what? Or is he some police constable or what?' he choked. He opened the pot of fresh mahua liquor and gulped it down. He had finished a couple of pots of toddy since morning. His hunger, however, had not died down. He could not stand the sight of Aunt Raji feeding sheera to Bhikho.

He had been close to Aunt Raji since the age of fifteen or so. She had taken great care of him. He would tirelessly take down pots of toddy from the trees. He was just a kid and would look like a monkey climbing the palm trees. He would be exhausted. Aunt Raji would feed him sheera rich with ghee. She would keep it ready from the morning. When he was very busy, she would say, 'Come, Uka, have some sheera.' He would put it off, saying, 'There are only five trees left, Aunt, and I will eat after I'm done.' Raji would wait for him in the kitchen. 'Poor boy is just a kid and yet he slogs like a workhorse. Shouldn't he be eating more often?' she would say and when he used to enter the home with the containers for storing toddy, she would grab him by the wrist and almost forcibly make him sit down to eat. She would sit near the stove and make him sit on a thick timber platform, which used to be her gigantic bed. She herself would sit on the clay-covered floor. She would add more ghee to his plate. 'See the way she speaks now: "Eat from the dish kept for you if you want", as if I am a dog or a cat! Should I be living here any more?' he spat in distaste. He got up, gathered dried fronds and leaves, and lit a fire. The fog was still very dense. There were no signs that it would disperse soon. Though the sun shone

The Bilge Water 169

on his head like a fireball, it was chilly due to the fog. One could hardly find any sunlight. 'Why does he refuse me the boats? What will he do with all those vessels? Why has he taken those two pots of mahua liquor? To stick them up his ass? He does not know that I can gulp two huge pots just like that...now what will she do with Uko? Uko is merely ghamat—bilge water—waste water...she has no use for him now....' Aunt Raji knew that Uko was fond of mahua since his childhood. He would go without food or drink. Hence, he would be starving most of the time. Even then, Raji would order for fresh pots of mahua liquor for him. 'Hey, for whom are you buying such expensive liquor pots? Has anyone kept you?' women she knew would enquire. 'Oh no, nothing of that kind, they are for my Uko, the ghamat. I have to spend on him, you see, I have to find fresh mahudo for him. Poor chap, he does the work of ten men all by himself. It gives him some relief. So even if it is difficult to obtain, I make it a point to buy it for his sake,' Raji would say. When Uko would return from fishing, she would have kept the pots ready. She would barbecue freshly-slit fish after stuffing them with fresh green vegetables. Uko would eat it as he gulped down the liquor. Uko was like a tiny king. He would have a great time with mahudo. He would chatter about fishing. 'Hey, Aunt Raji, I don't stop fishing till my huge fishing vessels are overflowing with fish! My huge fishing vessels are huge like Aunt Raji too! She moves on the sea just like Aunt Raji rustling in her ghagra as she walks!' Raji would smile affectionately and say, 'Watch your tongue, young man! Once you start drinking, you lose all control of it. Don't be shameless!'

'Don't smile so cunningly! You are large and so feminine! My vessel too is like you! She moves the way you move! She is unique like you!' Uko had named his boat 'Rajki'. His partners in fishing would curse him behind his back: 'The bastard goes around as if the boat is his father's. Luckily, Raji is not his woman.' 'Even if he sees a speck of dirt on the boat platform, he is furious and screams at the top of his head if we are late in scrubbing. He says, "O my Aunt washes herself religiously and is always so clean! My boat should remain as clean!" Does he really think that the boat is Raji? He calls it Rajki, now you tell me.' 'But have you seen Aunt Raji? Like the boat, she is large and womanly! You want to marry her; I swear! You want to cuddle up and sleep beside her during winter, and say to hell with fishing!' His assistants would have boisterous fun like this.

Raji was like that. No sooner had she gotten married, her husband went off on an expedition only to return after twenty years. She was barely fifty. She was broad and enticingly tanned. Tattoos of all kinds covered her, and her sparkling complexion caught everyone's eye. She looked dignified, like a Portuguese lady. She had a sharp tongue, and yet was very warm. She lived as if she was enduring her life and her mature attractiveness, with Uko 'Ghamat' by her side. It seemed as if Uko was her man and she used to care for him as she would her man. Aunt Raji was quite aware of her beauty and she used to keep a safe distance from people who drooled over her and made fools of themselves around her. A couple of years after Bhikho had left her, many influential and rich men wanted to keep her. Though he had two wives at home, the village Patel wanted to keep her. 'Why have you kept that jerk, Uko Ghamat? I will gift you three of my boats, my ship, my sprawling farms, and deck you in gold and silver jewellery from top to toe. Why the hell are you living with Uko? Of what use is the bilge water to anyone, anyway?' Jokingly, acquaintances would bring such proposals indirectly to her. Raji would be livid: 'There is no one like my Uko Ghamat...he was a prince in his previous birth. What a fine young man he has turned out to be! I would clasp him and beget his children every year! What do you know of him? You spindle-legged ones; how can you even think of keeping me? When Uko walks, the whole earth shakes! Once in many births do you get someone like Uko. If Uko asks me, I would be his without thinking for a moment. If he can't keep me, I will keep him in my home!'

'Who looks after Uko? Raji. So, who will keep Uko? Raji, of course,' she would shout, thumping her chest. Raji pandered to Uko's wishes and took care of him. 'Her husband is out on the seas, she is all alone in the gigantic house. She is ripe and ready and who knows what she is doing with him in her home. He is her keep, I am sure. No one in the village has such a huge farm as her. Nobody in the village has such a magnificent house with fifteen rooms. Uko is in for a real big fortune: a huge farm, huge house, and on top of that, a really big woman! But why in the world is Raji interested in him? The big shots in the village have big farms and mansions. Though she is not yet old, she is not a young virgin either. He is such a huge hunk, and he is all young, raw, and green...why does she need anyone else?' Tongues in the village would wag all the time. Raji would overhear such talk and would enjoy the undercurrent of frustration and envy. 'Yes, everything is for Uko,' she would say. 'You sleep with him or what?' somebody would ask. 'I would do anything Uko asks me to. If he tells me to sleep with him or marry him, I will not think for a minute. He is a bit naïve, but he is such a huge hunk!' she would say, smiling and biting her thick pink lips.

Uko was staring at the empty pots. Raji was happy with Bhikho Malam. She was feeding him sheera from a copper plate. When he recalled that image, his fingers tightened around the pot. Angrily, he flung the pot at the great Ravantadia palm tree in front of him. It shattered and the pieces flew in different directions. The fireball of the sun rose in the sky but was lost in the dense fog. 'Why on earth has he come?' was the only thought that gripped him. 'Where should I go now? Should I walk away with the fakirs and mendicants, or should I go join the singing-beggars? Should I go back to my village? I would survive by selling stolen goats and fowl.' He contemplated going back to his village, which had a lighthouse in it. There was great disquiet in his mind. He had heard the old women in the village talking: 'Who is his mother? Does he have a father? Who knows? They found him on one such foggy morning among these boggy weeds. He survived because the waters subsided. When they were cutting the weeds, they found him. Some said he is from Vaarau village. Some said he grew up on those Khaja Khaya streets. Whose child is he? They say "Everyone's", and then they say, "Nobody's child!" He would sleep anywhere. Those Portuguese soldiers looked after him for a while. They would have made a soldier out of him. But he would curse them! The poor chap will spend all his life in misery! Poor waif!' When he quarrelled with Aunt Raji, his whole life and the world would seem empty and distasteful to him. All sorts of thoughts would cross his troubled mind. 'How will that woman manage without me? Damn it!' His eyes would turn red and then bitter and brackish water would start flowing out of them. He was craving tea; he hadn't had a cup since morning.

On winter mornings, he would lie around in the boat. Aunt Raji would shout and raise a commotion to wake him up. 'Hey you! Uka...you senseless ghamat! The tea is ready, don't you want to get up and have it?' she would shout and tease from the wharf. 'Somebody wake up my bilge water! The White Master is still asleep, the shameless one!' The fishermen sitting on the wharf untangling the nets or drinking would laugh, 'Raji, neither our mother nor our wife would ever wake us up like this, and your ghamat seems to be quite a lucky guy!' 'Shut up, bastards, or I will thrash you... he works on my boat and manages my farm! Poor chap has no one of his own,' she would say. 'Just look at Raji! Don't we work on the boats? Don't we go on the high seas? Whom else do we work for? We go for our mothers and women too, but no one has ever come to wake us up or offer a cup of tea like this to us! Don't make us open our mouths! Yes, yes, it's fine. Your Uko is a prince....' The fishermen who had nothing better to do would laugh enviously. 'Such a gorgeous woman! Why don't you look after her, you sons of bitches! She keeps on saying, "Oh he looks after my business and my farm." Wouldn't be he looking after her ass too? She too must be up to something, for sure. Her man has been away for so many years.... I have even forgotten what his name is...oh yes, Bhikha Malam, the great sailor! He has come back. He must have kept a black whore for himself in Africa…and over here, Raji has kept Uko. He looks after everything, the farm, boats, business, and the woman too,' they would hoot, drunk on mahudo liquor. Uko returned home and sat on the bed. The cloth strips of the bed had sunk down and it looked like a cradle. The leaves of the badam trees had turned red like red cranes, as if indicating the approaching fall. The dry winter wind had started howling. Bhikha Malam was reclining royally on thick mattresses outside the house. Friends and acquaintances from the village had turned up to meet him. They were drinking mahudo liquor and munching on almonds, walnuts, and cashew nuts. No one saw Uko Ghamat. He went into the house on shaking legs. The house was noisy. The women from the village were chatting inside. Some of them glanced at Uko from the corner of their eyes, and smiled to themselves. They said in a sly tone, which Uko could clearly hear: 'O dear, the god of the ocean is a real and living god. So what if he has returned after twenty years…otherwise who else is so fortunate to have this huge farm, this thriving business, and a fabulous woman like you! It was in his destiny, so he came back. Even after twenty years…!' Uko was startled. He headed straight to the orchard. Aunt Raji was having a great time chatting with the women. She saw Uko and said, 'Hey you, why are you running around? Why don't you kill the cock?' She gave him a carving knife. Uko took out a large blade he wore around his neck. He took the cock near the big timber trees in the orchard. Then some old woman from Raji's family approached him and said, 'What are you doing? Give it to me,' and snatched the cock from his hand. The hag circled the cock around Bhikha Malam's head seven times. 'He has returned after twenty years and he is still having ill luck, so I am doing this for his good fortune,' the old woman said. Uko was enraged. He went up in flames. 'Where the hell was this fucking son of a bitch for twenty years? Why the fucking hell has he come back?' He furiously held the wings of the cock under his feet, and with a single stroke, he slashed the cock. The black cock struggled. It was a strong cock. He had been eyeing this cock for a long time. He used to tell Raji, 'Raji, this is an excellent cock. Let me kill it, it will be delicious.'

'You think you are a great White Master, you bastard?' she would say. 'It is a sacred cock that I plan to sacrifice to the sea god.' All her sweetness would disappear and she would change the topic.

'For whom have you taken the vow, Aunt Raji?' Uko would ask teasingly.

'Stop jabbering, you idiot. I have taken the vow for my bull. What do you have to say to that?' Raji would smile with bitterness.

'And who the hell is your bull?' Uko would stare at her.

'Oh, he is a big sailor! He takes a huge boat to the sea!'

Uko would smile coyly. 'Then fulfil your vow by circling this cock around my head. I will quickly cut it up. Fishing is closed for today and we can have excellent dinner.' Raji would refuse. 'Okay... Okay...Aunt,' he would say and hug her. 'Oh you are my auntie, please let me cut it up! Oh you are my woman, please let me cut it up... please, please, please....' Raji would push him away. He would stumble and giggle, drunk on mahudo. 'Oh Aunt, you are so immense and so slippery! Can't even hug you properly!' Raji would come over , acting coy, as Uko would double up with laughter. 'Behave yourself Uko, you cunning one!' she would say. He would get up when he saw Raji. 'I want to tell you something, Aunt, if you promise not to scream! I want to get married to you, and carry you away, I swear. I really want to!' he would say eagerly and sincerely. Raji would stand before him and glare at him sharply. 'Oh dear me!' she would say, 'Here I am, come and get me!' Uko would rush to her and try to grab her. 'Oh my Aunt dear, see I have grown so tall!' Both of them would play and the banter would exhaust Raji. She would sit down on the floor. She would push Uko away. Her coloured glass bangles would break. Her tall hairdo would come off. Raji would be overwhelmed by affection and maternal love. She would stare at his attractive face and say to herself, 'This is how a husband should be, so dear and loved. My husband has disappeared on the seas while my Uko is so good!' Women would tell her, 'You will end up falling for Uko! What are you up to? Why do you take care of him so much?' Raji would pretend to get annoyed and reply, 'Bastard, does he want to cajole me with a cock? Why should I get into all this trouble?' Uko would mumble, 'I really want to carry you away and you don't even realize! What if I were to drown and die one day? You won't even know! Then marry algae and weeds!' Raji would be moved and run her fingers through his hair and say, 'Let your enemies die! My Uko will be hale and hearty. Why do you utter such inauspicious words?' She would then fetch a cock and circle it around his head and say, 'Oh sea god! Keep my Uko safe and sound!' and have him kill it.

Uko killed the black cock. His limbs and blade were covered with blood. He washed it off with water and scrubbed it with clay. 'You White Master! You haven't eaten anything since morning. You have been just drinking and wandering around. Just look at your face! How crestfallen you are! I have been watching you since the morning,' Raji mumbled. While killing the black cock, Uko had sliced his own thumb. He had slashed it with great rage. 'You haven't even had a cup of tea since morning. Just because I have been very busy...have some tea, my dear!' Raji said affectionately, looking at his anguished face. She went inside, troubled in her heart. The earthen stove was burning furiously. She prepared tea with green tea leaves and mint. Uko was sitting outside, pressing his wounded hand. Bhikha Malam was looking at him angrily from the corner of his eyes. Raji came with the tea served in a big clay cup. She stood near him, arms akimbo. 'What the hell are you up to since morning? People from the entire village have been coming and going and I have been busy. Why can't you manage on your own? You are grown up now! Why are you making faces?' Uko had just started to sip the hot tea when Bhikha Malam grumbled, 'You seem to pay too much attention to that thieving bastard! And keep saying what a good man he is! Poor, poor chap and all that! Cut it out!'

Uko was enraged. He flung the cup to the ground. It shattered. He got up and started to walk off towards the boat. 'Why the hell are you yelling? You blackguard!' Raji shouted loudly. She took one look at Uko's face, and her heart sank. She went into the house, her ghagra rustling. 'So you have become a great sailor and all that! When you were on your voyages, who do you think looked after your boats and farms? You should feel ashamed abusing that kid!' Raji was greatly agitated. She felt like telling him, 'What have you come here for? You should have stayed where you were with your African whore! After all, you must have found that black woman more attractive than me!' The women gathered in the house said, 'Your Uko is just too much! What has happened to make you feel so hurt? What has Bhikha said?' Raji's eyes filled with tears. 'He has looked after the farms, boats, and also me for more than twenty years! And Bhikha takes him for an ordinary servant! Who is foolish enough to work like a workhorse for free?' The women fell silent. Raji's old aunt was also present. She was a woman with great practical knowledge. She had wished that either Raji would keep Uko or that Uko would take her away. However, nothing had happened for fifteen years, and now Bhikha Malam had returned.

Uko stomped his way to his boat. His pet dog followed him, wagging his tail. Uko kicked him away and started the stove on his boat to make tea. He filled up a whole glass with tea and sat down in the boat in despair. The waters in the wharf had receded. The sandy banks were now exposed. Waterfowl of all kinds had come out. They flocked on the clear area on the beach and were preening. The dappled fowls had fallen silent. There were puddles of clean water on the beach. The multi-coloured waterfowl and mud made the beach look ugly. The black-and-white winged sea hawks with coral red eyes were circling the foggy grey skies.

Uko had no idea when he fell asleep on the wooden plank of his boat. When his assistant arrived with the pots of mahudo liquor for the fishing expedition at night, Raji joined him. Raji's old aunt and Bhikha Malam had finished their lunch, but Raji could hardly eat a couple of morsels. When she saw Uko's assistant, she had kept her plate aside. 'How long should I wait for him now? That rascal must be really distressed. I don't know what came over him this morning. If I look after him, Bhikha gets agitated. He cannot stand the sight of Uko. Tell me, is it fair? The bastard loathes Uko. Does he have any idea what Uko might be doing?' Mumbling to herself, she came to the wharf. She had entered the clean water and fallen on her knees. She had shouted until she was hoarse. 'You son of a bitch, why on earth did you come into my life? It would have been better had you not come at all. I would have managed my life somehow.' Uko was snoring, drunk on mahudo. His assistant Jeevo Moto came and said, 'Hey Uko! Come down for lunch...why are you sleeping like a pregnant woman?' He coaxed and cajoled him into coming. 'I don't want to eat. Let me sleep, Jeeva Moto. You bastard, I will murder you....' Uko was frantic. 'Are you my mom or mother-in-law? Jeeva, had you not been my chief sailor, I would have given you a real piece of my mind.' Jeevo was his oldest assistant. He and Raji dragged Uko back home. Raji grumbled, 'This man has been drinking endlessly since morning. Why don't you eat something? I have cooked your favourite black cock!' Aunt Raji's brand new satin sari was wet. She had entered the water to reach his boat. Raji's appearance in her satin ghagra blew his mind away and his intoxication vanished. He wanted to hug her and weep, 'Raji...oh my Raji....' He looked at her with heavy eyes. He loved the way Raji smiled. She soothed him. He almost fell into the bed outside the house. 'I don't want to eat anything....' Raji cajoled him, and so did her old aunt, saying, 'Oh my son, oh my hero....' However, he did not budge. Bhikha Malam had finished his lunch and was reclining on a huge timber bed, chewing paan and waiting for Raji. 'You have become like a Portuguese ship. See how you walk! Go and sleep with him! Now that he has come back after becoming a great sailor and all that. Go lie down with him. He will eat and screw you and throw you away! He has been to a godless village and has become godless. You too have become like him!' Uko screamed. Raji lost her temper and punched him hard on the nose. Her red bangles jangled and broke. Her two hefty wrists were bare. She hit Uko in his ribs with her strong hands. Uko's nose started bleeding. Raji's old aunt and Jeevo poured some water on his head to stop the bleeding. Uko's eyes were overflowing with bitterness and anger. Raji went cursing and weeping into the room and threw herself on the bed with rage. As Bhikha Malam was in the last room, around ten rooms away from where this great commotion was taking place, he could not hear a thing. Raji's aunt cajoled Uko into lying down, saying, 'Oh come, my dear, you can eat later, lie down first.' Jeeva lit a large bidi and sat down to eat. Uko pulled a mattress close and huddled in the bed. Jeeva went away after eating. Raji's aunt said that as there would be high tide at night and as she had to go for the routine fishing work, she ate until she was full. She had the habit of napping in the afternoon. She went into a room and started snoring.

The cold wave towards the end of the Hemant season chilled the grey noon. It seemed as if the whole village was taking a break from the tiring routine and was having a siesta. The orchard was silent. Raji was lying on her bed in her wet clothes. She got up and went to the last room to change her clothes. Bhikha Malam saw her and snorted. 'You big fat wench, how much time you take! Why are you so late?' He got up suddenly and bolted the door. 'See how this man behaves!' she started and before she could complete the sentence, he pounced on her and grabbed her. Her wet clothes clung to her. She struggled and punched him to escape his grip. She tumbled on to the bed. 'So, I look fat to you now? Why did you return after so many years then? You are a large vessel yourself!' Malam was uncontrollable by now.

Uko, who was starving and trying to sleep, suddenly craved food. He flung the mattress aside and got up. The old aunt was sleeping in the lounge. Uko started moving from the orchard to the wharf stealthily. The window to Raji's bedroom was on the way. 'I don't care now; I don't want to stay here any longer. She has started hitting me now. Now I won't listen to her any more.' Raji's punches had hurt him deeply. As he started walking away from the house, he heard Raji's moaning and screaming, 'Oh Malam, not now, not now, we will do it at night!' She was struggling to get Malam off her. 'Oh I am not feeling well now, why are you biting me?' Raji's choli was in tatters. Malam had started biting her. Uko peered in through the window. He saw Raji struggling with Malam on the big timber bed in the dark room. His legs shook. He had goosebumps. He quickly started walking away. Raji managed to kick Malam off her. 'You bastard. You did not remember me for so many years and now the only thing you can think of is fucking? You have destroyed my new dress. What do you think of yourself? I am not going to allow you to touch me or sleep near me in my room! If you dare come near me, I will cut you up and stuff you with chilli powder!' Raji could even shove Uko away with great strength; Malam was nothing compared to him in strength. She managed to cover herself up; with great haste, she opened the bolts, and left the room in a huff. Malam, like a bull gone wild due to the heat, fell to the ground. He did not dare go close to Raji. 'A man who returns after twenty years should care whether it is day or night at least. Let him come closer, I will butcher him.'

There was loud commotion on the wharf at around two in the afternoon. The flocks of Siberian cranes started to fly about wildly. As they could find nothing to eat in the muddy waters, the fowl were pecking around in clear water. They started screeching. The sea hawk would swoop down upon a fowl and its feathers would fly all over the place. The sea hawk would take the fowl to the nearby woods. Feathers of fowl were flying around in the dry winter wind. The flocks of geese accompanied the fowls in their screeching. Uko was lying on the wooden plank of his boat. He was panting and disconcerted. Far away, the Mangalorean tiles on the roofs of huts in the village were burning red like Uko's eyes.

⁂

It was the ominous phase of the night. The arc of the setting moon slipped towards the horizon. The fog was extremely dense. The chilly winds started a shower of dewdrops. Uko, the bilge water, tried to sleep underneath three mattresses on the wooden plank of the boat. He was very drunk. He had inadvertently reached the middle of the ocean at night. He had no idea how deep the waters were. Even huge ships and oil tankers avoided coming this far into the sea.

He had come in a disturbed state from Aunt Raji's house in the afternoon. He had been lying quivering on the boat plank since then. He had guzzled mahudo incessantly without having anything to eat. His Aunt Raji was lying on her back on the huge bed with Malam on top of her...whenever he recalled this image, his anger knew no bounds. He was overcome with feelings of futility and emptiness. He had fallen asleep on his boat on the wharf in the afternoon. His eyes had given way to the heaviness of the lids due to the alcohol. He had snored until the evening. The opaque fog had descended and the lamps in the distant village had started flickering. The rising moon looked yellow on the horizon and it spread its muddy hue everywhere. He sat desolate, his whole body aching. His head was spinning. Crazy thoughts had entered his mind. The wild beasts in the woods near the wharf went about looking at him. He had just stolen a glance at what Aunt Raji and Malam were up to in the bed and come away furiously. He felt like strangling Aunt Raji. He was frantic. He sat on the plank in the boat smoking bidis. He felt hunger gnawing his belly. Jeeva Mota had kept a couple of Palva fish wrapped in leaves and ice for the fishing expedition during high tide at night. As Jeevo used to do all the preparations, he had kept things ready. Uko waited for his assistants before departing. But he thought that Aunt Raji would come anytime to call him. 'I don't want to see her dirty face any more! Why the hell had she fallen? for that bastard? Just because he returned after twenty years?'

Greatly distressed, he had entered the boat and pulled the handle of the boat machine. The bilge water under the engine glistened. The rumbling of the engine increased. He set the speed of the boat, adjusted the sails, and sat on the wooden plank. All alone, he sailed through the muddy, turbulent waters of the tide. 'I do not want anyone's property, damn it! All of them are blackguards and scoundrels!' He was filled with anger. He clutched at the sails and ceaselessly drove the boat, obsessed with thoughts of Aunt Raji. When he reached the huge sprawling bosom of the sea, he heaved a sigh of relief. The bilge water in the boat started rising and the engine started coughing. He adjusted the sail and increased the speed. The engine turned noisier. He lit the stove, took out the fish from the iron container, slit it, stuffed it with salt, and started baking it. He held the mahudo pouch in his hand and sat near the stove. The engine coughed and spluttered. He would occasionally adjust the engine or the sail. He sat munching the baked fish and sipping liquor from the pouches. Jeeva had kept around ten pouches on the boat. They came in handy. As he ate and drank, the boat had entered waters of unfathomable depth. Nothing could be seen in the glitter of moonlight in the dark and vast surface of the bottomless sea. The lights from the village had disappeared. The beam of the lighthouse was nowhere to be seen. Its light resembled a luminous dot far away. Its fiery head now seemed smaller than the eye of a sea hawk. 'Why did that bastard show up? I wanted to marry Raji.' His thoughts tormented him. The surface of the sea was disturbed by the turbulence at the bottom. Uko felt redundant, as if he was a nuisance like bilge water. When he used to fish, he would sleep on his boat. Recently, however, he had started sleeping at home. 'It is too cold out there these days,' he would say to himself.

He often felt like going to Aunt Raji's room. When he could bear it no longer, he would get up and go to her room. Raji had put huge bolts on the door. He did not dare wake Raji. He would return to his room, fling himself on the bed, and stay awake all night. 'Why do you bolt the room from inside at night?' he would ask her at daybreak and smile. 'What's the big deal? And, besides, how did you find out that I bolt the doors from inside at night? Do you return late from fishing?' Suddenly, realization would dawn upon her, 'You cheat, you better behave yourself...' she would scold him with sweetness in her voice. 'But tell me, truly, is it very cold these days?' he would say and laugh.

'Watch your step, you bastard! Had I a child of my own, he would be as old as you. You are horny but you are still small fry! Grow up first and then come!' she would say, blushing coyly.

Uko had started calling her 'Rajki' affectionately and she would pretend to get annoyed and say, 'Watch your tongue, who are you calling Rajki?' She would watch him sharply. 'I say, I am a grown-up man now! Marry me quickly! I am Uko and I am Rajki's husband!' he would shout, completely drunk. Raji would become coy. 'Oh, dear me, dear me,' she would say and feel embarrassed. They would play and fool around a lot. But of late, Raji had become pensive. 'It has been more than twenty years now, who knows if he will ever return...he would have probably found himself a mistress in Africa and must have had kids by now.... My Uko is really good, why not marry him?' she would think. 'How grown up and manly he has turned out to be, and he is getting horny these days. It seems he wants me nowadays,' she would say and smile to herself. She had turned forty-eight. She was counting Uko's age on her fingers. 'I am older than him by seventeen or eighteen years. He is almost thirty now, but he looks as if he is a man of fifty, hefty and mature. My god...!' she would end up sighing.

One evening, they were drinking together. They were fooling around and teasing each other. Uko hugged her tightly and said, 'Oh my Raji, you are sweet like honey. Oh, tell me, when will you marry me? I am no longer the naïve Uko Ghamat you knew!' He had come quite close to her. Raji was tired of cooking and sitting near the hot stove for long. She was drinking as she patted rotlas. 'Don't behave dirtily with me! Okay, okay, I will marry you! Leave me alone!' she had almost screamed. For many days, the fishing trips were turning out to be real successes for Uko. His boats would overflow with all types of fish. In her mind, Raji had been planning to marry Uko. 'I should marry him,' she thought. When Raji's friends had come to her place once, Uko had just returned from a fishing spree. Her friends said, 'Now you have grown up into a hunk. You are no longer a boy. Why don't you find a large woman for yourself? Or why don't you marry Rajki? Isn't she attractive enough for you?' They were in a playful mood. Raji was staring at Uko, overcome with feelings, putting one end of her sari into her mouth. Her heart was beating fast. 'Don't be idiots!' Uko had said. 'She won't marry me. She cares for me too much like a mother. I will find a virgin for myself!' he had said light-heartedly. 'Besides, she has grown fat like a Portuguese ship. I cannot even hug her properly. Such is your Rajki aunty!' Her crestfallen face had excited him even more. She seemed like a huge cargo ship on the verge of sinking. 'Bastard, now you call me an oldie and act distant, heh?' she said piteously. She was so upset with him that she had not spoken to him for a couple of days. Uko had to coax and cajole her for a long time, only then did she start talking to him. 'You were the one who wanted to marry me, you blackguard, you bloody rascal!' she said angrily. 'I also want to marry you! Come, let us get married immediately. Let me pull up a bucket of water; let us do the rites right away! Come, come. You silly boat, why are you getting grouchy?' He almost started dragging her and Raji had to struggle to escape his grip. Raji turned pale like a kevdo plant in the morning. 'Okay, okay, I will marry you....'

Uko thought he had reached the bottomless part of the sea when the engine coughed and broke down. He stepped into the pit of his boat and was startled to see that a lot of bilge water had crept in. He stared in shocked silence. He returned to the plank. He flung the anchor into the sea, picked up the filthy mattress and sat down near the stove with his pouches of liquor and fish. The moon hung in the sky like a huge yellow ball. It was an endless stretch of water and one could not discern direction.

Raji was angered by Bhikha Malam's behaviour. She searched for Uko in the evening. The low tide was slowly giving way to the surging waves of the high tide. She had told everyone she met around the wharf, 'Please send Uko home if you see him. Tell him his dinner is waiting for him; the bastard is very touchy.' It was getting very late. Uko did not turn up for his meal. Bhikha Malam and Raji's old aunt were drinking. Bhikha was visibly upset at the search undertaken for Uko. He had gone to the village at daybreak. At noon, just as he was about to catch a wink he had quarrelled with Raji. He was greatly dismayed. 'The whore is so worried about Uko! Does she sleep with him?' He met many of his friends and acquaintances in the village. They were overjoyed to see him. He threw a drinking party for them. He returned late. Someone murmured, 'Raji has kept Uko.' He flew into a rage. He drank without stopping until late into the night. Raji would keep mumbling, 'Where the hell has Uko disappeared? He has not eaten since morning.' She was agitated and kept walking in and out of the house, disturbed. 'If he returns late, he won't be able to see the road. And if he is drunk....' Bhikha was watching Raji's behaviour. His mind was in turmoil. 'See, she is troubled for Uko. As if that bastard is her husband! She feels nothing for her husband who has returned after twenty years! Uko and nothing but Uko is what she is thinking about!' The others had finished their dinner thinking that Uko would turn up any time. The high tide receded after some time. Uko's assistants returned from their work. 'Neither Uko nor his boat is to be seen anywhere. People on the wharf said that he has gone away all on his own with the boat into the sea. Now that the fishing trip is done, how can anyone go after him?' Raji's heart sank at Jeeva's words. She was stunned. The assistants were agitated and kept arguing until dawn. They went away, dismayed. 'When he shows up in the morning, we are going to thrash him...don't you try to stop us Raji.... Now let us go and sleep near our women!' Raji kept staring into the pitch-black fog that had descended upon her.

Raji threw herself on Uko's bed in his room, her eyes wet with tears. She worried about Uko while her aunt finished her meal. Malam waited for Raji in her room. He tried to sleep. 'Bloody wench! I will grab her hair and flog her mercilessly first and then ask her if she is willing to fuck. The whore is keeping that no-good bilge water!' But Raji did not turn up. Raji's aunt was lying on the big bed in the lounge and crying. Raji was sleeping in Uko's room and she had bolted the door on the inside. She was exhausted after the day's work. 'That filthy scoundrel did not think of Raji for twenty years. He was with an African whore that whole time. Now he comes out of nowhere and calls my pure-hearted Uko a thief and nuisance!' When the assistants had come down to inform Raji that Uko had made off with the boat, Bhikha had burst out in anger.

'Why have you kept that motherfucker? That thieving rascal! You are worried about him because you sleep with him. If not, why would you be so concerned? Why don't you see that he has run away with my best boat? Do not fool me! Just let him come, I will slash him with my blade!' he shouted in anger. Raji exploded, 'Who are you planning to kill? Here I am in front of you. Just try touching him. Who is he to keep me? I have kept him and will keep him seven times over!' A noisy quarrel broke out between them. 'Since when has Uko become a scoundrel and cheat? You are a bloody cheat! You were the one who had gone buggering around for twenty years! Now that you have failed, you have come back! I have been watching you since morning. You have been needlessly harassing that poor innocent kid! Where was the man in you when you were loafing around in Lisbon and Mozambique for years? You never thought about taking me with you even once! Get lost, you bastard...go away from my house! Take your fucking ship, thrust it up your asshole, and shake it! Uko is my man, real like gold! He is so young and yet he looks after the ship, the farm, and me. He has no one in this world. If he curses you, you will be destroyed!' she yelled and started to weep. 'I am not your woman, nor are you my man. Get lost from my home! You have been tormenting that boy since morning. You beat him up. But you are venomous. You have become godless after fucking your African whore for so many years!' She was shouting and while leaving for Uko's room she said, 'I am not his woman, nor is he my man. Even then, we will live together. Will eat, drink, and cry together. But if you utter a single word against him, I will be the worst thing you have faced in your life. You upstart, spoilsport...why the hell have you come here?'

Raji's aunt reduced Bhikha to ashes. She stretched out her aged hands and cursed him, 'This house and this ship now belongs to Raji. Get lost, you bastard! You go on your way and she will go hers. She has been living without you for twenty years, so it will make no difference to her. Go away and our troubles will end....' Bhikha was stunned into silence.

The chimney of the lantern was pitch-black. Raji's tears were bitter and anguished. They seemed brackish and poisonous. 'The bastard has become a big captain now...he is more like bilge water. Quite useless, let his ship sink on the high seas!' She was greatly worried for Uko. 'Poor chap! He would roll up his sleeves against the whole village for my sake! Had he not been around, what would a lonely woman have done? I would have hung myself. But that rascal Uko is an idiot too! He will always be ghamat! The jerk! Does he have to take permission to get someone like me? "Oh, will you marry me?" He should have caught hold of me and flung me on the bed.... Poor chap is so ingenuous. He was almost scared of me...how could he do that?' Raji almost smiled to herself. 'Let him come. I will drag him to bed now. I wasted twenty years for god knows what. Had I married him, who would have given a damn anyway?' Raji started yearning for Uko. 'How has he grown up now, huge hulk, just like a bull! But I am not old yet. But where the hell has the idiot gone with the boat? Just let me lay my hands on him.' Her kohl-lined eyes turned red.

Bhikha was lying in the last room, smoking his pipe continuously. 'Even though I've returned after twenty years, she doesn't care about me. What kind of women are these, these women from coastal areas? The women of Malabar were better. Even black women from Mozambique were better. They would worship totems to keep their men to themselves. Oh, the way they looked after their men! I should have stayed there!' He had taken the female owner of a pub in Mozambique named James. He had kept a Mopla woman near Malabar. The woman from Malabar had no idea that he had fought with James and come to her. At night, he obsessed over Raji. 'She must have kept that thieving rascal in my absence for sure,' he was convinced. He called over a couple of his sailors to pack his huge metallic trunks. 'Now your home is unholy for me. Your water is cursed for me. Anyone who comes back for you must be a real idiot!' His huge Arab vessel was anchored on the wharf. He had intended to sail off at midnight. When he went away, Raji heaved a sigh of relief. However, tears welled up in her dark eyes for no reason whatsoever. 'I waited for my Uko for twenty years and now he has betrayed me!' She was overcome with love for Uko. Great joy for Uko welled up within her. She remembered how she had punched him and had broken his nose. In all her trouble over Malam, she realized she had not paid attention to Uko. She broke down and sobbed. Raji's aunt consoled her by caressing her back with quivering hands. 'Don't cry, girl, that blackguard of Malam has now gone back to the sea. Why were you avoiding getting married to Uko? Now do not hesitate for a single moment. The village is anyway saying that you have kept Uko. Now turn it into reality.'

The waters of the high tide in the wharf were lethal. The lights of the Arab ship flickered far away in the darkness of the night and the sound of the engines could be heard in the distance. The square-shaped copper lanterns on the ship glimmered. They seemed like the eyes of some subterranean monster emerging out of the sea. Bhikha Malam's gigantic Arab ship left the wharf. Its huge motors churned the waters. It headed towards the heart of the sea.

Somewhere deep in the sea, the boat was anchored and was still. Many boats had left the wharf for fishing, but none had ventured this far out to sea. The lights on the boats were like fiery eyes in the foggy darkness of the night. Uko had guzzled a lot of liquor. He had eaten a couple of large fish. That gave a bit of relief to his rumbling stomach. He cursed Raji and lay on his side looking starboard. 'What's the use of Uko Ghamat now? Someone had abandoned me in the swamp weeds…you should let me drown then!' Uko felt that his life was futile. He fell into deep despair.

He was exhausted from the events of the day. He could not even stand up. Raji would enter his mind covertly like bilge water entering the boat without being seen. It was the ominous phase of the night. The bilge water in the boat was rising. The front tip of the boat stooped as the boat started to sink. When the boat had been anchored on the wharf, there was already some bilge water inside. Now as the boat was anchored mid-sea, more water had seeped in. The boat engine was covered with water too. The boat was sinking slowly. It seemed as if the boat would drown completely by the time the moon had set on the horizon. The fog was dense and thick. In the chilly winter night, no fishing boat was to be seen nearby. The wick of the flickering lantern in Raji's room was snuffed out and the house was drowned in darkness. Raji lay on the bed waiting for Uko to return like a boat sinking due to bilge water.

Translated by Sachin Ketkar

NANDU

DASHRATH PARMAR

I vividly remember my first meeting with Nandu. It happened under very strange circumstances. It must have been around eleven o'clock on a Sunday night. I had alighted from the last bus that shuttles to this place. The bus driver and the conductor had hurriedly disembarked from the rain-drenched bus when it reached the depot, and melted into the darkness. In a small town of an unknown hilly region, I sat on a broken bench at the deserted bus stand—all alone, wet, clutching my luggage to my chest. Maybe 'luggage' isn't the right word for what I had brought with me—a thela slung over my shoulder, a mattress and some clothes, and a bag that contained the sarkari papers of promotion that had brought me all the way here. The rain was intense and showed no signs of letting up. It had been sunny when I left home that morning. Even when the bus took off from the plains, there wasn't a sign that it would rain. But halfway through our journey, the weather underwent a sudden change. Cold winds gushed in, and at once it began to rain heavily. The driver had difficulty navigating and he slowed down, making our journey to the hills even longer. There were only four people in the bus, including me. I felt reassured by the thought that I would have company on my journey to the hills; I would get down and ask somebody about accommodation. But the other passengers alighted at different bus stops along the way and eventually I was the only one left—alone and helpless. For a moment, I was tempted to turn back but I couldn't bring myself to do that.

Feeling sorry for myself, I sat, helpless and directionless, trembling in the cold. Just then, a miracle happened. A boy appeared before me like a sudden cyclone. I was startled. Before I could say anything, he began to speak, 'Sahibji! Do you wish to stay here, thehar na chahte hain?' He was completely drenched and his voice trembled in the cold. The wind howled around us and muffled his voice, which made it difficult for me to understand what he was saying. But from the way he spoke it was clear that he was a hotel boy. I nodded in response. He promptly picked up my belongings and walked ahead.

'Did you come by the last wali bus, Sahibji? It was meant to arrive at nine. Looks like it got very late today. It must be the rain that delayed it.' He chattered on. Without saying a word, I followed him, holding my shoulder bag over my head. It was mostly dark around us, with occasional flickers of light on the roofs of some homes. Water splashed noisily—chhapak—every time we stepped into a puddle, and I would be unsettled each time that happened. We threaded our way under the intermittent street lights. We were flanked on both sides by houses where people seemed to be sleeping blissfully, evoking my envy. I continued to feel sorry for myself. Walking on a jagged path, and feeling exhaustion creeping up my limbs, I finally asked him, 'Abhi kitna door hai, how far?'

'Bas? Tired already, Sahibji? You see that yellow light over there? That's it, that's where we have to go.'

'Isn't there a guest house nearby?'

'This is a village, Sahibji, there's only this place by way of a guest house; the one I am taking you to.'

We finally reached. Illuminated by a yellow light, it was an old-fashioned one-storey house surrounded by thick vegetation. The fog and rain had hidden its name and one could only make out the words 'guest house'. Looking at its dilapidated condition, 'guest house' seemed like an ambitious term to describe it, but for a solitary and helpless person like me who had found a refuge in this hilly place, it was nothing less than a five-star hotel. The boy opened up a room for me and went out. I changed my clothes and lay down on the bed, my nostrils assaulted by the typical smell of the hills. I was comfortable in this place but exhausted and was gripped by a sudden desire to have tea. I went up to the door to express my wish. Before I could call out for the boy, he came right up.

'Sahibji, my name is Narendra. People call me Nandu. You can also call me by that name.'

I noticed that Nandu was only a boy, around twelve or thirteen years of age, five feet tall with slightly curly brown hair and sallow cheeks. His clothes seemed as though they hadn't been washed for a long time. Was this boy, who was as thin as a rake, the same fellow who had picked up my luggage with such ease and walked briskly ahead a few minutes ago? The moment I expressed my wish, he headed towards the kitchen. Within a few minutes he appeared with a cup of tea. I drank it up and once again lay down. I couldn't sleep till very late that night. The whistling winds and the sound of rain seeped in through the window and disturbed me throughout the night, not to the mention the droning of innumerable cicadas in the bushes around the house. I felt as if a pinjara cotton maker was thumping cotton all night.

It was quite late by the time I woke up in the morning. But I wasn't in a rush. I had to reach my office only by eleven o'clock. I came out of my room into the open space outside. It had been too dark the previous night for me to notice my surroundings, but now, under the gentle sunlight falling on the hills, the place revealed itself to me. In that small 'courtyard' of not more than ten feet, there were a couple of weather-beaten chairs and tables. One of the tables was occupied by two men who were busy drinking tea, dunking slices of toast in their cups. Across, at a slight elevation, I saw an old man sitting in a chair. He seemed to be the owner of the place. Because of the things strewn around on the table in front of him, I could only see his head. With some hesitation, I sat at the edge of a table. The next moment Nandu came running to me, 'Sahibji, tell me, what would you like to have with your tea? Idli, dosa, batata wada, poha?' I was impressed by the breakfast menu. I said, 'Ek chai aur idli'.

'All right, I will be back soon.' He dashed into the kitchen. I sat gazing at the rain-drenched mountain opposite. I suddenly remembered that I had not phoned home yet. I took out my cell phone from my pocket and called my wife. It sounded like she had been waiting anxiously to hear from me. She was delighted to know that I had found a convenient place to stay. While I was talking to her, Nandu arrived with breakfast. With astonishment writ large on his face, he stood waiting by my side. When I hung up, he said, 'Sahibji, tame Gujarati chho?' He had switched to Gujarati.

'Yes. Why?'

'You were speaking in Hindi yesterday, so I thought you were from some other state.'

'You also spoke in Hindi yesterday, no?'

'Yes, Sahibji, what to do, this is our livelihood, so we have to be cautious and speak like that with strangers. You can't tell from a face whether someone is Gujarati or not, right?'

Before we could chat further, the men at the next table yelled out for him, 'Arre Nandu, where have you bloody disappeared? Are you deaf?'

It looked like they had had a drink or two at the start of the day.

'Sahibji, you will be staying here, right? Let's chat more when you come for lunch later, barabar?' Saying that, he promptly left to attend to the men.

I returned to the guest house in the afternoon for lunch. There were quite a few others like me, who were already seated for lunch. There was another boy like Nandu, who looked older than him. Both of them scurried about serving everybody. The moment Nandu saw me, he came up and greeted me, 'Welcome, padhaaro, Sahibji!' and used the towel on his shoulder to clean the chair for me to sit. 'Do sit here,' he said. He quickly got a thali ready for me. While serving me he asked, 'You are a Gujarati, Sahibji, but from which part of Gujarat?' I mentioned the name of my district. He looked delighted, and barely able to contain his excitement, he continued, 'Really? I am from the same district. Which village though, Sahibji?'

I was also very pleased. This familiarity felt wonderful, seven hundred kilometres away from home in an unknown place. But the very next moment a shadow of sadness crossed over me.

'What happened? You seem lost in thought.'
'Nothing.'

I mentioned the name of my village softly. This time he jumped with joy. 'Arre, Sahibji, that's my fua's village, my father's brother-in-law. His name is Harjivan Mitha. I stayed with him until my seventh standard and then he got me this job here.'

'Which Harjivan Mitha?' I asked. I was trying to remember, but I couldn't recall anyone from my village with that name.

'You don't know him? Harjivan Mitha Raval. Many years ago, he used to hawk from a camel cart, and once, a sick camel bit off his right arm.'

I suddenly remembered. The entire village called him Harji thuntha, the armless. His image flashed across my mind—filthy clothes, coarse overgrown hair and beard, decaying black teeth, tobacco-smeared lips—and I was left with a bitter taste in my mouth. Harji thuntha was invariably called when a house was being built in the village. He owned around twenty donkeys and a camel cart. His main job was to ferry bricks and mortar. It did not bother him to do the rounds for anyone in the village, but if someone from our vaas or quarter went to him, he'd bark at us. He would do the work, but act as though he was doing us a favour, as though we were not paying him. He would get off his donkey without caring about breaking the bricks, and hurl abuses at us. If this was not enough, he made sure not to touch our money. We would have to put the cash on the ground, and he would use his stick to move it and then would lift it with his left hand.

Before I could tell Nandu that I knew his fua, a thought flashed across my mind. Nandu, who had so far shared information about himself, would seek more from me, and what would I then say to him? I am the kind of person who would rather suffer in silence than reveal my caste. I suddenly remembered something that had happened a long time ago, when we had gone for a vacation to a hill station near our city. We had gone to a dharamshala, an inn-like accommodation in the premises of a temple. We were almost given a room to stay, but when I had to reveal my identity, the 'manager' talked to somebody in his language on the phone, and refused to provide us accommodation us, saying, 'Sorry, Sahib, the room has been booked already. It was a mistake on my part.'

If Nandu continues to ask me questions, and I'm forced to reveal my caste to him, would he continue to treat me with the same regard that he has shown thus far? Would he not share the same values, the samskara, of his fua? I was in a difficult situation. I looked around. Nandu had left to serve the others. With no alternative in sight, I buried my 'self' in food.

I was somehow able to escape his questions that day, but Nandu continued to chase me. My belongings were in the guest house, so I had no choice but to go back. I had even considered sending the peon to bring my belongings over. I could stay in a corner of the office, but the office was so poorly maintained that I had to change my mind. I had requested my staff to suggest a place to stay but the response hadn't been very positive. Perhaps they had figured out my caste; they also said I wouldn't find a better place than the one I had. I could have taken a place in the plains, near the court. But it would have meant going up and down thirty kilometres on a hilly track every day, so I dismissed that idea as well.

I was baffled by my own thoughts. Why was I scared of a servant, for God's sake? But I was also not comfortable lying about my caste; that would mean being untruthful to my own self. I was reminded of my wife on such occasions. She always said that there was no point in being a paragon of truth, like Satyawadi Harishchandra. A small and harmless lie is not equal to committing a sin. Didn't Yudhisthir himself use half-lies in the Mahabharata?

Her arguments would leave me speechless. But my temperament would not allow me to lie, and so I found it almost sinful to hide my caste, my jaat, today.

I was restless at work. I called a staff meeting, but it didn't do any good. Tired, I returned to the guest house in the evening, although my appetite had vanished. I trudged in, dragging my feet.

Nandu seemed to have been waiting for me. He came rushing to me: 'Why are you so late, Sahibji?'

'It was my first day at the office, that's why.'

'Never mind, do sit. Let me serve you garma-garam food!'

'No, I don't feel like eating.'

I moved towards my room. He followed me hesitantly. I entered the room and closed the door. He must have turned back.

When I came out into the courtyard in the morning, Nandu greeted me, 'At a young age, I have managed to see a lot. But nothing like our village, Sahibji, I tell you!' He began singing paeans to the village. I thought the boy was young but astute.

'You are quite right, Nandu, but I have hardly stayed in our village. I stayed at my grandparents' when I was in high school and then in a big city once I got a job....'

'So what, Sahibji? Tell me honestly...have you ever enjoyed yourself anywhere else as you did in your village?' He asked while placing a cup of tea on the table.

I did not respond and merely sipped the tea.

'What's your name, Sahibji?'

The cup quivered in my hand. With my heart drumming, I told him my name. I waited for the next question. It's a question that gets asked one way or the other. I waited for quite a while, but nothing happened. I was disappointed but also surprised. If what I had dreaded had been postponed, I should, but obviously, be happy. Why was I feeling despondent then? I felt as though this was some kind of a game which I was expected to play. I should tell him on my own that this is how it is, and that this is the truth. Nobody could then accuse me of hiding. And that'd be a test for him as well and....

'Nandu—'

'Yes, Sahibji?'

'Do you know Becharbhai Jeevabhai Parmar of your fua's village?'

'No, Sahibji. Who is he?' He asked, astonished.

'That's my father.' I looked at him from the corner of my eye but his expression wasn't what I had expected to see. Without waiting further, I left and went directly to my office.

Once there, I couldn't concentrate on my work, and I didn't return to the guest house for lunch. An enormous feeling of guilt gripped me. This was an innocent twelve-year-old boy. His fua may have been a staunch casteist person, but it's possible that that has not had an impact on the boy. Caste discrimination is stronger among adults, but a young person, staying so far away from home, is not likely to harbour such feelings. I had not revealed my identity to him in the right way. I decided that I would tell him clearly in the evening and remove any feeling of discomfort between us. In fact, I decided that even before he begins to form prejudices against a particular person or community, I will explain everything to him. He must have waited for me all afternoon, and perhaps was still waiting.

I continued to work till late in the evening. Once it got dark, I hesitantly set out in the direction of my lodging. The yellow light of the guest house was visible from a distance. I thought Nandu would come rushing to me, as he usually did. In order to face him, I regained my composure, but when I went closer I realized that all my assumptions were false. Busy attending to other people, Nandu refused to even acknowledge me. He seemed completely immersed in his work, and his expressions were imperceptible. I sat at a corner table by myself. I lifted up the thali, hoping to draw his attention. I moved it back and forth, making some noise. I wiped it with my handkerchief a couple of times as I waited for Nandu. But he did not look in my direction. After serving the others, he went straight into the kitchen.

The evening turned into night; the hilly darkness outside enveloped in the incessant hum of the cicadas....

THE BLACK HORSE

MONA PATRAWALLA

Deep in the dense foliage and the bamboo groves of Ahwa-Dang lies the village of Vansda. Inhabited mainly by Adivasis, the village also has Koli, Kandi, and Anavil communities. About five miles from Vansda is the village of Manpur, where Bamansha Daruwalla lived in his timber and bamboo mansion. In Manpur, among the five to seven Parsi households, Bamansha's was the richest. He owned an enormous liquor shop in Vansda as well as more than a hundred bighas of land. In his large house, set amidst thick bamboo groves, Bamansha lived on his own like a huge owl.

As the ferocious winds of Vaisakha blew, the village in summer felt like a blazing furnace. The extreme heat made even the dense green forest appear an unpleasant brown. Only the flame of the forest trees, dressed in saffron, that stood in the midst of bamboo, teak, and mahua trees provided some relief to the eye. The kesudo trees resembled the bright blaze in the forest. The dust blown up by the whistling winds clashed with doors and windows before settling. In the still afternoon, the clear skies filled with the cries of kites and vultures.

On Friday, at about eleven o'clock, Bamansha set off for the weekly market at Vansda, riding his Arabian horse. Every Friday, he went to the market riding his horse to buy non-essentials. He rode with the air of a person who could buy the whole market if he wished to. Dressed in a white unbuttoned bush shirt, trousers, and a Parsi-style turban, with a twelve-bore gun on his shoulder and holding a horsewhip and a bamboo stick, he rode along haughtily on his black horse. His sinewy horse was as snooty and irascible as its master.

Holding onto the reins, in the dead heat of summer, Ratiya scampered alongside the horse as if he was racing with it. The aged

Ratiya, of course, could hardly keep pace. His throat was dry, and running on the hot tar road had cracked the soles of his feet. At times, when the horse trotted faster, dragging Ratiya along, Bamansha whipped its back, making the horse run even faster.

'Master! Water!' Ratiya burst out and collapsed near the shop of Abu, the butcher, at Vansda. He knew that his master would purchase five kilograms of meat, and he would have to carry it all the way back to Manpur. Thinking that a little water would be necessary, he mustered up a little courage to beg for water.

'What? Water?' Bamansha yelled angrily, staring fiercely at Ratiya. 'Is your old man going to give you water over here? And, by the way, what work have you done to feel thirsty? Come on, carry this meat and run along. You can drink water at home. Swines, all of them.'

And the thirsty Ratiya put the heavy bag of mutton on his shoulder and started trotting along with the horse on the road to Manpur. As soon as Bamansha reached home, Ratiya collapsed in a heap. Thirst and exhaustion caused him to foam at the mouth and he lost consciousness. Bamansha did not like this and shouted for Ratiya's wife Rukhdi. 'Rukhdee...Rukhdee. Where have you disappeared to? Come quickly!'

Rukhdi came running. 'See what is the matter with this swine. Go call Budhiya.' Ratiya was gasping as if he was breathing his last. Rukhdi went running to fetch Budhiya, her son. They picked up Ratiya and went to their hut.

'The dirty wild boar. Does not seem he will work again. I will have to look for a new horse,' Bamansha grunted and then settled down in an armchair.

As the hot blazing daylight receded, a chill gradually set in. The cool night returned with the scent of wild flowers. Everything was silent, except for the rustling of teak leaves. In the dense forest, lanterns from faraway huts flickered like the eyes of a female beast. From the faraway Adivasi habitats came the primeval sound of the pounding of drums. In the bamboo forest, nocturnal beasts roamed around. At about nine, Budhiya went up to Bamansha sobbing. 'Master, my father is dead.'

Bamansha was nibbling at a piece of roasted mutton, holding a glass of mahua liquor in his hand, and relaxing in the armchair. He did not reply for a long time.

Budhiya wept, 'Master, my father is dead.'

'So? What can I do?' Bamansha asked brashly. 'Go bury him then. Do you think I am going to weep over him?' Bamansha gulped down more liquor and gazed at the sky.

'Master, I need some money for his burial.

'What? Bamansha tensed in his armchair at the mention of money. He looked at Budhiya angrily, 'No money-shoney from me. You people are always begging for money; today for this, tomorrow for that. Do you think money grows on trees at my place?' Budhiya kept standing.

'Master, we have nothing left in our house,' Budhiya pleaded.

'Am I responsible for everyone here? Get away, you swine. Just dig up a pit and bury him. To bury someone you don't need all the paraphernalia of cloth and such things. You are talking as if some big emperor has died!' Bamansha shouted.

'Master, I fall at your feet. Have mercy. Give me eight or twelve annas. I will work for you and return every single penny.'

Not a bad idea, Bamansha thought, if you get Ratiya's well-built horse-like son in place of an infirm Ratiya for a few annas. Bamansha got up and, taking some coins from his coat pocket, threw them in front of Budhiya. 'Here, take these eight annas. Come straight to work tomorrow. Got it?' Budhiya nodded and went quickly towards his house, wiping his tears.

Three days after Ratiya's funeral rites, Budhiya came to work. Bamansha made himself clear, 'You will not get three days' wages.' Budhiya nodded in consent. That evening, Budhiya went with a bundle of grass to the stable. There, the brawny black horse with flaming eyes was waiting. The horse was a fierce creature. There was a nest of pigeons in the stable and the horse had chewed up a couple of fledglings that had fallen from the nest and, since then, the horse was hysterical. He would go mad at the sight of any person other than his master. Moreover, he would behave as brutally as Bamansha. It was with a lot of difficulty that Ratiya had managed to feed the horse and even the slightest error on his part would make the horse kick wildly. However, Ratiya was not as aggressive as Budhiya. Budhiya was well-built and short-tempered. He placed the bundle of grass near the horse, but as the horse could not reach it, the animal neighed and kicked violently. Budhiya dodged it nimbly. The horse became even more furious on seeing that his kick had missed its target. Both stood glowering at each other. The horse's red eyes infuriated Budhiya and he picked up a bamboo stick and flogged the horse. 'Very strong, heh?' Budhiya mumbled and spat angrily as he went out.

It was midnight and a chill had set in. Budhiya could not sleep. Then he had a strange dream involving Bamansha's horse. Budhiya dreamt that on entering the stable, the horse was chewing his own limbs. On seeing Budhiya, he kicked Budhiya's belly, tore it open, and thrust his head inside.

Budhiya woke up, anguished. His heart throbbed and he perspired profusely. He understood nothing. He flung the vilest of abuses at the horse and went out to light his bidi. As he was smoking, he was still very much disturbed by the thought of Bamansha and his horse.

Budhiya's throat was parched. He pushed open the door and went inside his hut. He raised the wick of his lantern and in that feeble light he saw that his mother was not in her bed. He still felt disturbed. He drank water, went outside, and sat down. The thoughts of Bamansha, his mother, and the horse were criss-crossing wildly in his mind. He knew the truth about his mother's relationship with Bamansha. He was more afraid of Bamansha than the black horse.

Budhiya started believing that his father had died because of this animal. He wondered how his aged father had managed to keep pace with the terrible brute. The thought sent shivers through his spine. Right from his childhood, Budhiya abhorred Bamansha. At the slightest mistake or even without having committed any mistake,

Bamansha used to clobber him with the horsewhip. Images of those barbaric acts drifted before his eyes and continued to haunt him. He lay down and slipped into a reverie.

After a scorching day, the night brought slight relief. When the first cock of the morning crowed, piercing the dense silence, Rukhdi stealthily entered her house. She blew out the lantern and slowly latched the door. The sound woke Budhiya. As though he understood nothing, he remained huddled up. He was sleepy. Occasionally, the crowing of the cock pierced the darkness of his mind.

It was Friday and, just like his father, Budhiya had to run along with the horse to Vansda. His soles were cracked due to the terrible heat and he could hardly put his feet on the ground. In the evening, at around seven, when he was drinking, he wept at the sight of his feet. In his mind, he abused Bamansha and his horse. Then he heard Bamansha crying out for him. Setting his liquor aside, he staggered up to Bamansha's house.

'What, you swine, started drinking already? Who will feed the horse? Your father? Go inside and feed the horse. And you better fetch water from the well for the horse.'

Budhiya felt both the horse and his master were equally venomous.

He wanted to vent his hatred for Bamansha on the horse. He collected hay and placed it before the horse. Once again, the animal could not reach it. Budhiya had placed it behind the horse. The horse started neighing out of sheer frustration. Budhiya brought water from the well and threw it near the animal's mouth. He also poured the water carelessly around the stable. The horse, whose anger was rising, stared at Budhiya. Budhiya made obscene gestures at the horse, cursed him, and went out to his hut.

It was ten o'clock at night. Because of his run from Manpur to Vansda, Budhiya's whole body ached. He was terribly exhausted and needed some rest. As he lay down, Budhiya remembered his father. He was twenty-five or twenty-six years old and Ratiya had been sixty-five. The memory of his father's death swam before his eyes. His father had been panting like a horse. He had been foaming at the mouth and craving water. His mouth and eyes had been open and helpless. Budhiya's eyes burned. Though he was sleepy, he was only able to huddle up and lie still. Then suddenly, he heard the latch open and he got up. He rushed out into the darkness, finding his way through shrubs and bamboo grooves towards Bamansha's house. He wanted to enter the compound, but instead, waited outside and smoked. He went towards Bamansha's house pensively. In the dim light of a lantern, he caught a glimpse of Rukhdi and Bamansha. They were intoxicated, playing with each other lewdly and laughing lustily. Budhiya did not know whether to stand there or walk away with his cracked soles and broken heart but finally decided to walk back home. He felt like murdering Bamansha. He also felt that he could not forgive his mother. Fatigued and tormented, he lit a bidi and swallowed its smoke as if he was swallowing fire. All kinds of thoughts crossed his mind. He fetched a pot of liquor from his hut and started gulping it down. His mind and body were both tormented. He was physically drained, and whatever strength was left, it was shattered at the sight of Bamansha and his mother.

He imagined Bamansha and Rukhdi revelling in a bestial orgy. Sometime later, their heads transformed into the head of a dark horse. Budhiya broke free from this nightmare. But it continued to haunt him. The shrill crowing of the cock pierced the silence again and again as unpleasant thoughts about Rukhdi and Bamansha rose and fell in his mind.

In the afternoon, Rukhdi was out of breath as she washed utensils. A pale-faced Budhiya sat near his hut, leaning against the wall. He had not slept the night before and had had nightmares. He vented all his anger on Rukhdi. Because they quarrelled bitterly, Rukhdi did not go to Bamansha's place at night. Bamansha's passion caught fire. The next morning, he beat Budhiya mercilessly for no fault of his. Budhiya started drinking mahua liquor on an empty stomach. Bamansha had ordered everyone in the house not to give Budhiya anything to eat. Every time he lay down and closed his eyes, the image of Bamansha and Rukhdi flashed in his mind.

It was about nine o'clock at night. Bamansha had gone to sleep with Rukhdi. Budhiya was starving. He lit a fire and roasted some peanuts. He sat with his liquor and nuts, staring into the darkness. Along with the thoughts of Bamansha and Rukhdi, thoughts of the black horse agitated his mind. Suddenly, as if he had made up his mind, he got up. He pulled out a burning piece of wood from the flame and stealthily moved towards Bamansha's house. Moonlight showed him the way. He stole into the stable. The horse immediately turned his head and looked with fiery eyes at Budhiya. In the pale moonlight, the horse recognized Budhiya. With the burning piece of wood in his hand, Budhiya went near the black horse with bated breath. The horse immediately became alert. Before the horse could do anything, however, Budhiya thrust the burning piece of wood at the animal's genitals. The horse's loud neighing pierced the silence of the night. Budhiya slipped out of the door of the stable and reached his hut. The horse was in terrible agony. He neighed loudly. But Bamansha, fed on mahua liquor and chicken, could not open his eyes. However, Rukhdi woke up, frightened. Picking up the lantern, she went into the stable only to see the horse neighing with unbearable pain. The loud uproar finally woke Bamansha, and in drunken stupor, he beat up Rukhdi and the horse, without having the slightest idea of what was going on.

✧

Bamansha reached home from Vansda late at night. The horse was limping due to the burns near his thighs and genitals. Bamansha had gone mad when he had seen the wounds. He suspected Budhiya. The first thing Bamansha did upon returning home was to look for his whip. He started flogging Budhiya who had been sitting quietly near his hut, smoking a bidi. Budhiya pushed the old man on to the large water container. Seeing Bamansha fall, Rukhdi could not control her laughter.

At night, Budhiya took Bamansha back to his house and left him there, grumbling and drunk. Budhiya smoked a bidi as he walked back. The feeble light from the lantern lit up his hut. 'You did well in not coming or the master would have killed you. Who did that to the horse?' Rukhdi stared at Budhiya.

Budhiya gulped down some liquor and spoke without the least hesitation: 'If you want to do the same thing to that Parsi someday, just let me know.' Rukhdi was shocked at his words. She went inside. A dreadful scream arose from the bamboo groves behind her hut. She shivered and raised the wick of the lantern. She heard angry grunts from Budhiya just outside her hut.

There was a loud commotion inside Bamansha's compound. The horse had caught Rukhdi's huge white rooster by the neck in his mouth. On hearing the wild shrieks of the dying rooster, Budhiya and Rukhdi ran towards the stable. In order to free the rooster from the horse's mouth, Budhiya got hold of an iron bar and started flogging the horse on its back and the legs. On hearing the din, Bamansha came running. He was shocked to see Budhiya flogging his favourite horse mercilessly. He fetched his whip, which he had kept in salt, and began lashing Budhiya's back. The whole compound was filled with Budhiya's shrieks and Bamansha's shouts.

As the sun came up and the dewdrops quivered among the spinous shrubs, Budhiya lay wallowing in pain. There were lashes on his whole body and he was bruised black and blue. As Rukhdi was nursing Budhiya, she did not go to Bamansha's house to cook for him. She was Budhiya's stepmother, but she had raised Budhiya ever since he was a child. She was deeply hurt by Bamansha's atrocity.

At night, the half moon hung in the sky. Bamansha was seen slowly riding his horse. He had gone to a veterinary doctor to treat his horse's burns and scars. The horse was of pure Arabian breed and did not once let out a cry of pain throughout the journey. They went slowly towards Manpur; Bamansha flinging terrible curses at Budhiya.

Bamansha's house lay still below the pale-yellow moonlight. There were noises from the distant huts. When he saw that his house was dark, he turned his horse towards Rukhdi's hut. He knocked at the door and shouted, 'Rukhdeee.' Rukhdi, who was sitting near the bruised Budhiya, shook with fear. Budhiya woke up on hearing the loud shouts which shook the whole hut. Rukhdi ran outside. 'Why is it so dark in my house?' Bamansha screamed furiously at her.

'Master, Budhiya is very ill,' Rukhdi replied in a trembling voice. Bamansha flared up at her words. When he came to know that Rukhdi had not even cooked that day, he was furious. He dragged Rukhdi by her hair. Budhiya, lying on a mat made of palm leaves, heard Rukhdi screaming for help and his blood began to boil. Fire started flowing in his veins and he cursed Bamansha and his horse.

It was well past midnight, but Rukhdi had not returned. Bamansha had forced her to drink and continued to use her till she passed out. Budhiya's head was throbbing, and he managed to stand with great effort. He pulled out a hatchet from the roof of the hut and started for Bamansha's house. Though his legs wobbled, he was determined. Bamansha's house was quiet and Budhiya's hatchet shone in the moonlight. 'Today I will finish him,' he decided. With his mind and body on fire, he reached the stable.

The horse was not in the stable. From the day Budhiya had attacked him, the horse had refused to stay inside the stable. Bamansha had tied the horse to the mahua tree just outside the stable. As Budhiya slowly moved towards the stable, the horse's eyes flashed at the sight of Budhiya's hatchet. The horse recognized his old adversary. The enraged horse kicked sharply. He struck his target. Budhiya screamed as blood spurted from between his thighs. The light in his eyes died slowly.

In the morning, there remained bits and pieces of the rooster that the black horse had chewed up.

Translated by Sachin Ketkar

MAAJO
PANNA TRIVEDI

Clickety-clack, clickety-clack...the noisy train slowed down as it reached Gujarivaas. At the edge of Gujarivaas began a bridge that went over the river. The train usually slowed down when it approached Gujarivaas. For a few moments, its noise drowned out all the sounds in Gujarivaas. As always, Sanno's hands paused momentarily over the dirty utensils she was cleaning with ash and water drawn from an old green weather-beaten handpump. Transfixed, she looked at the tracks. Binni, her head down, was rummaging through the garbage. Eight-year-old Maanko stopped for a few seconds before resuming 'driving' his old tyre, imitating the sound of a car. On the left side was doho, an old man squatting down on his haunches, playing cards with a few others. He took a deep and long puff of his bidi. Cursing his fate, he resentfully tossed a jack of spades. Next to the muddy puddle, right after the garbage pile, lay Shaniya, passed out drunk. When the train rumbled in, he woke up with a start. As always, six-year-old Paro began hiccupping at the sound of the train.

This is what Gujarivaas went through every day—among discarded tins and plastic boxes; empty bottles of mineral water; the hazy smokiness of bidis; tobacco stains; the ruckus around kings, queens, jacks, and jokers; old tyres hanging from tin roofs; empty cement bags; scrubbed and starched saris outside people's homes—the surroundings remained unchanged as the years progressed. Now you could see satellite TV dishes resting against corrugated roofs of certain homes. If anything really changed, it was the advertisements painted with permanent colours on walls that threatened to collapse at any moment, panting under the weight of the advertisements that reminded people to build toilets and use them.

When the train whistled shrilly, Tara, who lived in the third house in the vaas, rushed out, shouting: 'Oye Maajo, see, it's the queen. Alee, Maajo, see, it's your queen train.' Tara ran up to Maajo and stopped. 'Not queen, but king... K...i...n...g...say king! Arre, my raja has come, the Raajo of Maajo,' squealed seventeen-year-old Maajo as she stood near the train, fluttering her eyes, her manner coquettish, waving her hand at the passengers in the train..

The train jerked to a halt. Maajo's playful eyes became alert. They scanned each coach, one by one, until they came to rest upon the one carrying regular pass-holding commuters. Her eyes searched impatiently for Raajo. With 'goggles' covering his eyes, Raajo stood near the door. 'Oh...he hasn't found a place to sit even today!' Maajo's eyes lit up. She prayed in her heart for him to find a place to sit so she could feast on his entire body. So what if that lasted but for a second or two! On seeing this boy with a bag slung over his shoulder, Maajo called out loudly, 'Oye Shah Rukh, oye Raajo, oye oye.' Maajo waved at him but her hero turned away. Maajo ran a few steps after the train. The hero was soon far away.

Maajo would have continued to stand there, but her gaze fell on a Bisleri bottle with strings tied at both ends. Amidst swarming flies, a middle-aged man was defecating. Despite Maajo's presence, he continued to squat, as if Maajo was not Maajo, but another man. She turned around and muttered under her breath, 'Can't you sit a little further away?' Maajo's mind was too preoccupied by the train to notice his retort: 'Did you inherit this land from your father?'

Maajo's face was flushed pink. How could it not be? Her hungry eyes had finally managed to spot her hero! Whenever Maajo managed to see that young man, she went through the tasks of the rest of the day with renewed vigour. She could be slogging all day, but her delicate body felt no exhaustion. She would not only help her own mother, with whom she starched and dried old clothes, but also the other women of Gujarivaas. In the evenings, she would sift through old sarees with zari borders and remove the borders. Her most productive day was Thursday, the day of Guruvaari. Unfortunately, the Guruvaar Bazaar was open only once a week, so for the rest of the week, she would sit down with heaps of old clothes wherever she found a spot. Lest someone filch laces and borders, she made her little sisters Sanno and Binni also attend to the job, and that way, trained them. Maanko was too small to be of any help to their mother. And their father had no time left after gambling and drinking. If it took his fancy, he would, on a rare day, do some work. But that was of no help to anyone. He spent more than he earned, and sat puffing away on bidis bought with her mother's money. If he gambled away all the money he had, he rained curses upon Maajo. When he was heavily drunk he would sometimes forget that he was Maajo's father. He would then say, 'You have everything that can bring money…go find somebody.'

Maajo felt that night had descended too early that day. In the darkness, as usual, she went with Sanno to Mangi's place to watch TV. Seeing her sister ready to leave, Paro, as usual, began to bawl. Having no other option, Maajo held Paro's finger and took her along to Mangi's house. She walked fast.

Maajo waited as eagerly for the night to fall as she would for the day to begin. She lived with a dream. She longed for a TV bigger than Mangi's at her own house. Then she would watch films all day and night. Never mind if ants crawled out of the walls of her house and bit her; she wouldn't budge even if they sucked her blood as much as they liked. She thought of the girls travelling by the queen train in the morning. How beautiful they looked, with pant-shirt-mobile-purse and silky and shimmering Punjabi suits and colourful dupattas. Maajo wanted to wear high-heeled sandals and, with a mobile in her hand, sit next to her hero on the train and chug away into the distance.

Of course, she did travel by train. One Sunday every month, she got on a train with her mother to purchase damaged or inexpensive cloth, laces, and borders from Surat and Mumbai. The mother and daughter travelled with their wares along with other women of the vaas. All of them travelled without buying a ticket. They would sit with their bundles near the toilet, shaking with fear. They would sit where other people walked, next to their feet. If the ticket collector turned up, some of them would hide in the washrooms. The ones left outside had to bear the brunt of cuss words. When it became unbearable, Maajo's mother would get belligerent, saying, 'Strutting around just because you have a job….' But on being threatened she would become quiet. The ticket collector would threaten to throw out their bundles or kick them out at the next station. Then her mother would plead, 'Sahib, show some mercy, we are not going to eat up the seats, why are you doing this to poor people?' The back-and-forth would continue, and if it showed no signs of abating, she would take out a fifty-rupee note from inside her blouse. The sahib would ask for ten times more and finally settle for one hundred rupees. 'Why would you do this, Sahib?' Pleading, her mother would replace the note she had given him with a hundred-rupee note. The sahib would take the money and continue swearing at them. Addressing the people who had bought tickets, he would say, 'They want a joy ride, bloody women…dhandhawalis.' The allegation of prostitution would make Maajo's mother lose her temper, and she would yell furiously, 'You haven't bought me nor have I sold myself to you…. Bastard! Do I survive on the mercy of your fathers and grandfathers?' A terrified Maajo would cling to her mother. Deep in her heart, she desperately wanted to sit in a first-class compartment and leave her mark on a seat there.

When she entered Mangi's house that day, there was pin-drop silence. Everyone was watching TV with their mouths shut. In the congested and small space, Maajo made room for herself and sat right in front. It was dark but their eyes were used to identifying shadows. The only light that flickered was from the television. A faint light in the corner flickered every now and then when the wind blew. The film on the screen was *Mr. India*. Maajo had watched it before and yet her eyes were glued to the TV. The viewers' laughter merged with Mangi's father's phlegmatic cough in the dark room.

In the movie, an entire human body melted into a blob of red. Maajo would also disappear into shades of red. In her mind, images from another film mixed with this one. Her hero had become the prime minister, and yet made time to pick up his Manjari. Manjari...Manjari...the name reverberated within her a million times. The queen train flashed before her eyes. It was moving fast, racing towards her. Raajo gets down at Gujarivaas. 'Manjari...Manjari...' he shouts and comes towards her. She stands far away, in a corner. In an anxious voice he says, 'Why aren't you responding, silly girl? I have come to pick you up. To rescue you from this hell. Hold my hand, Maajo. So what if you were born in Gujarivaas? You have a right to dream. Not Maajo, but Manjari. You are my Manjari....' He holds her hand and leads her to his black, shiny car.

Maajo felt embarrassed by her thoughts. The movie was interrupted by commercials—of home loans, life insurance, purified water, deodorants, hair-smoothening shampoos, weight-reducing cornflakes, energy-enhancing Bournvita, and utterly butterly Amul....

'Your mother didn't come?' Mangi's voice pierced through the darkness and reached her. Maajo kept mum. Should she tell her that her mother's arms were swollen from scrubbing clothes or that her back hurt from her useless husband's beatings, because he had wanted money to gamble? Everybody knew what had happened... the walls of Gujarivaas hardly left any chance for privacy. Despite the walls, the vaas was naked, all of it. Maajo behaved like she had not understood the question and continued to watch the film. 'Chhu ke dekho ek baar, makkhan hai yaar.' Touch her once, she's like butter, yaar. Vidya Balan was on the screen, wearing a short frock and skipping rope. Paro was imitating her, repeating the words. This was one of her favourite advertisements. Maajo elbowed her to shut her up, but the darkness swallowed up the gesture. Paro suddenly asked loudly, 'What is butter like?' Maajo pinched her. Paro shut up. Soap, shampoo, deodorant, and then it was back to *Mr. India*.

The hero would disappear and reappear. But Maajo disappeared without even moving. A sky-wide expanse spread itself inside her. She kept thinking of the short frock in the advertisement. Maajo remembered that her 'frock' also stopped short above her knees, its buttons at the back had come off, and the frill in the front had come undone. She had been somehow holding the frock together in her hands. Now, she let it slip from her fingers. She looked around her in the dark and slipped off her sleeve to bare her shoulder, like Vidya Balan. She imagined herself in a bathtub in a posh bathroom. She sank with her soft butter-like body into the fragrant soap bubbles.

Suddenly, someone laid a hand on her bare shoulder and stood up. Terrified, Maajo screamed. Someone said, 'Arre what is going on? Did an ant bite you? Ants, baap re, so many of them!' Maajo trembled. She turned around. Everyone was watching *Mr. India*. A strange sensation ran through her body. Even when she headed home she felt as if she was being chased, and that someone was pawing her shoulder.

⸏

The *Gujarat Queen* train passed by the next morning, as always. Maajo caught a momentary glimpse of Raajo. She almost jumped out of her skin. She extended her hand and called out, 'Oye, oye.' The train slowed down as it came closer to the bridge. Maajo ran with the train. Tunelessly, she sang, 'Badshah, oh Badshah....' but the young man sitting by the window held a kerchief to his nose and shut his eyes. Maajo's song became softer, until it gradually became inaudible and finally died down.

Maajo felt as if his kerchief had not just blocked out the foul smell of the vaas, but herself, and her kind. She stopped running, infuriated. She picked up a fistful of sand and hurled it at the moving train but it flew into her eyes. Maajo stood for God knows how long, rubbing her eyes. She scrunched up her shoulders and brought them closer to her body to see if she smelled bad.... No, she didn't. But the next moment, she thought, it's not fragrance either, is it?

In that moment, all of Gujarivaas seemed to be reeking. Some foul odour seemed to have turned into a cyclone and swirled its smell throughout the place.

Maajo sat listlessly that afternoon. She neither helped her mother wash clothes nor did she do any of her own chores. She felt as if a fiery spherical object was hovering over her. The sharp smell of tobacco wafted in with the breeze.

'Maajo....'

Maajo turned around. It was Bhikho, Mangi's brother. He approached her and asked, 'What were you doing yesterday? When you were watching the fillum? Were you removing your frock? And someone's hand....' Maajo was stupefied. Bhikho laughed deviously. What had remained invisible in the dark was now apparent—a lowly ugliness. Bhikho came closer. He whispered into Maajo's ears, 'Do you want it? The same frock, the one you saw on TV? You can have ten of them, you know, not just one, in a few moments. I have a plan.'

Maajo's despondent face brightened slightly, 'How?'

'I know a person who can give you whatever you want. You know those bungalows that have come up where Govindnagar used to be earlier? He lives there. You have to go there and do what he tells you to do. If someone asks, say you cook for him. And that's hardly a lie, isn't it? That's what it is, your job is to cook food.... Sometimes, you will have to cook. But don't show attitude, okay? You will get a spare key to the bungalow. Their bathroom is bigger than our two houses put together. Bathe there until you are satisfied.'

Maajo's silver-ringed toes brushed against a new leaf emerging from the earth below her. Stamping on the leaf, Bhikho said, 'Look here, after Govindnagar, it's Gujarivaas's turn to be demolished. The municipality people can come any moment and raze it to the ground. Maanko is still very young, and you know your old father better than me. If the sahib is happy with you, he will provide you with a two-room apartment. Imagine! You can wave down at people from your apartment.' Bhikho realized that Maajo was warming up to the idea, and didn't let a second go to waste, 'So contraak final?'

'Hmm....' Maajo said. She caressed her arm. Her skin felt like butter. She smiled faintly.

That very same evening before the sun had set, Maajo accompanied Bhikho to the sahib's bungalow. The forty-year-old sahib inspected Maajo from head to toe. And then, looking at Bhikho, he nodded. Maajo was busy measuring the walls of the house in her head. Vases, carpets, paintings, mirrors, pure white translucent curtains, chandeliers....The sahib was giving important instructions but Maajo's eyes were surveying the house.

That evening, Maajo opened the bathroom door. Her eyes hardened immediately. She remembered the gunnysack-covered corner in Gujarivaas that they called a bathroom. A look of disgust spread on her face. When it wasn't raining it was possible to go to the riverbank and wash yourself along with your clothes. But on rainy days, there was no choice but to bathe in the bathrooms in the vaas. No matter how early you woke up and made your way to bathe with half-shut eyes, the scoundrels in the vaas would've woken up even earlier and would peep through the gaps between the sacks. Their eyes dripped with lust. The memory made Maajo want to spit but she gulped it down after noticing the smooth floral tiles of the bathroom she was in. That evening, Maajo scrubbed and scrubbed to such an extent that when she saw herself in the life-sized mirror in the bathroom, she couldn't help but whisper, 'Maa...jjo'. Her eyes grew wide. 'Wah wah Maa...jjo...look at you!'

⸝

The next day, another door opened, leading to a room with a pink bedspread.

Maajo felt suffocated. She wanted to run back into her thin-walled house and hide behind the clothes her mother had put out to dry. A shudder went through her body. Her eyes steadied upon the sahib's face. He wasn't that bad, she told herself, but her eyes would not listen to her. It was best to shut them. Some strange music was playing, but Maajo concentrated on remembering the sound of the whistling train. With her eyes shut, she imagined the train leaving

Gujarivaas. She brought it into the bungalow and took it inside the bedroom. The rhythm of her heartbeats matched the clickety-clack of the train. Maajo sat with her hair loose, mobile phone in her hand, next to Raajo. She held a kerchief over her nose. Like Vidya Balan in the commercial, she also skipped. With a leap, she was high up in the air and when she came down she landed in a quagmire of butter and sank deeper and deeper into it.

⌁

Maajo spent many evenings and nights in this manner—wakeful. Her body was now covered in soft and silky frocks with beautiful floral designs. When she wore a silk churidar and kurta with a dupatta that had tassels, the other girls in the vaas died of envy. No more did Maajo sit in the Guruvaar Bazaar market to sell laces; instead, she wore clothes with expensive lace on them.

Tara was consumed by jealously when she saw Maajo. Maajo's glowing skin convinced Tara that Maajo's raja will alight from the train and take her away some day. She said to Maajo, 'Alee Maajudi, how have you become this fair? Why don't you get me a job like yours, I'll be so grateful to you. You know that I cook food better than you....'

Maajo shivered. She avoided meeting Tara's eyes and said, 'You? Oh come on. You think this is easy? You have no idea. People who live in these big fancy bungalows are so moody. What they want varies with their mood. Sometimes they want bland food and sometimes spicy.... It takes time to understand. You need "tarening"... understand?'

Although Maajo had managed to give an answer, she could not meet Tara's eyes. She heard an expletive in her head and remembered the disgusted look on the ticket collector's face last week. When he had come to check the tickets, Maajo had stopped her mother from saying anything. She had taken out a few crisp notes and had given them to the ticket collector. However, she had also heard the word that had formed on the ticket collector's lips, 'dhandhawali'.

Meanwhile, Maajo's eyes grew heavy. She kept refusing, but Tara insisted on going with her. When Maajo refused to budge, Tara said, 'Swear on your beloved Raajo. You have to take me with you to the bungalow. I am not going to come every day. Just this one day, please.' Maajo finally gave up and agreed to take her. How could she not, after taking an oath in Raajo's name?

One morning, Maajo waited for the 'Queen'. It rumbled in and swiftly left. She couldn't spot Raajo. With sadness in her eyes, she stood for a long time, until the train disappeared from her sight.

Suddenly, she felt someone's touch on her shoulder. Maajo turned around, startled. Bhikho placed a bundle of notes in her hand and said, 'Maajo, your account is settled. Sahib has asked you to return the bungalow key.'

He came closer, and with a devious glint in his eyes, whispered, 'It's Tara's turn now.'

Maajo was dumbfounded. Even the thin walls of her Gujarivaas home seemed to have collapsed. She stared at Bhikho with vacant eyes. Was Tara more beautiful than her? The image of a full-bodied Tara flashed before her eyes, and Maajo felt like her own body had begun to reek.

Bhikho noticed the pain in Maajo's eyes. He mustered up his courage and said, 'Maajo, if you like, I….' Maajo looked up. In an unsteady voice, he continued, 'There's someone…but…but…'

'But?'

'He's somewhat old…would you like to cook for him?'

'Hmm...sure.'

That night, with Paro holding on to her finger, when Maajo made her way to Mangi's house, she felt the 'Queen' race through her. Paro sang and danced and kicked things out of her way as she walked, oblivious to the world. 'Yeh makkhan kya hai yaar?' she asked, 'What is this butter?' Maajo abruptly stopped. Paro looked at her, dismayed. Maajo looked into Paro's eyes and replied, her voice caught in her throat, 'Butter? It's very bad, Paro. It is black in colour. Bas, once it touches your tongue it doesn't come off. It gets stuck like a thorn in the throat and it pokes all day and night....'

Maajo tightened her grip on Paro's hand and walked into the deepening darkness.

THE TWENTY-FIRST TIFFIN

RAAM MORI

'Neetu….' Mummy's shrill voice interrupted my chat. I left the drawing room and went straight into the kitchen.

'Mummy, please stop calling me Neetu. You know my name is Neetal. You seem to conveniently forget things. And then you make a point of repeating the same mistake. When my friend visited me recently and heard you yelling, "Neetu…Neetu…" it turned into a joke in college. People have been calling me R. K.'s mom since then.'

I stood there, seething with anger. Unruffled and calm, Mummy briskly filled up tiffin boxes.

'Who's R. K.?' she asked as she counted the rotis.

'Oh God, R. K. stands for Ranbir Kapoor. Neetu Kapoor's son. Now, for heaven's sake, don't tell me you don't know who he is. This is not some random boy from my college, by the way. In any case, why am I even bothering to recite an epic to an ignoramus? Listen, Mummy, it's time you shed all your orthodox nonsense. It's as stale as the leftovers in your tiffin boxes. And please get a hold on your suspicious nature. All right, tell me now, why did you need me?' I asked, twirling my dry locks with a finger.

'It's past eleven, you see, it's time to quickly send off the lunch boxes. You know I cannot manage to prepare twenty tiffin boxes by myself. Obviously I need some help from you.' Her hands moved briskly as she tried to finish all her work.

'Mummy, you managed perfectly all this while. I happen to be at home only for the past ten days or so. How is it that you suddenly can't manage now and you feel tired? You know what, just stop all this tiffin-shiffin business. Please.'

'And tell twenty boys, "Sorry, I cannot supply you food from tomorrow"? Like that, abruptly?' She glared at me, leaving me perplexed.

'Your father has not felt the need to provide money for running this house; it's thanks to these tiffin boxes that he is able to invest and move around money in stocks and shares without worrying about household expenses. You are able to study in a fancy college because of these tiffin boxes.'

'Oh stop it, Mom. Are you saying that Papa is running away from his responsibilities? Or that he has not bothered to care for you? He loves you very much. He gave us this house, provides food to eat, clothes to wear, and his presence makes us feel safe.'

'Even a prison does all that,' she retorted. I looked at her, wide-eyed. Was her frustration with Papa peering out of her large, shapely eyes? I couldn't read them. I have come to realize that Mummy's eyes express nothing; they are simply dry and empty. And the lines on her flat expressionless face also don't speak to me. They always stay the same. My mother has been like this from the beginning: unkempt, unmoved, busy, and yet, a puzzle. On the other hand, I know Papa so well that I can almost predict his next sentence.

I have seen a certain kind of routine at home ever since I was a child. Papa would be constantly occupied. What comes to mind are his phone conversations, half-smoked cigarettes, white vest, and blue lungi. He would make calculations based on the financial projections he saw on TV, and buy and sell stocks and shares throughout the day, even at mealtimes, and turn to bed a tired man at night. As for my mother, she prepared tiffin boxes for twenty people day and night. She became the pressure cooker she cooked in. Her day began and ended in the kitchen. I often feel that Mummy has tied herself to this routine. When I picture her, what comes to mind is an indifferent woman, clad in a dull saree, hair wrapped up in a tight, stern-looking bun on her head, locks of grey hair around her face, an expanding waistline, and always reeking of perspiration. I remember that in the early days she used to prepare lunch for five people, later it became ten, and now it's twenty. I put aside the tablet and began to pack tiffin boxes in cloth bags. When all twenty were ready, I retreated to the drawing room and resumed chatting.

Mummy joined me in a few minutes. She switched on the television and began to flip through the channels.

'Mummy, don't you think you should dye your hair?' I asked, my eyes on the tablet as I talked to my friends.

'It's fine just the way it is. In fact, it's more than fine.' As she changed channels, a Ranbir Kapoor song appeared on the screen.

'Wow! Mummy, let it be. Don't change.'

She stood up and went towards the door to look for Bhanu dada, who ferried her lunch boxes to different locations.

'Neetu, it's very exhausting now. I can't cook more than this,' she said as she tucked her grey locks behind her ears. I threw a cursory glance at her, only to be lured back to the song on TV. Silence hung heavy for a while. I felt that she wanted to say something to me, but was perhaps waiting for the right moment.

'Neetu, will you open the window? It's so dark in here.' I pushed down the window stopper and nudged the windows open to let the light in. Just then I heard the sound of the main gate being opened. I didn't bother getting up, assuming that it was Bhanu dada who had come up to pick up the tiffin boxes. But he usually rang his bicycle bell when he arrived. In which case....

'Namaste. May I come in, ma'am?'

Wow! What a voice, exactly like Ranbir's. I put aside the tablet and peered out of the window.

A young man was standing outside our house. He seemed to be around twenty years old. Mummy looked at me and said softly, 'Neetu, you go inside....' Before I knew what was happening, the man had already entered the house. He sat down on the sofa. I kept staring at him. He was dressed in a formal body-hugging purple shirt that seemed more appropriate for a party, and black trousers. He had a pleasant and neat hairstyle and wore a formal wristwatch. His eyes were light in colour. He had a large forehead, chiselled features, and glistening, white, symmetrical teeth—the kind you see in the commercials for toothpaste. His skin looked as though he had just come out of a spa. In short, he was a veritable five-feet-six-inchetall package for marriage. My eyes rested on him without blinking.

As if he knew, he smiled at me and my mother and said, 'Hello, my name is Dhruv Majumdar. I am an engineer, and arrived yesterday in this city for six months of training in a company.'

My mother must have realized that I hadn't taken my eyes off him. I was about to say, 'Hi, I'm Neetal' but Mummy spoke up, 'Neetu, go and bring a glass of water.'

I muttered under my breath as I went into the kitchen. Mummy followed me. Before I could say anything she pounced upon me, 'At least keep a dupatta with you. We do a tiffin service from home; you never know when some boy will drop by to make a payment. Ever since you have come on vacation, they all seem to visit quite frequently.'

'Don't say anything more, Mummy. Please finish your job and go.' I felt embittered. This is what Mummy is like. If she wasn't yelling some four hundred times a day, she wouldn't know what else to do. While cooking, if she banged utensils or broke cups and saucers, it was a message to me to go to the kitchen. And this kitchen of hers is like a battlefield. Not a single thing is in its place.

I stood near the window looking at that fellow. My mother was sizing him up like he were a potential match on Shaadi.com; I was feeling uncomfortable. I was hardly of marriageable age, and here's my mother trying to....

'By the way, ma'am, my roommate uses your tiffin service. When I arrived yesterday, he was out, so I ate the meal you had prepared. I really enjoyed it. It was so tasty. And I am particularly fond of potatoes. Even the toor dal was delicious. The seasoning of the kadhi was also great. You know, I was really happy to eat such a meal. My sister-in-law used to make such food. Really wonderful.'

When I looked at Mummy's face, I was surprised to see a smile. What's more, her cheeks had turned crimson and her earlobes looked flushed! Was I imagining all this when I heard my pleased mother say, 'Thank you'? The expression on my mother's face made me feel dizzy. Of course, this guy was not merely flattering her. Her cooking had to be good, otherwise why would Bhanu dada increase the number of deliveries from five to twenty tiffins? I immediately thought of Papa. Mummy makes things even outside the tiffin menu. I wondered if my father had ever said something like, 'Wah, such good food....' Or if I had seen Mummy laugh or blush before....

I was lost in my thoughts when this fellow said, 'Ma'am, if you don't mind, would you prepare lunch for me as well? It's only a matter of six months. I really like your cooking.'

'Oh, a twenty-first tiffin?' In my head I could hear complaints while preparing twenty tiffins—the cacophony of her voice, the clashing utensils, the breaking cups and saucers, the mess, the perspiration of her body—and I saw her plonking with exhaustion on the sofa, saying, 'Neetu, I can't handle more…not more than twenty, this much is enough.'

I came out of my room to decline the request at once, but before I could do that my smiling mother said, 'Not a problem. I anyway make twenty. One more it is. I will give Bhanu dada your tiffin from tonight.'

I frowned. The boy paid for a month and left. Without counting the cash, Mummy went to put it in a drawer. I stood between her and the drawer.

'Mummy, what is going on? What is this?' I asked with exasperation.

She began to dust the drawing room. 'How does it matter? One more tiffin is not going to kill me, child.'

'Oh. Now you better stop yelling for me from the kitchen. And stop breaking crockery. You are a fine one to complain to me, "Neetu, I can't manage". You have added more work for yourself now.' I knew I was overreacting. I took the keys of the scooty and left home. When I came back home, I saw my mother smiling at me. Something nagged at me, the smile perhaps—I wasn't used to it.

From that day on, Mummy changed in small ways. Papa had no time to notice, but the changes didn't escape me. She had stopped shouting altogether. A once-cantankerous Mummy had now started to hum. At every mealtime, her enthusiasm to prepare the tiffins was different now. I would pack the tiffin boxes and put them away, but the moment I reached the twenty-first tiffin, she would say, 'One minute, Neetal, don't shut that one.' I would watch mutely while she dragged a stool from the drawing room and climbed atop it. She would take out the pickle jar from the top shelf, and after filling up a small box with slivers of mango pickle, she would close the tiffin box and gaze at it with contentment. These days, potato sabzi appeared more frequently on the menu, and the other day, I saw generous amounts of it in the twenty-first tiffin. Even the rotis that went into that tiffin had more ghee on them. I found all this really childish. I watched it all and felt it was all stupid.

As soon as the month ended, Dhruv would come home to make his payment. Without planning to, I had begun to ignore him. Mummy would make a special ginger tea for him, accompanied with some snacks. He would sit for an hour or so, chatting with her. I would peep at them talking and laughing together. Their friendliness made me uncomfortable.

And today, he's come up with a new thing. He says to my mother, 'Ma'am, since you cook with such commitment, why don't you start a small restaurant at home? I am sure it'll do very well.'

'I won't be able to sustain it even for six months,' my mother quipped, and the two of them laughed. It was a shock for me to see my mother making these smart comebacks.

I was beginning to feel impatient with myself as well as my father. An outsider has been able to change my mother so fundamentally, to make her laugh while we, the people who have lived with her for years, have failed. One day, sick and tired of Mummy and Papa's quarrels, I remember saying to her, 'Mummy what is the matter with you? You seem to pick a fight with Papa all the time.'

'Do I initiate the fights, Neetu?' she replied, with her usual flat voice and straight face.

'It doesn't make a difference, Mummy. Why don't you just learn to let go a little? He's really perfect.'

She had put her hand on my head and said with emptiness in her eyes, 'Beta, he's your papa, that's why he is perfect for you. He's a husband to me, and my evaluation is going to be different.' I remember how pale her face was then. But today, where has that pallor gone? At times, I keep thinking about Mummy and Dhruv.... I keep thinking, and my thoughts hit the blades of the fan and scatter throughout the room, wounded. I don't know what I'm supposed to think any more.

The biggest shock was when my mother began to dye her hair. She had deftly coloured her locks black, and as she looked at herself in the mirror, she had asked me, 'Neetu, how do I look?' What had not been possible through all my efforts was now achieved by that fellow's visits. While it was true that all the boys Mummy cooked for came home to make payments, Dhruv stayed the longest. Mummy would seldom chat with the other boys.

Dhruv is a really special case! Now Mummy wears her hair in a loose, low bun. Her sari is worn carefully, every fold in place, held together by a safety pin. And no matter how little time she has, she makes sure to wear a matching bindi on her forehead. She would steal a moment to check her reflection on a utensil as she cooked. And gone were the sounds of utensils being banged; a mellifluous humming had taken their place. I would often scream, 'Mummy what are you doing? Where's your mind? The roti is going to burn.'

'Neetal, why are you shouting? I am paying attention...' she would reply.

'Where?' I would ask with a meaningful glance, while she would happily go back to being lost in her own world. She would drag the stool and take out the sweet-sour gorkeri pickle and fill up the twenty-first tiffin.

I have noticed these days that on the last Sunday of the month, namely, Dhruv Day, Mummy takes longer than usual in the shower, and lingers over her reflection in the mirror. Although she would sit on the sofa watching television, she would be waiting for the sound of the doorbell. She would run the moment it rang. I was beginning to find all this quite intolerable. All these lights had begun to singe me...and that fellow constantly came up with new gimmicks:

'Ma'am, why don't you participate in MasterChef? We can put your cuisine on the international map.'

'Ma'am, you should also learn some foreign dishes, you know, progress....'

'Ma'am, do you use Tarla Dalal's cookbooks?'

Now I was the one screaming. I would knock down tiffins, break crockery, and bang utensils but Mummy seemed oblivious to all this.

One day, Dhruv did not come on a 'Dhruv Day' but in the middle of the week. He held a present in his hand. He sat with Mummy and they sipped tea and talked.

'Ma'am, today my training is over. Six months went by so fast, eating food prepared by you. I didn't even realize how quickly time has passed.... This is a small token of my appreciation for you.' My heart began to thud vigorously. So we will not see Dhruv any more then? Something bothered me. I gazed at him steadily. Mummy unwrapped the present. It was a recipe book of cuisines from different parts of the world. Mummy thanked him. The two of them sat quietly for a while. He swallowed the rest of the tea and stood up to leave. I felt as though I ought to see him off to the gate, but I asked myself the very next moment why I wanted to do so considering the fact that I didn't even like him coming to the house. As he left, he turned around, smiled at me, and left, closing the gate. Numerous cups and saucers broke inside me. I felt worried about Mummy. She stood in the drawing room, unmoving, for God knows how long. I could sense a funereal silence around me. The sun had set and darkness was upon us.

At night, Mummy was filling up tiffins in the kitchen while I was folding clothes in my room. 'Neetu...where the hell are you now?' I heard Mummy shout. I rushed to the kitchen. A saucer had slipped from Mummy's hand. I noticed that Mummy's hair was tied up in a stern tight bun. Her back was drenched with sweat and she was panting. Loose strands of hair clung to her sweat-drenched face.

I immediately filled up dal and sabzi in different tiffins. Mummy counted the rotis and began putting them in each box. When all the tiffins were filled up, Mummy went to the drawing room, dragging a stool with her. My eyes were downcast but I knew what she was doing. She brought the pickle jar down. With pursed lips, and eyes downcast, I struggled to speak, 'Mummy, you…but…he….'

My mother looked at me. Our eyes met, mother's and daughter's, and I could not bear her gaze. I looked away, beyond the window. Mummy also turned her gaze away. But I had noticed three lines on her flat forehead and a hazy mist clouding her dry eyes. Dark shadows had descended upon and between us—between mother and daughter.

CHUNNI

ABHIMANYU ACHARYA

Chunni dropped a sparrow at Shaili's feet. Shaili looked into Chunni's amber eyes. She had had her first glimpse of Chunni's feral nature about a month-and-a-half ago.

Shaili had broken up with Rahul since he was going to the UK to study. She had moved to Bangalore for an internship with *The Hindu*. With crime reporting, a different city, new people, and a foreign language, she felt she would need some sort of company. Chunni had been a friend. When she moved to Bangalore, she had taken her along.

Shaili had always loved cats. On Instagram, she had seen that Rahul had got himself a puppy in the UK. She had even commented on Rahul's photo with the pup, 'Aww…so cute and adorable!'

In reality, she had felt sorry for the pup. As if in response to Rahul's Instagram post, she had posted a photo of Chunni and herself; Chunni's claws being the main focus of the post. Shaili tagged the photo #Chunni #partnerincrime #onlycompany.

Chunni mostly lay on the sofa, barely moving. She was unbelievably lazy. Even on the day that Manoj came home, she barely stirred from her spot on the sofa.

The doorbell rang and Shaili opened the door. 'Hi!' Manoj greeted her.

'Hi, come in,' Shaili invited him in. As she was closing the door, Shaili caught the aunty who lived in the flat opposite hers staring intently. When the aunty's gaze met Shaili's, she stared in a peculiar way. Shaili could not meet her gaze. She hastily shut the door.

'I have brought some rum,' Manoj announced.

'Oh great! Thanks, although that wasn't necessary. I have some whisky. But we'll have rum since you got it.' Shaili led Manoj to the balcony.

She had come across Manoj on Tinder. She had downloaded the dating app shortly after arriving in Bangalore. Since she had just come out of a committed, romantic relationship, she did not want to be emotionally involved with anyone. That is why she had downloaded Tinder.

Manoj kept talking, and Shaili refilled their glasses—one peg after another. Her attention was on the tree outside her apartment. During the day, she could spot birds in its canopy; at night she couldn't see anything. Occasionally, she could sense birds taking flight in the shadows. She had spotted some sparrows in the tree a few days ago. In the darkness, she tried to see if they were still there. Manoj was saying something about his life. Shaili heard bits of it, but soon grew bored. She had little desire to know much about Manoj's life.

After the third peg, she waited for Manoj to do something—hold her hand, grab her waist perhaps, maybe even kiss her. But he didn't make a move. From the topic of films, he had moved on to music. Shaili was bored. Wordlessly, she slid closer to him. Manoj fell silent. Shaili, too, didn't say anything, and they sat in awkward silence.

Manoj drained his peg, as if to fortify himself for what he was about to say.

'Shaili…I…would like to say something to you.'

'I'm listening.'

'You know, for the last three days, I mean, ever since we began talking, I can't get you out of my mind. I think…you are…you know…I like you very much. Unlike other boys you may meet on Tinder, I am not interested merely in your body. I like you as a person.'

Manoj fell silent. His face reminded Shaili of the expression on Rahul's puppy's face.

'Thanks,' she said finally. 'Well, I have an early day in the office tomorrow. I think you should leave.'

'Yes, sure. We'll meet again.'

'Yes.'

'Bye.'

'Bye.'

Shaili shut the door behind him and immediately blocked his number.

The next day as she sat smoking in the balcony, talking with her mother on the phone, Chunni sauntered in. A cockroach scurried along the parapet of the balcony. Chunni crouched, ready to pounce. Shaili noticed just in time, and flicked the cockroach off the parapet. Disappointed, Chunni fixed her peculiar gaze on Shaili.

'Why do you want to harass the poor cockroach when you have cat food, sweetheart?' Shaili asked affectionately. She went into the kitchen and brought out a bowl of cat food, but Chunni was nowhere to be seen. Shaili peered over the parapet only to see her leaping from ledge to ledge—from the fifth floor to the fourth, and then to the third, until she reached the ground floor.

Shaili left her front door open. After some time, Chunni returned and leapt onto her spot on the sofa. Shaili placed the bowl of cat food near her and began to get ready for office.

The workload at the office kept her busy. Neither the crime rate nor her work decreased.

Of late, she was tossed between professors and their students. Several female students had come forward to accuse their professors of sexual harassment. A large number of faculty at one of the top colleges in Bangalore were among those named. However, no one could provide any hard evidence. She would take statements from the students and then, if they were willing, from the faculty members. She would write reports based on her interviews. All day, she was surrounded by news of rapes, murders, and robberies.

By evening, she would be drained. She would go home and fix herself a drink—a respite from the physical and mental exhaustion. Sometimes, when her exhaustion overwhelmed her, she would hug Chunni and let out a sob or two.

One day, as usual, Shaili was in the Metro, on her way to Majestic from Baiyappanahalli. She noticed a man standing in a corner, stealing glances at her every now and then. His stares were different from the way her neighbour had glared at her the other day. He continued to stare till she disembarked. She was overcome by a wave of nausea.

꜖

She met another boy on Tinder.

His name was George. He was a guitarist in a band. She had swiped right on Tinder because George liked Pink Floyd, her favourite band.

They talked about Pink Floyd when they first chatted. 'Which is your favourite Floyd number?' Shaili asked.

'Echoes,' George replied.

Aha! Shaili was pleased. They had a long conversation over the phone. Shaili felt that things were finally heading somewhere.

The conversation turned to George's guitar. He began to explain the workings of the guitar in great detail.

'Will you teach me to play?' Shaili asked.

'Sure. Do you want to a see a photo of my guitar?'

'Yes.'

George sent a few pictures in quick succession. They were all pictures of his penis. A fresh wave of nausea hit Shaili.

꜖

She had almost given up on Tinder. But then one day, she found Rohan. He was about eight years older than her. He was an English teacher in a high school. He wore his hair in a ponytail. Shaili had always had a strange attraction for men with long hair.

Shaili had clarified in the initial stages of their chat, 'I am not looking for a serious relationship. But that does not mean that I have any desire to see pictures of your private parts. Do you get it?'

'Of course! Don't worry. You will not have any reason to complain. And thanks for clarifying. At least we both know what to expect from each other.'

'Yes. I have only one expectation—to have a good time.'

And just like that, one day, Shaili invited him over. Unlike Manoj, Rohan didn't turn up with a bottle of rum. Before coming, he had asked her, 'Should I bring something?'

'Yes. Some chips. And cigarettes,' Shaili had replied.

Rohan came over, chips and cigarettes in hand. Seeing Chunni on the sofa, he went over to her, and caressed her head. Chunni rolled her eyes in pleasure.

'What is her name?' he asked.

'Chunni,' Shaili replied.

'She's really cute.'

'Yes.' Shaili picked Chunni up and placed her in another room. Chunni stared at her until Shaili shut the door.

As usual, Shaili led Rohan to the balcony. Drinks were poured and the conversation began. For some reason, Shaili found herself being interested in what Rohan was saying. Rohan didn't talk about himself. The conversation covered a range of subjects.

Rohan liked to talk about his students. He made comparisons between the current generation of students and his generation. His students were more advanced and smarter than Rohan's own generation. Shaili forgot to look at the tree and search for the sparrows. There was not a single moment of awkward silence. Like an artist filling a blank canvas with colours, Rohan filled the passage of time with his talking.

Gradually, he moved closer to her and slid his arm around Shaili's waist. She jumped and let out a giggle. It had been a while since someone had done that, and she had forgotten that it tickled. Rohan smiled and tickled her some more. Shaili laughed and playfully pushed him away. Rohan tightened his grip around her waist.

He left the next morning. Shaili began to dress for work. She was about to take a selfie with Chunni to upload on Instagram when she noticed the hickey on her neck. Smiling softly, she covered it with a scarf and took the selfie.

Rohan's visits became a regular affair. Whenever he came over, he would play with Chunni for a while, caressing her head. Then Shaili would lead him to the balcony.

One night, Shaili had a dream—as she was reaching out to caress Chunni's head, Chunni moved away. She went closer and reached out again. But Chunni became angry and sank her claws into her hand. Shaili woke up with a start. Rohan lay sleeping by her side. She checked the back of her hands but there were no marks. She went back to sleep.

⁘

She had just received a brief to write a report. A professor from a college in Kammanahalli had raped one of his students. The student had lost consciousness and was taken to a hospital, but had died there. With trembling hands, Shaili just managed to write the report.

She messaged Rohan: I am feeling really low. Come home.

She left office early that day.

It wasn't quite evening when Rohan came over. He had brought pizza with him: double cheese with pepperoni, her favourite. It was a large pizza and they couldn't finish it. She peeled the pepperoni pieces off the leftover slices and fed them to Chunni. Chunni was pleased.

After eating, they lay in bed together. Shaili reached for Rohan's hand and said, 'Thank you.'

Rohan smiled and moved closer. He placed his lips on hers. Shaili didn't know what to do. Rohan continued kissing her and she kissed him back. His lips drifted to her neck. Shaili grew tense. She held on to him tightly. His kisses grew more passionate. She stopped him. 'What is it?' he enquired.

Shaili could only stare back, eyes wide, lips pressed together.

Rohan held her shoulders and shook her, 'Speak up, what is it?'

As if in reply, unable to suppress the nausea that had been welling up in her all these days, she threw up. With a groan, she vomited over Rohan's shirt, his arms, her arms, the bedsheet—everything.

'What the....' Rohan pulled back angrily. He stomped into the bathroom. Later, he left without saying goodbye, slamming the door behind him. By now, the entire room reeked. Shaili sat up on the bed, staring at the vomit on the sunflower-patterned bedsheet, now flecked with bits of pepperoni.

She got up and went to the bathroom to change. She came out looking for Chunni. She wanted to cuddle her for comfort. However, Chunni was nowhere in the apartment. She went out into the balcony. Chunni was there, but she wasn't alone. A sparrow lay beneath her paws, struggling, its wings fluttering. Chunni ripped its wings apart and wrung its neck. The sparrow ceased its struggles and fell still. Chunni, too, seemed to be at peace. She quietly picked up the limp corpse in her mouth and laid it at Shaili's feet, as if it were an offering.

Shaili looked into Chunni's amber eyes. She felt as if Chunni was staring at her with a strange look in her eyes. Shaili could not bear that gaze. She turned her eyes towards the tree, searching for the sparrows.

NOTES ON THE CONTRIBUTORS

DWIREF (Ramnarayan Vishwanath Pathak) (1887–1955) was a prominent voice from what is called the Gandhian era in Gujarati literature. He had a deep engagement with both criticism and fiction and his short stories, especially 'Khemi' and 'Mukundrai', have been a staple of the Gujarati reading public for generations. Dwiref received the most prestigious awards in his lifetime including the Narmad Suvarna Chandrak for *Prachin Gujarati Chhando* in 1949 and the Sahitya Akademi Award for *Bruhat Pingal* in 1956. He was also the president of the Gujarati Sahitya Parishad.

K. M. MUNSHI (1887–1971) is synonymous with regional pride in Gujarat, for he popularized the idea of asmita. His trilogy of the Patan novels (*The Glory of Patan*; *The Lord and Master of Gujarat*; and *The King of Kings*) has recently been translated by Rita and Abhijit Kothari. Munshi contributed to every genre of Gujarati literature. He established numerous institutions including the Bharatiya Vidya Bhawan. He also participated in the Gandhian movement for independence and served as a Member of the Rajya Sabha as well as the Constitution Committee of India.

DHUMKETU (1892–1965) was the nom de plume of Gaurishankar Goverdhanram Joshi. In the early decades of the twentieth century, Dhumketu appeared like a comet in Gujarati literature, such was the force of his short stories. His first collection *Tankha* (1926) lent an enduring benchmark to the Gujarati short story. His stories have been translated into English by Jenny Bhatt in a collection called *Ratno Dholi*.

SUNDARAM (Tribhuvandas Purushottamdas Luhar) (1908–1991) was a leading voice in poetry and the president of the Gujarati Sahitya

Parishad. He is particularly well known for his collection of poetry, *Koya Bhagatni Kadvi Vaani ane Garibo na Geeto* (lit. Bitter Tongue of Koya Bhagat and Songs of the Poor, 1933). A freedom fighter and socially engaged writer in the first half of his life, Sundaram came under the influence of Sri Aurobindo in his later years and turned to more mystical literature.

JAYANT KHATRI (1909–1968) wrote extensively about the region of Kutch, where he grew up. His short story collections *Fora* (1944), *Vehta Zarna* (1952), and *Khara Bapor* (1968, posthumous) received warm reception in Gujarat. He was also a painter and painted symbols and images for his short stories.

SURESH JOSHI (1921–1986) left an indelible mark on the history of Gujarati literature by introducing an experimental and modernist mode of writing. His intervention in the sentimental and 'Gandhian' mode of writing gave rise to a new movement often associated with his name. His well-known poetry collections include *Upjati* (1956), *Pratyancha* (1961), *Itara* (1973), and *Tathapi* (1980). His novel *Chhinnapatra* has been translated into English by Tridip Suhrud as *Crumpled Letters* (1998).

BHUPEN KHAKHAR (1934–2003) was one of India's leading artists in Indian contemporary art. He received the prestigious Padma Shri in 1984 and the Prince Claus Award in 2000. Khakhar's works can be found in the collections of the British Museum; The Tate Gallery, London; and The Museum of Modern Art, New York among others. Khakhar's literary works, including short stories and plays, reflect his preoccupation with the common man with an ironic and humorous gaze.

RAGHUVEER CHAUDHARY (b. 1938) is a towering figure of Gujarati literature, and has participated in many civic movements of Gujarat. A recipient of the Jnanpith award, he started his career writing novels and poetry and later ventured into other forms of literature. He has authored more than eighty books and received numerous literary awards. He also served with many literary organizations. His novel *Amrita* (1965) explores the concept of existentialism. His 1975 trilogy titled *Uparvas, Sahwas,* and *Antarvas* won him the Sahitya Akademi Award in 1977.

ANJALI KHANDWALLA (1940–2019) wrote for adults as well as adolescents. An unusual writer and accomplished singer, Khandwalla is known for her collection of stories, *Leelo Chhokro* (1986), *Ankhni Imarato* (1988), and *Ghughat Ke Pat Khol*. Her collection *Areesama Yatra* was published posthumously in 2019.

DALPAT CHAUHAN (b. 1940) is an eminent Dalit writer and a pioneer of the Dalit literary movement originating in the 1970s. With several books to his credit, including novels, poetry and short story collections, plays, essays, and literary history, he has received prestigious literary awards from the Gujarati Sahitya Parishad, the Gujarati Sahitya Akademi, and the Narsimh Mehta Award.

VARSHA ADALJA (b. 1940) is one of the foremost women writers of Gujarat. She received the Sahitya Akademi Award in 1995 for her first novel *Ansar*, which is her most notable work. Adalja is a versatile and prolific writer who has contributed to almost every genre, including mystery novels and historical fiction. She holds important positions in the literary establishments of Gujarat and is currently working on her autobiography.

HIMANSHI SHELAT (b. 1947) is one of the most acclaimed women writers of Gujarat. She was conferred the Sahitya Akademi Award in 1996 for her short story collection *Andhari Galima Safed Tapakan* (1992). Shelat has actively engaged with marginalized groups, evident in both her non-fiction as well as short stories, yet her fictional world is vast and variegated.

MOHAN PARMAR (b. 1948) is an eminent Dalit writer and one of the most prominent names and acclaimed short story writers of Gujarat. With several novels, short story collections, and critical books to his credit, Parmar has been the recipient of the Uma–Snehrashmi Prize, Premanand Suvarna Chakra, and the Sahitya Akademi Award.

CHANDRA SHRIMALI (1950-2020) was arguably the first Dalit woman writer of Gujarat. A rare voice in Gujarati literature, she received several awards including the Savitribai Phule Dalit Mahila Sahityakaar Award. Shrimali's notable collections include *Chanibor* and *Chudlakaram*.

NEERAV PATEL (1950–2019) has been one of the strongest anti-caste voices from Gujarat. A bilingual poet and critic, Patel is best known for *Burning from Both the Ends* (1980, English poems), *What Did I Do to Be Black and Blue* (1987, English poems), and *Bahishkrut Phulo* (2006, Gujarati). He edited *Swaman*, a journal of Dalit writings in Gujarati.

BINDU BHATT (b. 1954) is a scholar of Hindi literature and a prominent novelist from Gujarat. She was honoured with the Sahitya Akademi Award for her novel *Akhepaatar*, and the Goverdhanram Smriti Award for her short novel, *Mira Yagnik Nee Diary*. Bhatt is also an accomplished translator of Gujarati and Hindi.

MINAL DAVE (b. 1960) is an associate professor of literature at Shree Jayendrapuri Arts and Science College in Bharuch. She has written one-act plays, short stories, and critical essays. She has also translated works from other languages into Gujarati. Dave's is an important voice with striking ethical clarity and literary quality.

NAZIR MANSURI (b. 1965) is a Gujarati novelist and short story writer based in Navsari. His recent novels are *Chandalchakravo* and *Veshpalto*, both of which appeared in 2009. His collection of short fiction, *Dhal Kachbo*, was critically acclaimed. He received the Katha Award for creative fiction in 1997 for 'Bhuthar' and it was a part of Katha 'The Best of the Nineties' Fiction. He is also the first Gujarati writer to win the Sanskriti Award for Literature awarded by the Sanskriti Pratishtan in 1999.

DASHRATH PARMAR (b. 1967) is an important and emerging voice in Dalit literature. He is the author of *Paarkhu* (2001) and *Be Email ane Salagvo* (2013)—both of which are acclaimed collections of short stories. He has won prizes for many of his stories.

MONA PATRAWALLA (b. 1972) is one of the most significant modernist and postmodernist voices in contemporary Gujarati fiction. Her fiction depicts the lives of the Parsis and tribals living in the Dang-Vansda forest region of South Gujarat. Her short story collection *Rani Bilado*, from which the story in this anthology is taken, was widely acclaimed. Her massive novels, *Ghorkhodia* in two volumes (2009), and *Andhar Pachedo* in four volumes, each volume subtitled *Vesh*, *Andharpadal*, *Aganpadal*, and *Andharpachedo*, all of which appeared in 2017, have been received very well by critics. Translations of her stories have appeared in periodicals like *The Little Mag*, *Indian Literature*, and *New Quest*.

SACHIN KETKAR (b. 1972) is a bilingual writer and translator. He teaches at the Maharaja Sayajirao University of Baroda, Vadodara. He is currently working on a critical history of Marathi literature. His Marathi poetry has been translated into several Indian languages. His books in English include *Skin, Spam and other Fake Encounters: Selected Marathi Poems in Translation* (2011); *Migrating Words: Refractions on Indian Translation Studies* (2010); and *A Dirge for the Dead Dog and Other Incantations* (2003). He won the Indian Literature Poetry Translation Prize awarded by Sahitya Akademi, for translations of modern Gujarati poetry in 2000.

HEMANG DESAI (b. 1978) is a bilingual poet, translator, editor, and critic working in Gujarati and English. He is an Associate Professor at the English and Foreign Language University, Hyderabad. His Gujarati translations of Arun Kolatkar's *Kala Ghoda Poems*, *Sarpa Satra*, and *Jejuri* have received critical acclaim. His forthcoming translations include Dalpat Chauhan's novel, *Vultures*, and short story collection, *Fear and Other Stories*.

PANNA TRIVEDI (b. 1979) teaches at the Veer Narmad University, Surat. She has received the Jay Dinkar Shah Award (2010), Dhoomketu Award (2014), and the Bhagini Nivedita Award, among others, for her poetry, short stories, and other contributions. She also translates from Hindi into Gujarati. Her notable collections include *Safed Andharu* and *Ekanto no Awaaj*.

RAAM MORI (b. 1993) is one of the youngest recipients of the Sahitya Akademi Award in 2017. His short story collections, *Mahotu* (2016), *Coffee Stories* (2018), and *Confession Box* (2020) have received resounding acclaim in Gujarat. He also writes columns, plays, and scripts for television and films.

ABHIMANYU ACHARYA (b. 1994) is the youngest writer in this anthology as well as one of the most promising stars of Gujarati literature. His debut collection of stories published in 2018 in Gujarati won the prestigious Yuva Gaurav Puraskar from Sahitya Akademi. He has also won the Sanhita Manch playwriting award for his play *Bhes* (Hindi) and has been twice long listed for TOTO Funds the Arts Award for his writings in English. He is a doctoral student of Comparative Literature at the University of Western Ontario.

ACKNOWLEDGEMENTS

Grateful acknowledgement is made to the following copyright holders for permission to reprint copyrighted material in this volume. While every effort has been made to locate and contact copyright holders and obtain permission, this has not always been possible; any inadvertent omissions brought to our notice will be remedied in future editions.

The English version of 'A Letter (Ek Patra)' of K. M. Munshi is reproduced with the permission of Bhartiya Vidya Bhavan, Mumbai 400 007.

'Jumo Bhishti' by Dhumketu. Reprinted by permission of Gurjar Prakashan.

'The Death of Maaja Vela' by Sundaram. Reprinted by permission of Sudha Sundaram.

'A Drop of Blood' by Jayant Khatri. Reprinted by permission of Kirti Jayant Khatri.

'Once Upon a Time in Nainmesaranya' by Suresh Joshi. Reprinted by permission of Pranav Suresh Joshi.

'Vaadki' by Bhupen Khakhar. Reprinted by permission of Dhaval Khakhar.

'Pyre' by Raghuveer Chaudhary. Reprinted by permission of the author.

'Indubhai Gayab' by Anjali Khandwalla. Reprinted by permission of Pradeep Khandwalla. First published in Rita Kothari (trans.), *Speech and Silence: Literary Journeys by Gujarati Women*, New Delhi: Zubaan, 2006.

'The Invasion' by Dalpat Chauhan. Reprinted by permission of Dalpat Chauhan and Hemang Desai.

'Name: Nayana Rasik Mehta' by Varsha Adalja. Reprinted by permission of the author.

'Doors' by Himanshu Shelat. Reprinted by permission of the author. First published in Rita Kothari (trans.), *Speech and Silence:*

Literary Journeys by Gujarati Women, New Delhi: Zubaan, 2006.

'The Unblemished One' by Mohan Parmar. Reprinted by permission of Mohan Parmar.

'The Stairs' by Chandra Shrimali. Reprinted by permission of the author. First published in Rita Kothari (trans.), *Speech and Silence: Literary Journeys by Gujarati Women*, New Delhi: Zubaan, 2006.

'Creamy Layer' by Neerav Patel. Reprinted by permission of the author.

'Congratulations' by Bindu Bhatt. Reprinted by permission of the author.

'Nightmare' by Minal Dave. Reprinted by permission of the author.

'The Bilge Water' by Nazir Mansuri. Reprinted by permission of Nazir Mansuri and Sachin C. Ketkar.

'Nandu' by Dashrath Parmar. Reprinted by permission of the author. Previously published in *Indian Literature*, Sahitya Akademi's bimonthly journal, New Delhi: Sahitya Akademi, ISSN 0019-580-4, Vol. 274, March–April 2013, pp. 117–141.

'The Black Horse' by Mona Patrawalla. Reprinted by permission of Mona Patrawalla and Sachin C. Ketkar.

'Maajo' by Panna Trivedi. Reprinted by permission of the author.

'The Twenty-first Tiffin' by Raam Mori. Reprinted by permission of the author.

'Chunni' by Abhimanyu Acharya. Reprinted by permission of the author.